ALL THESE STEPS LEAD DOWN

NELSON W. PYLES

ISBN: 978-1-7343897-2-2 (trade paper)
ISBN: 978-1-7343897-3-9 (ebook)

First printing edition: October 29, 2024
Printed by Cold War Radio Press in the United States of America.
Front Cover Design and Layout: Don Noble/Rooster Republic Press
Back Cover Photograph: Declan Pyles
Editing, Interior Layout, and Cover Text: Scarlett R. Algee
Proofreading: Sean Leonard

Cold War Radio Press
201 Lake Street
Ridgely, TN 38080

For Deb

"Nelson Pyles seductively leads us downstairs to his twisted torture party. The ideas are freaky and his endings deliver...a raucous reflection of his writing to date –a great retrospective of an entertainer having a blast in the genre, going after it all gangbusters, like a rock-and-roll werewolf grabbing the mic and belting out 'Brick House' his own damned way at a wedding party." —Michael Arnzen, Bram Stoker Award-winning author of *Proverbs for Monsters*

"*All These Steps Lead Down*, as the title suggests, is a collection that will spiral readers into murky pits; and down here, the eclectic range of stories will have you double-checking every basement shadow as you descend into its depths.

"Pyles offers up a dynamic set of stories where characters are hungry to share their secrets; readers will play witness to dark imaginings and confessions, but it's really the twisted humanity Pyles creates that becomes the star of such tales."— Sara Tantlinger, Bram Stoker Award-winning author of *The Devil's Dreamland*

"Pyles excels at plumbing the depths of mortal wickedness while never losing touch with his humanity or sly sense of humor, conveying empathy and pathos for even his darkest characters, who — most frighteningly of all — can't help but remind us of ourselves.

"A thrilling story collection for fans of *The Twilight Zone*, H.P. Lovecraft, *Creepshow*, and the classic EC and Warren comic anthologies." — Phillip Mucci, award winning filmmaker and comic book creator

"Do you dare to venture down those narrow and rickety steps into the dark imagination of Nelson W. Pyles? Serial killers, werewolves, killer bees, evil unicorns and hungry Elder Gods lurk down there, stretching out a claw, a stinger or a tentacle to wrap around your mind.

"There's something for every horror fan: short stories, flash fiction, factual essays and a radio play. Vengeance, terror, dark humour and even redemption abound. Descend those steps, Dear Reader. We dare you." —Anna Taborska, author of *Bloody Britain* and *For Those Who Dream Monsters*

CONTENTS

Introduction
9

Muerte Con Sabor a Fresa
13

Mrs. Morrison's Pie
34

Carol's Christmas (with Scarlett R. Algee)
46

When the Blood Runs Clear
58

The Lonesome Death of Phineas T. Croughly
78

Highway 90—A Radio Play
83

Hello, It's Not Me
106

Have Yourself
109

A Piece of Cake
114

All These Steps Lead Down
129

The Humanity of *Blade Runner*
138

Negotiations
148

The Trouble with Unicorns
157

Regards, Eleanor
159

Manners Count
161

Mallory
163

The Best Show Ever
166

The Wolf and Her Wife
170

Stories about the Stories
199

Publication History

Acknowledgments

About the Author

INTRODUCTION

Some of you reading this will know me as an editor and publisher. Some of you may know me as a writer. Friends, it's time I let you all in on a little secret.

I've never written an introduction before. It's my understanding that I'm supposed to say a lot of very nice things.

As it happens, I first met Nelson in 2015, when I was invited to write a story for a new podcast, *The Lift*. I ended up writing several *Lift* stories, as well as a few more for the podcast Nelson created, *The Wicked Library*. One of our TWL collaborations, "Carol's Christmas," is contained in this very volume (you like holiday-themed serial killing, right?).

I've watched several of these stories develop from ideas to finished works, and let me tell you: Nelson Pyles writes like nobody else. Who else could pen a story like "Muerte Con Sabor a Fresa," in which a man's quest to improve his physical body instead unleashes a new eldritch abomination on the world? (My existing aversion to strawberries has now grown to include protein powder.) Or "Mrs. Morrison's Pie," in which Death herself comes for Mrs. Morrison, only to discover that the good lady has a few conditions to be met first...

But Nelson's real strength is in writing about families—not happy families, so much, but perhaps more realistic ones than we like to admit. The radio drama "Highway 90" is a nightmare of a relationship, filtered through the lens of *The Twilight Zone*; hostility radiates through every word Peter and Melinda say to each other, right up to the end. In "A Piece of Cake," the adult children of an addicted mother come to terms with her flaws, and their own, over the titular dessert, while the story contains one of the most succinct descriptions of addiction I've ever encountered: *it feels good until it doesn't and you have to do it again.* And "Have Yourself"—well, who among us *hasn't* suffered through an interminable family Christmas party and wanted our relatives to follow suit?

To say nothing of the other stories in this vein: the unreliable narrator of "Hello, It's Not Me"; the perkily obsessed "Mallory"; the abused and abusive Jerry of the titular "All These Steps Lead Down." Because don't they? Ever downward, ever darker, toward a bottom you can't see.

Finally, editors aren't supposed to have favorites (this is a lie), but I do, and it's "The Wolf and Her Wife." Because family isn't always what you're bred from; sometimes it's what you make, what you find, what you're willing to fight and bleed for. That one is absolutely not to be missed.

Yes, my friends, Nelson Pyles is a damned good writer. But don't just take my word for it. Go. Go forth and read for yourself. Take in every nuance, every drop of blood, every strawberry-flavored scrap of death.

Just watch your step.

Scarlett R. Algee
October 8, 2024

ALL THESE STEPS LEAD DOWN

MUERTE CON SABOR A FRESA

1

Georgie Turner no longer cared if Daryl Madison was still alive. If Daryl couldn't give a call to say he wasn't coming to work, or quitting, or whatever, then Georgie shouldn't be expected to care. She thought about this as she sat in front of Daryl's apartment complex. She gripped the steering wheel tightly in frustration.

She looked across the sunlit parking lot. It was now midday on a Wednesday, and the lot was nearly empty.

Except for Daryl's car, sitting in its little assigned parking spot.

She scowled and called his cell phone for the tenth time. It didn't even ring, just went to voicemail.

"Hey, this is Big D. Leave a message, but I'll probably just text you back. Deuces."

Georgie hung up for the tenth time and punched the steering wheel. She was going to have to get out of the car and walk up to the door.

She got out of her car, slammed the door, and walked to the entrance to the building.

She listened to her shoes clap against the sidewalk and tried to let it calm her down. She liked meditation quite a bit, but it just wasn't working today. When it came to Daryl, her patience was already thin, and she really hoped he was home so she could do some screaming meditation.

That would do wonders to calm her down.

She stood in front of the exterior panel of the apartment mailbox and searched for Daryl Madison's name. Of course, it was the last one, and of course it said *Big D*.

She nearly punched it, but instead she pushed it hard just once. For fifteen seconds.

No response.

She then pushed it fifteen times in rapid succession.

She closed her eyes for a moment before deciding that she didn't have the patience to even talk to Daryl. Her eyes snapped open just in time to see a mid-twenties looking man with long dreadlocks and a nice grey suit open the door.

"Hi," he said with a big smile. "Are you trying to get somebody? The buzzers don't always work."

He held the door open for her. She blinked and returned his smile. She nearly gave him a curtsy as she walked into the apartment complex.

"Thank you so much," she said. She smiled at him and thanked whatever higher power there is that her building wouldn't have allowed a stranger inside. Still, whatever would work was fine with her. She just had to find the apartment, fire his dumb ass, and get on with her day.

Georgie knew his apartment number by heart and glanced at the numbered doors as she got closer to her destination. There on the left was Apartment 105. She stood in front of it and took a deep breath. The breath was for strength, but along with it came a smell the likes of which was unusual. It smelled like meat just before it rotted. She envisioned a steak in the fridge, forgotten and turning greyish. You could still eat it, but if it started to smell, you'd be shit out of luck.

She held her fist up to knock and hesitated a moment, then swallowed and knocked three times.

There was no answer, but she did hear something. A small mewling voice, but she couldn't make out what it said.

"Daryl?" she called out. "Is that you in there? It's Georgie."

She heard the mewling voice again, but she still couldn't make it out.

"Can I come in? Are you okay?"

She heard the voice a third time and she grabbed the doorknob. She gave it a turn and opened the door.

The apartment was dark. The lights were off, and the curtains had all been closed. The room was also hot, adding to the stronger smell of greying meat. She saw the green digital light on the stove in the kitchen. It was the only light in the place, so she went toward it.

"Daryl, I'm turning on a light in here. Where are you? Why is it so dark in here?"

The mewling sound was louder. It sounded like it was coming from the opposite side of the apartment. She found the kitchen light and switched it on. The kitchen was not what she expected. It reeked of rotten meat, but looked immaculate. She noticed that the oven was on, which would explain the heat, but not the smell. She turned the oven off; the plastic knob was hot and soft. It must have been on for days.

She walked to the refrigerator and opened it. The smell hit her like a fist. It was stocked with grey, bruise-colored meat and rotten vegetables. A thin pool of cold blood began to seep out of the fridge and collect on the linoleum. She gagged and slammed the door shut.

"Jesus fuck," she said in revulsion. She heard the voice again and now could at least see from the light in the kitchen that the small apartment was mostly clean.

Mostly.

Georgie started to walk out of the kitchen when she saw a large empty container of what looked like protein powder on its side, abandoned on the counter. It had a black label that read simply DENSITOL XXL-STRAWBERRY. She gave it a quick glance, frowned, and then made her way into the next room. The mewling sound was getting louder but not any clearer. She glanced at the wall near the front door and saw the light switches. Turning them all on, she saw nothing spectacular in the living room. It, too, was clean. She shook her head and walked to what she assumed was the bedroom. There was a bathroom to the left of the closed door. She knocked on the door.

"Daryl, are you in here?"

A sound came forth, nearly like a scream. She opened the door, but it only opened halfway. There was something heavy in front of it.

"Help me," came the reply. It had a wheezing, high-pitched sound, but was very soft and labored. It was the mewling sound she had heard, and it was coming from the floor.

Georgie reached her hand inside the room, feeling for the light switch, and found it. Light exploded in the room from the ceiling. She looked down and saw a leg blocking the door.

At least, it looked somewhat like a leg.

There was a shoe and a sock and a pant leg, but it looked...empty. The shoe was pointed up, as if something was holding it up. She pushed the door harder, expecting the pant leg to move, but it just wouldn't budge.

"Stop," the thin voice said. "Please help me."

Georgie squeezed herself into the room with some effort. She looked down at what was blocking the door and screamed.

2

The most unusual part of the paramedic rescue call for Priyanka Choudhry wasn't what the victim looked like—that, in and of itself, would trigger future nightmares for the foreseeable future. It was just how much the victim weighed.

The general statistics about the victim, Daryl Madison, was that he was five feet, six inches, and roughly about a hundred pounds. However, it took three paramedics and two firemen tremendous effort to get Madison onto the gurney, and even then they had to roll him onto it. They never raised it up; they had to shuffle it out of the apartment, and they needed additional help to load him into the ambulance, which nearly buckled under the weight.

Rolling the man onto the gurney proved to be nearly impossible. Madison was nearly flat. Most of his bones were broken in the most unusual ways, as if he had been crushed under something. How he was still alive and breathing was nothing short of miraculous.

Pri had determined from the amount of excrement around the body that he had been on the floor of his bedroom for nearly a week. The woman who had called 911 had said that Madison had been missing about eight days. By rights, due to the injuries and the excrement, Madison should have died from dehydration at the very least.

Looking around the apartment, anything vaguely resembling a clue as to what could have happened to him was nonexistent. The woman, Ms. Turner, said that she hadn't seen anything out of the ordinary at all. From her description, the apartment was dark, and she heard Madison crying out softly from the bedroom.

It seemed to be the only thing that made sense.

Pri sat on the edge of her bed and shuddered. She closed her eyes and saw Madison's tear-streaked face. His expression didn't change. Of course, how could it? The bones in his face had all been crushed, and he looked like a rubber Halloween mask without a head inside it. A deflated head that was still alive and suffering in a most unimaginable way.

She had left the hospital once they had managed to find a room (and a bed) that could hold him. There was another call that her and her partner went to from there, but she knew that she wasn't going to stop thinking about Daryl Madison for quite some time.

She crawled into bed and shut off her light. She waited a long time for sleep to come.

3

The research and development lab in Pentacorp's own industrial park was tucked away in a large facility in Eastern Pittsburgh. It was a half hour from Monroeville, and quite a lot of the employees lived there, game for the heavy commute. Truth be told, the job was challenging and difficult, but most would say rewarding.

Especially financially.

Georgie opted to not live in Monroeville, however, and lived in a semi-quiet complex in Penn Hills. The town was full of "yinzers" who got good and liquored up on the weekends and most weeknights. But the rent was inexpensive, and there was a guard at the door to keep the riffraff out...and some of it in, so to speak.

So, because of her proximity to the R&D facility, she had no trouble getting there before anyone in the department and simply waited for whomever the first person was to arrive.

And, unfortunately for Phoebe Armstrong, it happened to be her.

"Well, good morning, Dr. Armstrong."

Phoebe gasped and dropped her coffee. It splashed onto her beige pants and she yelped as the coffee poured onto the white tile floor. Her face went from shock to quick anger as she saw Georgie, feet propped up on a lab table. Next to her feet was a familiar-looking plastic container.

"Jesus H. tap-dancing Christ, what are you doing here?"

"I'm here to ask you some questions, and you had better have some really good answers for me." She took a foot and kicked the plastic container off the table and onto the floor. "Question number one: Why the fuck was this in one of our employees' apartment?"

Armstrong looked at the container and her eyes narrowed.

"Daryl," she muttered through her teeth.

"Oh, don't you mean 'Big D'?"

Armstrong blinked and glared at Georgie. There had been a long-standing animosity between the two women, but it was absolutely about to get worse.

"First of all, fuck you. That's first. Just want to get that out of the way." Phoebe folded her arms and leaned to one side. "Secondly, we were authorized to start human testing. You authorized human testing, so what do you think 'human testing' means?"

"Human testing means finding volunteers or college students to sign waivers and give them a few bucks here and there. You know, so if something bad happens, they can't sue us and aren't attached to the corporation. Daryl was a fucking employee."

"Daryl is still alive apparently, and he's also an adult who happened to sign the aforementioned waivers. I'm not stupid, George. All the bases were covered."

Georgie kicked her feet off the lab table and stood up. She walked slowly toward Phoebe.

"Except, of course, for the base where the subject stays in the goddamn testing facility to be monitored and doesn't massively overdose on the test drug because it's a goddamn test drug."

Phoebe sank slightly.

"Well, okay. You got me there."

"When I found Daryl, he looked like a deflated balloon." Georgie pulled out her cell phone and showed Phoebe a picture.

"Oh balls," Armstrong said.

"Indeed. And it took several people to get him onto a gurney. He was unbelievably heavy."

"Like, how heavy?"

"It took five men to get him into the ambulance. Why?"

"That's pretty heavy, yeah," Phoebe said and turned away. She whirled back around to Georgie. "We have a problem."

"I would love to hit you right now," Georgie said quietly.

Phoebe ignored it.

"We need to get Daryl here to the lab ASAP."

"Is this something you can fix?"

Phoebe looked at her and frowned.

"I'm just hoping it's something that can be contained."

4

If there was one thing Daryl loved more than anything, it was the taste of strawberries. He had loved it ever since he was a child, and when the opportunity came to not only try a new weight-building protein powder, but also choose the flavor, he jumped at it. Well, maybe wasn't entirely true; strawberry was the only flavor that seemed to mask the actual flavor of the powder, or so he had been told. "Flavor was a secondary concern," Dr. Armstrong had said.

But to Daryl, it was necessary if he was going to do it and stick with it.

And hot damn, it tasted great!

Daryl had been underweight most of his life. He was tall, but always so damn skinny. He'd tried everything, and really hated the protein shakes most of all. They tasted terrible and never added any weight. He was still hovering around the same 100 pounds he'd been ever since high school. Dr. Armstrong had noticed his efforts and pulled him aside.

"I think I can help you."

"Yeah? How? Nothing works. Nothing has ever worked."

He was near tears, which was embarrassing since they were in the company lunchroom. He had been eating a cheeseburger and fries.

"I've spent the last six months eating shit like this," he said, holding up the messy burger. It dripped grease and mayonnaise. "And not a single pound."

"Come to my lab after you get done with work today," Dr. Armstrong said and got up from the table. She paused, looked at him, and said, "I can help you."

He never would have guessed that help would have been strawberry-flavored.

He never would have guessed that one day he'd be silently begging for death.

Daryl didn't know what day it was. He couldn't hear, he couldn't see, and he couldn't speak. He was unaware of anything, except that he was still alive somehow and the only taste in his mouth was sour, vaguely strawberry and vomit. He knew he was alive, but didn't know how or why. He couldn't even remember what had happened to him.

He had taken the protein powder home and read the instructions carefully. They were very simple instructions; eight ounces of water, juice, or milk, and a scoop of the powder before working out. Only one serving per day.

One.

Dr. Armstrong had even gone so far as to underline the word *one* three times, as if Daryl was too dumb to follow the directions. He laughed as he mixed his first batch. Grinning, he took a breath when he was finished and took a sip of the thick shake.

The texture was unlike the other protein shakes he'd had. It was somehow heavier, but not in a bad way. It was thick and delicious. Dr. Armstrong had suggested water over milk, but Daryl preferred milk and, boy, had he been glad he used it. The shake was amazingly delicious. He smacked his lips and looked at the shake, all pink and frothy.

It was refreshing too. It didn't feel like a chore to drink it. It was thick, but also smooth. Not quite greasy, but it really slid down his throat easily. The strawberry taste was sweet, but not overtly so. It was the best strawberry anything he'd ever tasted. He picked up the container and looked for the ingredients to see if it was artificial or made from natural flavors.

There weren't any ingredients listed.

He shrugged and downed the rest of the shake in one gulp.

As he put the empty plastic cup on the counter, he let out a loud belch. He chuckled and wondered what would happen if he mixed up another batch. Dr. Armstrong had said he had enough to last him for two months if he followed the instructions.

That had seemed like forever ago.

Where had he gone wrong?

Maybe the second shake that day was what started it. Or maybe the other shakes that followed in the hours and days that followed. It didn't seem bad at the time and, Jesus, it tasted so goddamned good.

By the second day, he was actively craving it. When he wasn't drinking one, he was thinking about it. He had four on the third day. By the end of the fifth day, he had consumed eight.

He'd also begun to gain weight. He had stepped on the scale in Dr. Armstrong's lab fully clothed and weighed a paltry 98 pounds. She had recommended that he give it a week before starting to weigh himself, and although he didn't follow the instructions for taking the powder, he did almost follow that direction. It was the very end of day five. *Pretty much a week*, Daryl thought.

He got up off the couch with a bit of difficulty. He felt stiff, but really didn't know why. He lumbered into the bathroom and stepped on the scale. The large digital numbers loaded up, and what he saw he couldn't believe.

"One hundred sixty-five pounds?" he said out loud. He looked at his reflection, and other than looking like he had a hangover, he couldn't see the weight. He took off his shirt and stepped off the scale. He looked himself up and down in the bathroom mirror and didn't really see any difference. If anything, he could see his ribs more clearly than before. He realized, looking at himself, that he hadn't taken a shower in a few days.

Or left the apartment. Or even gone to work.

He debated getting into the shower, then decided against it.

He felt a pang of hunger. He hadn't really eaten anything either. Just the shakes.

Maybe he needed a shake, and then he'd take a shower.

By the seventh day, it was difficult to even stand, but he managed to make it into the bathroom. He was shirtless and still looked as gaunt as ever, but he felt so...bloated. He staggered into the bathroom and turned on the harsh fluorescent light.

He looked even more gaunt than before. His shoulder blades looked like they were about to poke through his skin, which was looking a little grey. His eyes appeared to have recessed into their sockets. His teeth, which had always been a point of pride for him, looked as if they were false gag teeth from a novelty shop, a darkish yellow. He stuck out his tongue and it was black.

He backed away from his reflection and tripped over something. It was the scale. Almost as an afterthought, he stepped on it, although it took more effort than it should have. He put a hand on the wall to steady himself and he heard the sheetrock crack under his hand. He steadied himself carefully and looked down.

The scale said "ERROR" in black flashing letters. He sighed and stepped off the scale. It took a moment, but it eventually reset to zero. He stood back on it again and, once again, it read "ERROR," and this time he heard the scale crack. He gingerly stepped off and grabbed the sink counter, which groaned.

"What the hell," he muttered. He steadied himself and walked out of the bathroom, leaving the light on. He slowly made it into his kitchen and opened the container of powder. He knew it was low, but what he saw wasn't low, it was practically empty. There was maybe a half-scoop left.

His eyes welled up. Dr. Armstrong would be furious with him, if she wasn't already. He'd already gone through a two-month supply in, what, a week?

Daryl staggered over to the stove, nearly falling. He caught himself and nearly upended the stove. He looked at the green clock and saw that it was six forty-five in the morning.

What day was it?

He had closed the blinds and curtains days ago. He hadn't watched television or checked his phone. He struggled to think of what he had been doing and couldn't honestly remember. His eyes began to grow wide with panic. Without thinking, he shuffled back over to the counter and picked up the container. He opened it and, with great effort, put the container up to his face. He opened his mouth, crying.

He emptied what was left of the powder into his mouth, and he coughed and choked trying to swallow. He dropped the container back on the counter and staggered out of the kitchen. He was sobbing and trying not to fall as he headed back to his bedroom.

He needed help.

He would get his keys and try to drive himself to the hospital or to the lab, but he needed help. Daryl worked his way into his bedroom, throwing the door hard into the wall. He turned to swing the door back around to get the keys from his coat, but as it slammed closed, he heard a snap come from the floor. He tried to look down, but the floor had already risen to meet him.

He had fallen, but it seemed surreal, like a dream. Daryl was on the floor, but he was still looking at his bedroom door, as if he had fallen through the floor.

For a moment he thought he had dropped to his knees, until he noticed that he couldn't even see his knees. When he looked down, he saw his shoes and his pants and a pile of greyish leather spilling out in between them. It took a quick poke of a finger to realize the grey leather was, in fact, part of his leg. He pinched some between his fingers and pulled. It was very thick, and the fact that he felt it made him a little nauseous.

What happened to my bones?

He felt his torso fall backward. As his head hit the carpet, he heard a sound like a heavy wet blanket being dropped onto a concrete floor. To his amazement, he realized it was his own head. He tried to sit up, but couldn't. He tried to scream, but all that came out was a mewling sound. His eyes darted around until even they were unable to move. His breathing became shallow as he felt his body seemingly sink into the floor.

No, not seemingly.

Daryl no longer had any concept of time and had no idea how long he had laid there in that condition. He would come in and out of awareness, each time not able to feel, hear, or speak.

But he could taste, and he wished he couldn't.

He remembered someone coming to save him. Was it Georgie?

Who was Georgie?

He didn't know, because that was a lifetime ago.

Or just a few minutes.

All he did know was the taste of rotten strawberries and a growing wish for death.

5

Georgie was still furious at Daryl, but looking at him now—or whatever was left of him—made her shudder. She sat outside of an exam room in the lab and watched as Armstrong and two other scientists examined his body.

Daryl was inside of what looked like a giant petri dish. He was naked, but also completely without form. He looked like a cataclysmically deformed grey puddle. Where his face should have been was a gaping, toothless maw and two bruise-colored indents where his eyes had been. There would be an occasional ripple in the flesh and something that sounded like a moan, but not much else. He was alive by some miracle, and although his size wasn't changing, his weight was increasing.

Georgie stared at the thing that was Daryl until Armstrong smacked the plexiglass window with the flat of her hand. Georgie started and glared at her. Armstrong mouthed, "Come in here, bitch," and walked back over to Daryl.

It took a moment, but Georgie put on a white hazmat suit, and entered the airlock into the examination room. Armstrong waved her over.

"Okay, what has no bones and weighs fifteen hundred pounds?" Dr. Armstrong asked.

"How can you make a joke?"

Armstrong frowned.

"That's not a goddamn joke. It was a legit question. Daryl here currently weighs around fifteen hundred pounds. All his bones are gone. Absorbed, along with his teeth, nails, eyes, and hair. This is fascinating."

Georgie shook her head.

"How is he still alive? Has he said anything?"

"Near as we can tell, he's still alive for the moment because he isn't done yet."

"Done?"

Armstrong nodded. "He's changing. Transforming into something."

"Into what?"

Armstrong shrugged. "Your guess is as good as mine." She smiled, then added, "Actually, no. It isn't as good as mine, but I got nothing right now. Running some more tests."

"What's in that stuff?"

Armstrong smiled. "Science. You wouldn't understand."

Georgie's eyes narrowed. "Why don't you goddamn try me."

"Well, the 'stuff' is a complex chemical compound that has been decades in the making. It's gone through several different test modes. It's a myriad of—"

Georgie took both of her hands and shoved Armstrong against a wall. She held her there and turned her head to the other two scientists in the room.

"You two, get out of here right now."

The two looked at each and then left through the airlock. Georgie held Armstrong against the wall.

"I always thought you were into the rough stuff, George, but we're at work."

"What is in that protein powder, Phoebe?" Georgie said through her teeth. "This isn't some small side effect. This is physiologically altering his fucking molecular structure!"

"What's impressive is that it smells like rotten strawberries," Armstrong said. "And even though we didn't use any natural strawberries in the powder, its smells like real-life strawberries."

Georgie blinked.

"Are you crazy?"

Armstrong brought her arms up and pushed Georgie off. Georgie staggered backward and tripped over her feet, landing hard on the tile floor.

"I am pretty far from crazy," Armstrong said, standing over Georgie. "And I'm not stupid, nor am I one of your flunkies. You may have hired me, but I don't answer to you."

"Well, who do you answer to then?" Georgie growled. "Because you seem to be absolutely off course."

Armstrong smiled and walked over to the tank where Daryl's grey gelatinous form twitched. She ran a hand over the Plexiglas tank almost lovingly.

"I am exactly on course." Armstrong twirled and stopped, resting her hands on her hips. "Big D has done so much better than I thought he would. Just wonderful. We're even ahead of schedule."

Georgie started to get up off the floor.

"Schedule?"

"I didn't stutter."

"You had told me that this was something to be contained," Georgie said, standing up. She brushed herself off as Dr. Armstrong stood in front of her. "But now it's on schedule?"

"Ahead of schedule, yes. See, there were a few things we used as an additive for the powder that worked so much better than expected. And the fact that he polished off the entire five-pound container in a week..." She stopped for a moment and cackled loudly.

"But you had given him instructions that he clearly didn't follow."

"True, but this was the expected result. It just happened faster with him. Guess he loves strawberries a whole lot, am I right?"

"The expected result?"

"Look, can I level with you?" Armstrong reached out and took Georgie by the shoulders. "Since we're so close to the end of this experiment, I feel like we've really bonded."

Georgie roughly pushed Armstrong away from her. "You are fucking insane."

"My sanity is irrelevant." Armstrong flung herself into Georgie, both tumbling to the tile floor. "But what *is* relevant is that this experiment is about to rocket ahead."

Armstrong rolled on top of Georgie and grabbed her head with both hands. It was hard with the vinyl hazmat suit, but she began to pound Georgie's head against the floor.

Georgie counted to three as she tried to fight off Armstrong, but things began to darken when she got to five. The pain in her head began to subside and everything blurred into blackness.

6

Georgie awoke with a splitting headache. She realized she was on the floor and reached to the back of her head. There was a growing lump and a bit of dampness that she assumed was her own blood. She opened her eyes and saw she was still in the lab examination room, except now she wasn't wearing the hazmat suit.

She sat up and looked around the room. It was just her and Daryl, still twitching in the giant tank. She struggled to her feet, grabbing a nearby examination table for support.

"Hello?" she called out. "Doctor? Anyone?"

There was no answer, not that she expected one. She sighed and turned slowly to the tank.

The faceless, formless Daryl just sat there, twitching or breathing or whatever it was he was doing.

"How about you? You still in there, you poor bastard?"

The form did nothing.

"You know this is all your fault, right?"

She walked to the edge of the tank and looked inside. There he was, Daryl, in all his grey fleshy mush and rotten strawberry stench. A stupid little man who made one stupid mistake too many. She felt pity, revulsion, and hot rising anger. Her hands closed into fists.

"Stupid son of a bitch." She leaned over the top of the tank. "I don't know if you can hear me, but if you still had a face I'd punch it. I'm not without sympathy, but I hope whatever you're going through is painful as—"

A thick grey tendril shot out of the tank and caught Georgie under her chin, knocking her on her back. It happened quickly and left her jaw throbbing. She sat up and the tendril was still in front of her, weaving back and forth like a cobra about to strike.

Her eyes widened with horror as the grey mass pulsed and throbbed inches from her face. She watched the mass, roughly the size of a fist, widen and expand into the shape of an oval. It grew to the size of her head, and she began to whimper.

"Daryl...please..."

From inside the clear plexiglass tank, the grey mass that was Daryl began to rise and spill out over the sides. It poured out onto the floor, and the sheer weight of it made the tile floor creak and crack.

From above, the exam room PA clicked on and Phoebe Armstrong's voice boomed into the room.

"Oh, George, this shit just got real."

Armstrong then began to cackle.

Georgie began to clamor backward away from the oval tendril, her eyes never leaving the pulsing thing. The tendril followed her, maintaining the same distance, neither advancing nor falling back. Behind it, more and more of the grey flesh spilled out onto the tiles. The cracks began to snake toward Georgie more and more.

"Oh, Big D is getting so much heavier now. He's about twenty-five hundred pounds right about now. Looks like that floor isn't going to hold him much longer," Armstrong's voice boomed.

"Why is it so heavy?" Georgie nearly shrieked, still backing away and rapidly running out of room.

"Density, stupid," came the reply. "The formula was designed to do a lot of things, and putting on weight was one of them. So part of the physiological change was restructuring the particle density of the subject. Do I need to explain that to you?"

"Yes, goddamn it!"

Armstrong let out a small laugh.

"Knew it," she said. "So goddamn smart, aren't you? Well, since we're in a lab, and a learning lab at that, guess you're going to learn something today. First, Daryl's mass remains the same. However, his density and volume has been increased. His bones, hair, and nails have been absorbed by his changing physical makeup."

Georgie reached the wall and stopped. She was shuddering as the grey form was now completely out of the tank and covering most of the floor, save the oval tendril pulsing in front of her face.

"What the fuck does that mean?" Georgie said through her teeth.

"It means the experiment is working."

"This is what you were trying to do?" Georgie glared at the tendril which still hovered in front of her. "You were supposed to be making a protein shake."

"I know what I was supposed to be making," Armstrong said through the PA system. "But this was always the goal. Always the plan."

"What plan?"

"An Elder God made flesh," Armstrong said. "An Elder God brought back."

Georgie tried to slide to her left to get to the door, but another tendril shot out, blocking her path. She tried to go to the right and the same thing happened. The grey mass creeped closer to her and she screamed.

"Please, Daryl, don't!"

"Daryl is gone, George," Armstrong said. "Daryl was just a vessel. This is a god, you see. A hungry god. Daryl was weak and stupid."

At this last phrase, the grey mass stopped and retreated slightly. A low rumble began to shake the room, and the grey mass vibrated. It felt like an earthquake, but Georgie didn't think that was the case.

From within the grey mass came a sound like a flattened tuba rising in volume. Along with the sound, the shaking increased. Georgie managed to get to her feet and the mass continued to pull away from her. She staggered over to the door and tried to open it, but it was locked.

"Damn you, Armstrong! Let me out!"

The PA speaker crackled.

"You don't really think that's going to happen, do you?" Armstrong said. "You've pretty much become the newest thing in the experiment."

Georgie began furiously pounding on the door, screaming. Her voice was eventually drowned out by the sound coming from the grey mass. Chunks the ceiling began to fall. They landed on the tile, which was also cracking. The ceiling chunks that landed on the grey mass were absorbed into it.

Georgie stopped screaming to look behind her and saw that the grey mass was trying to form into a different shape. It was pulling itself together, it seemed, and the loud tuba sound was starting to change pitch. The low bass rumble wasn't so low, and it started to sound less like a tuba. It almost sounded to Georgie like...

"Daryl?"

The sound changed to a sputter and almost sounded like a word.

"What are you trying to say?" Georgie asked. "You're still in there, aren't you?"

"Why isn't it eating you?" Armstrong said over the speakers.

The sputtering continued as the grey mass tried to form a different shape. It was mostly in one place now, almost like a ball of cookie dough. The shaking was starting to subside, but the room was still shaking. Georgie, still terrified, moved closer to the mass to look at it.

"It's reforming," Georgie said aloud. "Daryl is trying to put himself back together."

"Bullshit," Armstrong said. "How the hell do you know?"

The grey mass, which was now a large grey ball, began to reform itself into something that looked slightly human. There were two leg-like things and a discernible torso, two malformed arms and a large blob where a head would go. It twitched and pulsed, and was now starting to sound more human. It sounded like it was saying the letter O.

"Daryl, can you hear me?" Georgie asked. She reached a hand out toward it. A grey stumpy arm-thing reached out in return as it continued to twitch and pulse.

"It's not Daryl, stupid," Armstrong hissed. "Daryl is dead."

Upon hearing this, the grey, twitching, changing thing reacted. The reaching arm-thing dropped to its side, and a gaping maw appeared on the head-like ball on the top. It was a crude mouth, and although the sound was coming from the entire mass, the mouth was meant to be the focal point.

"NAAAAAT!" it boomed. "NAAAAAAT DEEEEEAAADAAAAH!"

Although the sound was deafening, it was clear enough to Georgie, who stood with her hands over her ears.

"I think Daryl disagrees with you, Phoebe."

"FEEEEEEEEEBEEE!" said the Daryl-thing.

7

Dr. Phoebe Armstrong didn't hear the bastardized version of her first name come through the intercom system, but felt it come through the wall. She looked through the two-way glass at the grey mass that had once been Daryl—apparently still *was* Daryl—and shuddered.

How could he still be in there? This process was specifically designed to overtake the host and eradicate it completely. That was the whole point of the density, literally consuming every facet of the original host until all that remained was the beautiful Void.

...the Goat with a thousand young...

In lieu of the beautiful Void, however, goddamn Daryl was still hanging in there for some reason.

And whatever was left of him was pissed.

Every fiber of her being was screaming at her to run as she watched this living God on the other side of the glass. This was both everything she'd ever wanted and nothing like what she'd expected. It was horrifyingly beautiful, this thing she created. She watched it try to reform itself to resemble the human host from which it had spawned and fail.

Perhaps the Void was trying to release the imprint of Daryl, and this was its way of exorcising the human stain. She smiled at this thought and decided she would sit down to watch this transformation to the end. This was a miracle she was watching, after all. A miracle of her own design.

She was a Godmother in the very literal sense.

"FEEEEEEEEEBEEE!"

Her smile disappeared. A large grey lump slammed against the reinforced plexiglass. It splintered and bowed in, coming within a foot of Armstrong's face. She screamed and threw herself backward, landing on the floor.

The lump pulled back, taking the broken web of plexiglass along with it. Armstrong looked in wide-eyed horror as the chunk of plexiglass was absorbed into the Void. She began to scoot backward as the Void vibrated, pulsed, and moved toward the new opening.

"FEEEEEEEEEBEEE!" it repeated.

Again Armstrong screamed as the Void—her creation, her child—wrapped itself around her legs. The tendrils of grey continued to envelop her as her vocal cords were strained to failure. She made desperate pained mewling sounds as over half of her body was not only covered in the grey flesh, but absorbed as well. It wasn't painful, but that didn't take away Armstrong's awareness of what was happening. She clawed desperately at the grey matter until her hands were taken and absorbed. She became aware that she could hear in her head what the Void was thinking.

Mostly it was hatred toward her, and that didn't stop the urge to scream as she slowly became part of the Void. She would become the Void along with Daryl, and as she began to relax, that one word...Void...began to ring in her head. She stopped fighting and allowed herself to become a God.

To become.

8

Georgie watched the damned thing consume Armstrong, and although she wasn't sad to see her go, Armstrong was the only one who had any inkling as to exactly what the hell was happening. Georgie was still in a locked room with a mutated thing that just ate the only person that had any idea of what to do about it.

She stood watching the Daryl-thing half in and half out of the room. It began to ooze back into the exam room. She noticed that the mass of it hadn't gotten any bigger, but it was moving slower.

And moving toward her.

"Daryl, just listen, okay?" Georgie pleaded. "I can help you."

"DAAAARRRLLLLFEEEEEEBEEEE!"

Georgie was now backing away from it as it came closer and closer. She watched carefully as it was fully intact and following her as a lumpy ball.

Not even trying to look human anymore, Georgie thought.

The more it moved across the floor, the more the floor creaked and cracked. She wondered what would happen if the floor collapsed under its weight as she tried to get Daryl far enough away from the control room to try and escape through there.

The Daryl-thing seemed to sense this and divided itself into smaller, lumpier balls to fill in the space between Georgie and the control room.

"Bastard," Georgie said.

"BAAASSAAAAD!"

"Daryl, I have to get to the control room to help you. Can you let me through?"

The Daryl-thing divided again into four smaller balls, all connected by a thinning grey tendril, forming a semi-circle around Georgie. Each one was shaping what looked like a head. A mouth-like slit formed on each one, and although the sound came from everywhere, the faux mouths moved in unison.

"NOT DAAAAARRRRRYLLL NOT DAARRRLLLLFEEEEEEBEEEE." It wasn't as loud or as booming, but it was still coming from the entire thing that was Daryl.

"Okay," Georgie said, putting her hands up, trying to address all four identical versions. "You're not Daryl or Phoebe. Who are you, then?"

All four mouths opened, and a pained bellow came from everywhere. Each mass throbbed, and the four things reconverted into each other. It was both repulsive and fascinating to Georgie. She took the opportunity to make a break for the control room. The bellow began to clarify, and the volume reached a quiet level. The thing spoke a single word.

"Void."

The sound of the voice stopped Georgie dead in her tracks. She had made it into the control room and turned to look at what had just named itself.

"Void," it said again. Georgie thought it sounded like it was trying the name out to see if it liked it. She watched it pulse and move; it seemed like it was preening. The pale grey pallor seemed to darken as it moved around the lab, and a low humming began to emit from it.

It bumped into the plexiglass tank and Georgie watched as the thing...Void...began to cover it and consume it whole. Within a minute, there was a circle-shaped exposure for the steel-reinforced floor beneath.

Georgie heard the control room door open behind her and a sudden gasp. She turned and saw one of Dr. Armstrong's lab assistants, a pretty young woman, not quite thirty, with a hand covering her mouth. She was still in her hazmat suit from earlier. She was also carrying a small pint of fresh strawberries.

"What the hell is that?"

Georgie turned back to the Void, which was now consuming a side lab table, still humming and now repeating its name like a mantra.

The thing stopped and began to move toward the control room.

Georgie regarded the young lab assistant and her strawberries.

"Void," it said, now adding, "God."

"Apparently, that is Void," Georgie said. "And God. I see you've brought it a snack."

"Um, Dr. Phoebe thought Daryl might like...actual strawberries."

Void heard the word and began to twitch. It moved closer to the control room.

"God. Void. God. Void."

Void was directly outside the control room. It reached a dark grey tentacle out, found the intercom control panel, and began to absorb it. The steel floor beneath began to groan from the weight.

Georgie chuckled and patted the assistant on the shoulder as she pushed past her. She made her way to the control room door and opened it.

"Good luck with that," Georgie said, and walked quickly out of the control room.

9

The lab assistant watched Georgie leave and looked quickly back as the dark grey thing that she thought was still Daryl came within inches of her.

"Um, do you know where Dr. Phoebe is?"

She held out the pint of strawberries.

A thick tendril slapped the strawberries out of the assistant's hand. She gave a small yelp and noticed the tendril was now wrapping itself up around her arm.

"Void," it said. "God."

"I'm, uh, Cheryl," the assistant replied. "Hi."

MRS. MORRISON'S PIE

Mrs. Morrison was too busy to die. Not that she didn't take the threat of death seriously, but she didn't have the time (or the patience) to wait around for it either. The urge to finish the things she had begun was overwhelming sometimes, but she had always been one to satisfy her urges.

It was an early, cold, and snowy Thursday morning. With two pies in the oven and three grandkids still in bed sleeping, Mrs. Morrison did not, in fact, have any time to die. She thought this as she hummed a very out-of-key version of one of her granddaughter Penny's favorite songs. For the life of her, she couldn't say what the song was, or who sang it, but the chorus was very catchy. She reminded herself to ask Penny what the song was, and maybe if she could send her the song on her 'puter. She was still trying to figure out how to use it, but she was getting better every day. Penny, who was twelve, seemed to really enjoy introducing her grandmother to new and useful things on the old Acer computer that surprised everyone by still working.

"You need some new tech, Gram," Penny had said the day before. "I can totally trick out your computer if it weren't so..."

"Old," Mrs. Morrison said, smiling. "If it weren't so old, is that right?"

Penny laughed.

"I was going to say 'out of date,'" she said, hugging her grandmother. "Old is one thing, but out of date is a lot different."

She hugged her granddaughter back tightly.

Mrs. Morrison thought of this as she opened her oven to see how the pies were coming along. She felt the wave of heat in her face, and the smell followed. The pies smelled delicious, and she smiled. They were both buttermilk and were still not brown enough on the tops. She closed the oven door and set the timer for another five minutes. She looked at the old Kitty Cat pendulum clock on her wall, its tail beating out the seconds.

It was a few minutes after 3AM.

Five minutes would do just fine.

The coffee maker began to spit out the final bits of water into the now-full pot next to the sink. She went to the fridge and pulled out a small creamer in the shape of a very cute cow—a recent Christmas present from her youngest granddaughter, Prudence. Little Pru had gotten the money by borrowing from Penny and Paula...and a little extra from Mrs. Morrison on the side. She had picked out the creamer, blissfully unaware that her grandmother didn't use creamer. Still, it was so cute, and today, at least, she was going to use it.

She made sure the cream was still good (you couldn't trust the grocery store sometimes) and put it on the little table next to the fridge. Everything except for the pies was ready. Now, just the waiting.

She glanced at the clock, and before the time registered, there was a very gentle knock on the door.

It was time.

She walked carefully down the hall to the front door. Through the thin curtain she could see the silhouette of a woman standing there, moonlight behind her. She could see the snow being blown around by gusts of wind and she smiled.

She unlatched the lock carefully and opened the door, standing back to allow the visitor inside.

The woman stepped in quickly and closed the door behind her, then turned and faced Mrs. Morrison.

She stood well-dressed in a black pinstriped business skirt with a jacket. She had a pale complexion and deep red hair pulled into a tight bun. Thin-rimmed spectacles hung from the tip of her nose, giving her the look of a schoolmarm. She appeared to be about forty-five, but her eyes seemed much older. She gave Mrs. Morrison a genuine smile.

"How lovely to see you again, Mrs. Morrison."

"Very likewise, Ms. Black."

"It's Blake, actually," came the response, with a hint of a laugh.

"Of course it is," Mrs. Morrison replied, equally amused by the old joke.

Ms. Blake didn't appear to have a single snowflake or bit of moisture on her person. Mrs. Morrison noticed this as well, but said nothing except, "Please, come in."

Ms. Blake nodded and walked down the hallway to the kitchen as if she knew her way around the house. Mrs. Morrison watched as Ms. Blake regarded each picture on the wall, then stopped at one in particular.

"This is new," Blake said. "How very adorable."

The picture in question, Mrs. Morrison saw, was the one of her three granddaughters from last year's Christmas with her son, James, and his lovely wife, Francine. They were all in their pajamas, except for Pru, who was mostly naked, and all of them were laughing. Someone had stuck a huge bow on Pru's head.

"That was taken last year," Mrs. Morrison said, smiling. "Before the accident."

"Yes," Blake said. "I was very sorry to hear about that, Mrs. Morrison." She looked at her host.

Mrs. Morrison nodded. "I've made coffee," she said quietly.

Blake nodded and continued into the kitchen. As Mrs. Morrison walked past the picture, she absently brushed her fingers across it and followed her guest.

Blake took a look around and inhaled. "Buttermilk pie?" she asked, a smile poking at the corner of her mouth.

"I recall it was your favorite of all the pies," Mrs. Morrison said. "Please, have a seat."

Blake sat and put her purse on the floor next to her as Mrs. Morrison walked to the coffee pot, turning off the oven on her way.

"It certainly remains a favorite," Blake said. "Although you've made some pretty wonderful pies over the years."

Mrs. Morrison returned to the table with two coffee cups with saucers in one hand and the coffee pot in the other. She placed the cups on the table, and Blake took the top one. She placed it in front of the empty seat and smiled. Mrs. Morrison poured coffee in Blake's cup and then her own. She set the pot on the kitchen island in the center of the room and grabbed an oven mitt.

She opened the oven and pulled out the pies one at a time to cool on the island, then tossed the oven mitt between the pies and sat down.

Blake was holding the cow creamer and smiling. "Gift from the youngest?" she asked.

"Of course," Mrs. Morrison said proudly.

"Absolutely darling," Blake said genuinely, pouring cream into her cup and watching as it came out of the little cow's nose. She chuckled, snorting a little. She offered to pour some into Mrs. Morrison's cup.

"No, thank you."

Blake put the creamer down.

The two women looked at each other, letting the silence sink in before either raised a cup to drink.

Blake sighed.

"Tired?" Mrs. Morrison asked.

"You know that I am," Blake said.

"And yet, you come each year," Mrs. Morrison said, taking her cup and sipping.

"I have to," Blake replied. "You know that I do."

"It would be something akin to a miracle if, perhaps, you didn't," Mrs. Morrison said. "Maybe just one year, skip it. You certainly don't come for the pie."

At this, Blake laughed.

"Well, it certainly is a consolation," she said.

"Before we get started, I have to know something," Mrs. Morrison said. "Did you know?"

For a moment, Blake didn't know what she was talking about, but she caught on rather quickly.

"Your son and his wife," Blake said.

"Yes," Mrs. Morrison said, nearly through her teeth. "Did you know it was going to happen? Was it you?"

Blake took another sip of coffee.

"It wasn't me," she said, putting the cup down. "I promise. I found out after the fact. I only have one..." Blake struggled to find the words.

"Victim?" Mrs. Morrison offered.

"No, not victim," Blake replied. "You're hardly that."

"My Harold was."

"Neither was he. You know how this works."

"Yes, I do. More than most. I just needed to know it wasn't you, that's all. I cursed your name for quite some time, forgive me, but I didn't think it was you. Still, I needed to be sure."

"I understand," Blake said. "But it doesn't change anything."

"Oh, but it does."

"How so?"

"Our meeting last year. Do you recall?"

"You know that I do."

"Then you know why I've changed my mind."

Blake sighed again.

"Sigh all you want, but it's simply not going to happen," Mrs. Morrison said.

"How long have we been doing this?" Blake asked.

"A while."

"Thirty-five years. That's how long. No one has ever gone that long. Ever."

"I have," Mrs. Morrison said, smirking.

"Yes, you. Only you."

"Well, I'm on a roll."

"So it would seem. But you can't do this forever."

Mrs. Morrison was going to say something and then stopped herself.

"You think you can," Blake said.

Mrs. Morrison shook her head.

"No, and I don't want to either, but this is different. Much different. And it's not my fault."

"How do you figure?"

"You," Mrs. Morrison said, sounding angry for the first time. "You and your...kind. Taking and taking, always. On your terms. Only your terms."

"Except for you," Blake said.

"Because I know better. Because I'm stronger. Because you goddamn robbed me," Mrs. Morrison said through her teeth.

Blake said nothing.

"And you know it's true. That's why I'm still here. That's why I'm still not coming. And because of what you did, I'm not going this year either."

"I told you, it wasn't me."

"It was you. Your ilk. Whatever you call yourselves."

"We maintain..."

"Balance," Mrs. Morrison interrupted. "Your goddamn balance. You don't want chaos, in spite of the fact that chaos is all you do. Chaos, grief, sadness. How is that balance?"

"There is no light without dark," Blake said without conviction.

Mrs. Morrison sniffed.

"Whether you believe that or not, Mrs. Morrison, that is balance. For there to be joy, there must be sadness; for there to be life, there must be death."

"What about *my* balance? What about the balance of those three little girls? Can you honestly tell me that there is a good thing that can come from them losing both of their parents so early in their lives? Was there some kind of balance when you took my Harold from me and left me to raise my boy alone? And then you took him too? Where's the balance there?"

"The scope of the balance isn't for me to say," Blake said.

"Totes bullshit answer," Mrs. Morrison said.

"What?"

Mrs. Morrison glared at Blake for a moment, then softened.

"It's something my Penny says when I tell her she can't do something," she said. "I'll say the dreaded 'Because I said so,' and she'll say, 'Totes bullshit answer, Grandma.' Under her breath, of course."

Blake looked at her stone-faced for a moment and then began to laugh. After a moment, Mrs. Morrison did as well.

"Mrs. Morrison, I don't know what to say to you. Even after thirty-five years, I don't know how to explain balance like this to you. I've tried."

"I know you have. I remember the first time you said it was like trying to explain the color blue to an ant."

Blake laughed again.

"That was where I made my first mistake with you."

"Quite," Mrs. Morrison said, getting up. "I think it's time for pie, don't you?"

Blake nodded.

Mrs. Morrison took two pie plates down from a shelf over the sink and placed them on the now somewhat crowded kitchen island. She also grabbed her pie cutter, which was another Christmas gift (this one from Paula, who was somewhat of a growing math legend in her school. She had found the pie cutter and server online that was the shape of the word "pi," which Mrs. Morrison found endlessly amusing.)

"So, you're tired of this?" Mrs. Morrison asked. "Well, I am too. And because of that, I am willing to make you a deal."

Blake seemed surprised. "A deal?"

"Yes, a deal. No more games. No more early morning visits, no more arguments about balance."

Blake nodded.

"You interested?" Mrs. Morrison asked.

"Yes, very much so."

"Good. Here's your pie. Take a bite first and then we'll...negotiate."

She placed the pie and a fork in front of Blake, who greedily began to eat. Mrs. Morrison sat down and did the same.

"Delicious as usual, Mrs. Morrison," Blake said.

"Thank you. More coffee?"

"No, no thank you," Blake said. "Tell me about this deal."

"You're excited about this, aren't you?"

Blake paused before answering. "I...wouldn't say excited. Interested, perhaps. As you know, we aren't exactly supposed to make deals per se, but..."

"But I'm an exception."

Blake nodded.

"And tell me why I'm an exception."

Blake's face turned red and she shook her head.

"No, after this long, you can tell me. I already know why, but for this deal to work, you have to tell me."

Blake slumped. "Because I've always...felt guilty."

"Yes. Yes, you have, because you know I've been right."

"No, not right," Blake corrected. "That's not exactly the right word. You were...honest."

"What do you mean I wasn't right?"

Blake shoved another piece of pie into her mouth. "You weren't upset that I took your husband. You were upset that you couldn't go with him."

Mrs. Morrison looked stunned.

"You didn't want to be left to raise your son alone. You were afraid. So I was surprised when I came back for you and you refused."

Mrs. Morrison allowed a single tear to fall from her eye.

"I suppose that's true, to a certain degree," Mrs. Morrison said. "It was a selfish thought, I'll admit that. But after I had time to think about it and you showed up, I couldn't do it. I wouldn't do that to my son. He was devastated. He didn't deserve that twice, and you knew it."

"I suppose I did," Blake said. "And that's how we began this...tradition?"

"It was nice to know some of the little legends were true," Mrs. Morrison said, smirking.

"What was the first game? Do you remember?"

"Jenga," Mrs. Morrison said proudly. "I beat the pants off you."

"You have always beaten the pants off me, so to speak."

"Every time."

"I know you cheated on most of them."

Mrs. Morrison looked away for a moment. "I'm not going to admit to that," she said quietly.

Blake smiled. "You don't have to," she said. "Because I allowed it."

Mrs. Morrison looked at Blake.

"You did?"

"I did," Blake replied, biting another piece of pie. "Like I said, I felt guilty. But I'd always hoped that you'd eventually get tired."

Mrs. Morrison nodded.

"Last year, I got tired. I was going to come with you this year. Honest. But I can't now."

"Why not?"

Mrs. Morrison raised an eyebrow.

"My granddaughters need me," she said. "It's not about what I want anymore. It's about what they need, and they need me. I'm the only living relative they have, and I'll be good and goddamned if they're going to be raised as wards of the state."

"And so, you have a deal?"

"I do."

"Well, let's hear it. Maybe I will have some more coffee. But allow me to get it, please."

Blake stood up and collected the coffee pot from the island before Mrs. Morrison could protest. Blake poured a little into Mrs. Morrison's cup and then refilled her own. She sat back down, resting the pot on the small table.

"Thank you," Mrs. Morrison said.

"Please, continue."

She took a sip of her coffee, and Mrs. Morrison cleared her throat.

"I will come with you. Free and clear, no games of chance, no argument. We won't even have to play a game tonight. But I have three conditions."

"Only three?"

"Only three."

Blake waited as Mrs. Morrison took a sip of coffee.

"One," she began. "If any of the girls are on some list to balance anything, they are to be removed so they can live a long, full life."

Blake nodded.

"Two. I wish to go in my sleep. I don't want to know the date or the time. But I don't want to suffer. Please, no long-term illness. Just take me like you took my Harold."

"And three?"

A small grin formed on Mrs. Morrison's face. "You will wait twelve years to do it."

"Twelve?" Blake asked.

"Yes, twelve. No more, no less. In twelve years, Pru, my youngest, will be eighteen and likely in college. Each of the girls has rather substantial inheritances from both of their parents and from me when they turn eighteen. They'll be set for the rest of their lives once I die. Pru deserves to at least be an adult before I die. I want to see her graduate high school. I want all three of them to have as happy a childhood as I can provide for them before I get too old. I don't want them to have to care for an old woman. Twelve years accomplishes that rather nicely, I think."

Blake said nothing. She just looked at Mrs. Morrison.

"No tricks," Mrs. Morrison added. "I'll be, what, seventy-eight? Still able to do things, right before things go south for an old woman. I'll go quietly in my sleep. It's a bargain."

"I'm not sure about this, Mrs. Morrison," Blake said finally.

"I could set up the Monopoly board now," Mrs. Morrison said. "I don't have to cheat to kick your ass in that game for all the times we've played it."

Blake chuckled and blushed a little.

"You wouldn't have to come back here for the next twelve years," she continued. "And once I go, I'm sure I can find a way to make you a pie in the after-wherever."

Blake smiled warmly and shook her head. "I'm afraid there is no pie there."

Mrs. Morrison scoffed. "No pie? Jesus."

Both ladies laughed.

"I'm going to tell you something, Mrs. Morrison," Blake said. "I saw your Harold, after he came with me. He is a very nice man. I went to him to ask his advice about you once. All he did was laugh and say, 'Good luck with that.' I asked him what he meant, and he said, 'My Cheri will come with you when she's good and ready, not before.'"

"He said that?"

"He did."

Mrs. Morrison smiled. "No one knew me better."

Blake took the last bite of pie and washed it down with the remains of her coffee.

"Mrs. Morrison, the pie and the company were wonderful, as always. I'm going to miss you."

Blake stood up. Mrs. Morrison stood up as well, but she looked puzzled.

"Miss me?"

"Yes, I am going to miss you. Mostly, I will miss your pies."

Mrs. Morrison's mouth hung open.

"So, I have a condition myself, if you don't mind."

Blake explained her condition, and Mrs. Morrison nodded.

Then she smiled.

Blake walked to Mrs. Morrison and did something she had never done in thirty-five years.

She embraced her tightly.

"I will see you in twelve years, Mrs. Morrison. No more, no less."

Mrs. Morrison reached around and hugged the woman back. "Thank you, Ms. Blake. Oh, thank you."

Blake whispered into Mrs. Morrison's ear. "Actually, my name is Ms. Black." She chuckled. "I just hated that you guessed it all those years ago, Mrs. Morrison."

Mrs. Morrison giggled, still hugging. "Thank you so much."

"You should try and get some sleep, Mrs. Morrison. I can show myself out."

"Nonsense," Mrs. Morrison said. "Come with me."

The two women walked quietly through the hallway, arms linked, until they came to the door.

"Well, I guess this is it," Mrs. Morrison said.

Blake smiled at her.

"Mrs. Morrison, you have always been a woman who likes to finish things that you begin," she said. "And you have finished this splendidly. I wish I would have known you under different circumstances."

"Perhaps one day we will, Ms. Blake," she replied. "And then you can call me Cheri."

"I'd like that very much."

Blake walked out the front door and disappeared before Mrs. Morrison had completely closed the door. There was nothing but snow, wind, and moonlight.

A few hours later, a certain Miss Prudence Morrison padded carefully down the stairs and into the kitchen, where she saw her grandmother fussing over her beloved kitchen island. The kitchen looked neater than usual, but out of the corner of her eye, she noticed two coffee cups on the little table next to the fridge.

And the cow creamer.

Pru squealed with delight.

"You used the little cow!" she said. Mrs. Morrison whirled around and began to laugh.

"I most certainly did, Pru!" she said as the little girl ran full steam to her. "And it was absolutely adorable!"

"Did it look funny? Did it look cool when the cream came out of his nose?" Pru asked.

"It's a *she*, darling. Cows are ladies, bulls are guys."

"But was it funny?"

Mrs. Morrison hugged her granddaughter tightly. "I'm still laughing about it, yes."

"Yay!"

"What do you want for breakfast?"

"I smell pie."

"You want pie?"

"I always want pie."

"Funny you should say that. Go have a seat over there."

Pru walked herself over to the little table and pulled out a seat.

"Do you want the dirty cups, Grandma?"

"That would be wonderful, thank you."

Pru collected the coffee cups (leaving the saucers, of course, because in spite of being told otherwise, she didn't believe cups and saucers belonged together) carefully and walked them over to the sink, where Mrs. Morrison set them down. Pru then hustled over to the table and hopped up on a chair.

Mrs. Morrison cut a piece of buttermilk pie for Pru and also grabbed a small cup of milk. She set both on the table in front of Pru, then grabbed the little cow.

"Watch this," she said as she poured a little cream into Pru's cup of milk. The cream streamed out of the cow's nose and Pru laughed. Unlike her sisters, her laugh was unrestrained and wild as a child's laugh should be (at least, that was Mrs. Morrison's opinion.)

"Now, let me tell you what you're doing today. I think you're going to like it."

"Just me?" Pru asked through a mouth full of pie.

"Well, your sisters too. You're all going to learn how to make pie."

Pru's eyes went wide. "Really? I mean, real pie? Not that crap pie with the light bulb?"

"Don't say crap," Mrs. Morrison said. (This was an argument started last year when her son had gotten Pru a toy baking oven for her birthday. This was also when she learned the word "crap.")

"Sorry."

"And yes, real pie."

Pru smiled.

"Awesome."

"I'm glad you think so," Mrs. Morrison said. "Because I need you three to help Grandma with a favor for a friend of mine."

CAROL'S CHRISTMAS

WITH SCARLETT R. ALGEE

Hey you. You all there? Just nod if you understand me. Oh sugar, I said nod up and down... There you are. You remember me? No?

Aw, baby girl...I'm Carol. Remember from school? All floodin' back yet? Carol Dumas.

I was here visiting my folks, in a manner of speaking. Anywho, I made a stop to visit you all special. See, I'm what some folks would call a serial killer. Except, not a conventional one. I prefer *murderer*. Serial murderer. It sure don't roll off the tongue, to be sure, but it's a bit more accurate. And lucky you, darlin', you're my Christmas present!

Well, that's getting a little ahead of ourselves, isn't it?

There's very little forethought to when it's time for me to take someone out. Not *out* in the causal sense. Out as in like a light. All the way. It's all spontaneous.

Anywho...

After thirty years, my favorite kill is the last of the year. Well, right next to the New Year's kill. Every kill in between is great too, but the Christmas kill is special.

Which means you're special. Extra special.

Why?

Well, I'm glad you asked...if only with your eyes. Hahaha

Every good Christmas tradition should, and does, have a good story attached to it. As it so happens, I have three. Now you just lie there all properly bound and gagged and I will regale you with your Christmas stories. Tucked in? Good! I hope you like these three stories.

They will literally be the last thing you hear.

1.

Past Presents

December 2, 1987

Dear Diary,

I woke up this morning a sixteen-year-old. Whoopity doo. And what I got for my birthday is this journal. God knows why—I didn't ask for it. I didn't ask for anything. I don't care. I don't write and I don't want to write about what I don't care about. I don't know why I don't care. It's funny, it's like I actively don't care about anything. Like, at all. I have friends at school, but no best friends. Not even actual friends. Just people I know. People I grew up with. A lot of them are just... I don't know. Messed up. They write poems, if you can believe that. "High School Suicide Locker" poetry, I've called it, and it seems to fit. It's all about boys, which is hilarious. Nobody writes anything real. It's all stupid. Everything.

What am I supposed to put in this thing? My inner thoughts? Boys I like? Bad mouth my parents?

My parents are okay, actually. They love me. They always make sure I'm okay—well, they ask. I have no reason to think they don't care. They do. The problem is me. As I get older, I'm finding the problem with me is simply *me*. And I don't even think it's a big problem. I just simply do not care.

So, this journal may not be updated very much because I don't care. I might care more if I got to stay home from school today, but not likely. Time to go.

December 3, 1987

I'm not calling you Dear Diary. I'm writing to myself—no need for formalities.

Something interesting happened. Well, interesting for me anyway. After I wrote, I found myself thinking about it and rereading it. Maybe I'll keep it up a bit. It's something I guess I enjoyed? I dunno.

I told my mom and she nearly exploded with emotion. (Maybe there's a better way to word that because, ewww.) In any case, I certainly felt something for a change. Maybe I'll keep this up. We will see.

I've been sixteen for a full day. No noticeable difference from fifteen.

December 4, 1987

It's Friday afternoon and I'm on the bus ride home. I'll have to write quick. I got into a small fistfight. No, really! I was waiting in the hall for the bell to ring—it was a really long day—when Danielle Dolce decided to choose this moment to mouth off to me. Why? I have zero idea. I'm pretty quiet. I don't make any waves and I just drift along unnoticed for the most part.

But not today.

She walked by and shoved me against the lockers, face first. To be honest, it didn't hurt, but I did drop all my books. I turned to her and she just stood there, laughing with her stupid-ass friends. I must have scowled at her, because she asked in her very best school bully voice, "What are you looking at?"

I have a few answers for that question that I think are pretty funny. You know, like, "Not much," or something sarcastic, right?

I couldn't remember any of them. I don't really know what happened, but something in me just kind of switched on, I guess. I jumped on her and just started punching her in the face. Again and again.

I'm looking at my hand and it's raw and still bleeding a little. It should hurt, but it doesn't. It feels...awesome? That's a little weird, but I feel good. Like, really good. Maybe it's because I didn't take any shit from someone, or, I don't know. But I felt something. That's good, right?

I'll have to explain this to my parents, and I'll probably leave out the part where it felt good.

I'll probably be in trouble, but I don't know. I'll just enjoy it for now.

-later-

Oh
My
God
Not grounded. Not in trouble. I explained everything to my folks and they were proud of my for defending myself. My hand still hurts, but it also still feels good. I'm glad I wrote this down because I reread it five times already. It feels that good.

December 25, 1987

So I haven't written anything in a while, but a lot has happened. For one thing, I have a new reputation in the school. Not as a slut, which is kind of nice since that's what seems to be the biggest thing girls get tagged with... No, I'm now known as a tough chick apparently. I've hit the former school bully girl three times now. She keeps screwing with me, although I think after this last time she's done.

However, this time I got in trouble. I know why, and I suppose I deserved it. But not as much as she deserved it.

A couple incidents were a little bit low key, just a shove here and there, a shitty comment. But this last one. I guess I reacted a little more intensely than I should have...

We were playing floor hockey in the gym. She's in goal and I'm trying slap my puck in and she calls me a bitch. I laugh at her and make the goal. I laugh harder.

Then she called me something a little worse than a bitch. The one with the C? Words don't bother me really. It's all context, or so my father tells me. But this... I don't know. I suppose I sort of snapped, because I ran at her with the hockey stick. I full-on swung it at her head, and it connected on the side of her neck. It didn't knock her over, so I just started swinging away like the stick was an ax. Nothing focused really, I just started smacking her with it again and again. She was stuck in the goal and fell down, curling into a ball inside the goal.

I started kicking her. I threw the stick and put both hands on the top bar of the goal to get better angles while I kicked her. Funny thing I noticed was that I wasn't angry. I mean, it wasn't the first time I hit her. I guess I would have had to be, right? But the more I hurt her, the better I felt. It was like taking a deep breath and exhaling slowly...

I wonder if there's something wrong with me, because I felt absolutely fantastic.

So, I got suspended right before winter break. I guess two weeks off before having two more weeks off was supposed to be a punishment. Dummies...

The folks were a little upset, but as of this morning, it's a damn fine time here at the house. Aside from clothes and stuff, they got me a membership at a karate school. That should make stuff interesting. It's supposed to teach discipline.

It couldn't hurt.

April 5, 1990

Well, look what I found! There are a few years of missing items in the diary here, y'all. (And a new twang. Unexpected side effect of going to school in Georgia.) So, what to update y'all with first?

I'm a black belt in karate, and jiu-jitsu, and working on Aikido. I like martial arts.

It's very good for discipline. It's also really good for big expenditures of energy, and I can really hurt people who have it coming. And I can hurt them for longer periods of time.

Sadistic? I don't think so. I've learned to be careful. But I will tell you something, I still enjoy hurting people. I've just gotten better at it. Now, before you judge me (I'm still not calling you Dear Diary), I'm not crazy. I'm only hurting people who deserve it. Really. This school is full of people needing a whoopin' or worse.

I'm still deciding what kind of hurt "worse" is, but I think I'll be able to figure it out eventually. It's funny though...in my criminal psych course, I'm becoming aware that a lot of what I harbor could be considered signs of some kind of criminal leanings. I do have what the folks call a violent streak, but I've learned to keep that under hat, so to speak. That's what the martial arts was for initially. Good ole' Dani and the hockey stick probably would have still happened...but control is an even better coping tool. Especially when you want to dish out more hurt.

I find that I like the hurting part. Doesn't mean I'm crazy or deviant. I mean, I'd know, I reckon; I'm pulling an A in the class!

I'm really glad I found this diary. I'll have to thank Mom.

May 15, 1990

I killed someone tonight. I'm not going to freak out, but I am going to tell my little book (you, in other words), and I have to put down how I feel.

I feel alive. I feel like this is what love should feel like...but love for yourself. I don't know if that makes sense at all. Maybe that's why I need to write this down. The details don't matter. The person, we'll call her One. She was really in the wrong place at the wrong time. I don't hate her then or now, but I also don't feel either way about it. Maybe that's cold. I hadn't planned it, but what is fascinating to me is how rational and calculated it became once I decided to do it.

I really think that the process suits me. I don't feel any guilt and I am so alive right now. I can't tell anyone, of course. Ever. Just you. And I'll be burning you soon. But, until I do, I'm telling you...this is a vocation. This is a rebirth of sorts. I went to a revival meeting down here, and watching how all the other folks reacted...that's what I feel on the inside. There isn't going to be any swooning or fainting on my end, and if ever there was proof there ain't no God, I reckon I might be it.

She didn't go quietly, I'll tell you that much. I need to learn how to refine the process. Strip it down to its basic elements. (An engineer or an architect?) Can you reverse-engineer a murder?

I guess we'll find out, y'all.

Anywho, I reckon this lil' diary needs to become ashes before it becomes a liability.

It was fun while it lasted.

—Carol

2.

Invisible Future

I see myself one day in the near time to come, but different versions of me. Sometimes all at once, sometimes changing mid-thought.

There is no way one can peer into the future because, really, there is no future. Just the here. Just the now. Just the me.

Just the you.

It doesn't matter who you are. Danielle Dolce had a future. Probably imagined it for years before her actual future abruptly punched her clock without warning.

To be fair, there had always been a warning. It's the same warning we all get. Some of us hear it and some of us choose not to hear it, but that warning is always there, big as Jesus.

You aren't promised to be here later.

No one promised her, and if they did, well, they were lying.

One day, I'll either get caught or I won't. Sometimes I think about confessing, although that makes me laugh. It's possible that it would make other people laugh too. That's how good I've gotten.

If I filmed every single murder I've done, narration voice over the entire goddamn thing, they'd still have to think about it. And that isn't arrogance. That is a cold fact. That's pride in a job well done. Earned, y'all.

When I killed that girl in '90, it was like learning to fly under own power. The first time. Popped my own cherry, as it were. Even when I had sex for the first time, one week later, it wasn't half as satisfying. Like sex, it got better each time I did it, but nothing is better than the first kill.

That girl in 1990 was legitimately in the wrong place at the wrong time. At least, as far as she may have been concerned. I thought her place and time was perfect. A gift from the universe. Called me a cunt, which, to be cliche, is a trigger word for a lot of women. I reckon it was for me. Hell, still is, as far as I'm concerned.

It ignited a fire in me that simply will not extinguish. It is a glorious fire that I want to burn until I die at a ripe old age.

You see, there is no legacy I want to leave behind. It's not important that anyone know what I was other than Carol Dumas, architect and gardening enthusiast. Hot yoga attendee, possible spinster, cat owner. She made a killer buttermilk pie and always was good for great donations to the local church in Lawrenceville, Georgia.

Because, from the look in your eyes, you know. For as long as you live, you know.

That's legacy enough.

That's the here and now.

The you.

The me.

3.

Present, Tense

You nodded off on me. That was rude. Come on and wake up, now.

To be honest, I'm a little surprised that chloroform I picked up online actually worked. It ain't something you can just go buy off the shelf at the corner drugstore anymore, you know?

I guess you really can get anything on the internet these days.

The bleach, the trash bags, the sheet of plastic...none of that was a problem. It's winter and I'm back in town. I'm cleaning house, I'm weatherproofing. It's even gonna be kind of true, when I'm done with you.

Your eyebrows kinda popped up when I said "bleach" and "trash bags."

Interesting.

But I digress. I see you lying there with those big eyes, wondering why. Why you. Why this. Probably why me.

Crying won't get that duct tape loose, just so you know. It's the good stuff. I've had too much practice not to have picked up on people's little tricks by now. So you just sit there—come on, I'll get you up, there you go—and we'll have a little talk. Of sorts. Murderer to helpless victim, like. The you. The me. The why.

The why. Heh. I said you were special, remember? I don't think you know just how much.

I admit, I never really intended to come back here. You can't do what I do, for as long as I've done it, and get comfortable having the same dirt under your feet too long. You learn to like the move.

It wasn't about you, originally.

I didn't expect to get that phone call, you know? The one to my real phone, not one of my burners. Only two people have—had—that number, though neither of 'em ever used it much. So when I saw a call at 10PM that wasn't from one of them, I knew something had gone mightily awry.

This is a hell of a goddamn time of year to find out a drunk driver's killed both your parents.

The first thing I did—after I woke up right good and said yes, yes, of course I'll come, I'm on my way—was smash the fuck out of that phone with a masonry hammer. On the drive down, I dropped the pieces off the interstate bridge. Because I wouldn't need it anymore, and because there's no such thing as too careful.

Not that I've been saying much to my mom and dad these past few years, you know? I couldn't exactly be the dutiful daughter who called in every week, not without leaving a trail. And nobody ever said anything, not Mom, not Dad, but sometimes I think they suspect, just the same.

Suspected. Goddammit. I didn't even really feel much of anything, other than being kind of pissed at how they died. It's been two weeks, and they're both buried, and I'm still just numb with this little glaze of angry, like it's something that'll flake off before too long. It's always been easy to just go numb. But still. My parents, you know? They were decent people. They didn't bother nobody. They didn't deserve that.

They loved me. I'm pretty sure of that. They always looked out for me, and I tried to love them back, some. Back when I was a tot who still thought Santa'd bring me a pony under the Christmas tree, I might have even managed it for a little while. It sure was never their fault that the love thing didn't ever really take with me.

Heh. That pony. I asked every year. Closest I ever got was a goldfish when I was ten. There's not much to love about a goldfish, they just eat those flakes and shit their water and startle when you tap the glass.

Anywho. Smart people, my folks. Figured out I'd made my own self comfortable, so there ain't some big inheritance coming. The house is being sold and the money given to their favorite charity. Which is the Humane Society, in case you wondered.

Oh, I know. Lot o' people'd be real mad, real torn up, losing out like that. But I'm not bothered. Truth be told, I like not having anything to tie me here.

Not after I finish with you, anyway.

You're hyperventilating. Do I need to tell you why that's not good for you? Besides, I'm just coming up on your part in the story...Danielle.

Despite what you might think, I hadn't really thought about you in quite a while. Places to go, people to kill, you know? I just remember that the last time you came up in conversation, my mom said you'd hooked up with Tommy Slate. I remember being surprised that she was surprised. I distinctly remember not being surprised. I figured y'all suited each other. The bitchy school bully and the dumbass dopehead football jock. In fact, I fully expected her to tell me there'd been a shotgun wedding, 'cause I know for damn sure y'all two would've bred a mean little bunch of brats. You've got the kind of blood that runs true.

But I guess Tommy got tired of you fast. More likely, he discovered that he liked the girls who didn't bitch about his pain pills and his nose candy. Least ways, I'm glad he dumped you before he took up the shake and bake method. I'm told he went out with a bang.

At least he was courteous enough to leave you for me.

It almost didn't happen, you know. Us meeting up like this. If I hadn't decided that the middle of the night was a good time to peel the hell out, now that I've stayed long enough to do the right thing by my folks, I wouldn't have needed to pull in to the 24-hour QwikMart for a grape drink and some barbecue chips and one of those five-hour energy shots. And you wouldn't have slouched over the counter and cussed me for disturbing your little 3AM nap.

I honestly never had you pegged as a convenience store clerk, Dani. Never thought you'd be a flunky, just a boss-type in some job where you could rule over people like the queen bitch you always thought you were.

Mighty don't always fall very far, does it?

I knew who you were right away, of course. Kind of surprised me that you didn't recognize me. I know it's been a few years, but I don't reckon I've changed that much, 'cept for maybe my haircut. But you...

I knew your parents had taken you off for some plastic surgery after what I affectionately think of as the "Hockey Stick Incident." And it looks good, it really does. For your age—well, our age, I guess—you can barely tell much of anything happened.

Except that little dent in the bridge of your nose. I'd know that dent anywhere. I should. I put it there.

And I knew right then that you'd be the one this Christmas. Just looking at your face made my hand hurt in that good way again. You know, the one I punched you in the face with the first time? Hot damn, things do come full circle.

And here I am, ready to do a little plastic surgery of my own. I might salvage a decent Christmas for myself after all. I'm sure it's what my folks would want. They always did like to make sure I was okay.

Unlike yours, apparently, since you're the one living out here in the sticks in a trailer.

Oh, don't get me wrong. It's really a nice trailer. Just another one of those things I wouldn't have expected out of you. But hey, that's good. Keeps me on my toes.

It sure as hell wasn't any problem to follow you out here. After you cussed me, I went back to my loaner car and cut the headlights and popped the top on my soda and just sat there sucking the salt off my chips till you locked up at four and came out. You were so damn glad to be out of that place, you didn't even notice you'd walked right past my car. Hell, you didn't even notice me till you were out front trying to get the door unlocked.

That kind of hurt, Dani. It really did. For a few seconds. You always went out of your way to pay attention to me before. I thought about just dropping you right there; a good roundhouse kick would've done it. But that would've been over too soon and would've spoiled my fun before I got started, and I wouldn't have gotten to test the chloroform.

Besides, I admit, I am enjoying your little Christmas lights. They're festive, though I think you kinda skimped out on 'em.

Ah, but I've wasted enough breath on the why and the you and the me. That little energy shot's got me pretty wired. Must be why I've talked so much. But the more I look at your face, the twitchier my punching hand gets. A couple jabs for old times' sake would be just the thing to warm me up, and that cute little notch in your nose looks so lonely.

Oh. Oh yeah, it's just like I remember. Better, maybe. Don't let anybody tell you nothing's better than sex, because I can name off quite a few exceptions, and feeling the skin of my knuckles split against your cheekbone is at the top of the list right now. Just the right amount of pain, the right amount of hurt. Lord, I have missed this.

Aw, damn, Dani. Again with the crying. I'm working up to killing you here, I didn't come out here for you to ruin the goddamn moment.

Yeah. That's it. Dry it up fast. People tend to do that when they see the ice pick. The screwdriver. The hand drill. Sometimes I use 'em in order. Sometimes I switch 'em up and use other tools. Other times I like to be a little more...hands-on.

Oh, your cheek's looking sweet. Hang on a minute and let's get the other side to match. Aren't you glad I gave you that gag to bite down on?

There. That's better. No, don't turn your head. Look at me. Look at me.

That's a good girl.

I said you were special, didn't I? I'm about to get started and realized I haven't really told you why.

You're precious, Danielle. You were a bitch to me in school and a bitch to me tonight, but you're precious. Even if you called me the C-word and shoved my face into a locker. I don't love anybody, but I can appreciate the gift you're about to give me.

See, I can only do this once. This one murder in this one place. Because there's only one of you. It makes each of my kills unique and special, but also a little sad, because I know I'll never have this moment again. I won't be able to recapture how good this feels right now. It keeps me going. Seeking. Chasing that high, I guess, and never finding the same one twice. If I could bottle this, what's about to happen, I would treasure it forever.

Just know one thing.

I don't hate you and I never did. Not then, and not now. Quite the opposite; if I were capable of love, I'd love you. One of the few things I would actually love, and this? This is the highest form of my affection.

Merry Christmas, Danielle.

Now. Let's see what we can do about your nose.

WHEN THE BLOOD RUNS CLEAR

1

Fathi Betesh watched the prisoner sleep, suspended by his wrists in the cold, stone cell. He hadn't been sure if the prisoner was asleep, or if he'd simply passed out. Betesh rubbed his chin and listened carefully.

Snoring.

A thin smile broke out on his face, and he turned from the door window and walked down the hallway to the interrogation room.

There was a table set up with all sorts of tools, three chairs, and three men standing at attention, waiting for him.

"Relax," Betesh said in Arabic. "We are not an army here."

The three men remained at attention.

Betesh sighed.

"Very well," he said. "What do we know about this prisoner?"

No one spoke.

"You, tall one. Answer me," Betesh said sharply.

"Sir," the tall one spoke. "He is American. He has resisted all attempts of interrogation. We know his name and where he is from, that is all, sir."

Betesh nodded.

"Well, we shall see how he resists now," he said, walking toward the table of tools. "These will not be necessary. Clear this room. I have my own methods."

The three men immediately began to clear the table. Betesh left the room and walked the hallway back to the prisoner's cell. He looked through the window, and this time, the prisoner was awake. His toes were one inch from the floor. He hung by his wrists, which were behind his back, wrenching his arms back in an unnatural position. He was bent nearly in half. He was looking up at Betesh through the window.

And he was smiling.

"Are you my new interrogator?" the prisoner asked quietly.

Betesh said nothing and walked away. There'd be time for talking soon enough.

2

"Tell me about this man," Betesh said. He was seated in a bright open room in a rather comfortable chair. Before him sat a much younger man in a hard wooden chair with a file folder covered and smeared with dirt. The younger man handed the file to Betesh, who took the file and dropped it on the floor.

"Your name. Ahmed, yes?"

The younger man nodded. The look on his face was one of sheer terror. Betesh smiled.

"Ahmed, if I wanted to read the file, I would have asked you for it. Part of what makes what I do frustrating is indirect answering. I told you to tell me about this man, yes?"

Ahmed nodded.

"I am sure your file has everything I need to know. I want you to tell me about him. What is not in the file."

Ahmed swallowed hard. Betesh laughed.

"I am not interrogating you, young man. Relax, we are on the same side."

"I...don't know how to say what you want."

Betesh nodded.

"Tell me about him. You have interrogated others, yes? What makes this one different?"

Ahmed took a deep breath.

"He does not scream. He does not cry. He is...emotionless. He reacts to pain, but he doesn't beg for it to stop."

"I see. What does he do?"

"Sometimes, more often than not, he prays."

Betesh nodded.

"To whom does he pray?"

Ahmed again swallowed hard.

"Sir...we have no idea."

"I beg pardon?"

"We don't understand what he is saying," Ahmed said. "He starts low, almost guttural, and he builds in volume, but...the words..."

"Have you written these words down?" Betesh asked. "Are they in the file?"

Ahmed shook his head.

"We... I tried." Ahmed said. "But they are phonetic...they are almost nonsense words. At first we thought he was making them up...from the pain, you know?"

Betesh knew. Often times during an interrogation, the pain and horror of what was happening to the subject would cause a mental breakdown of sorts. They would begin to cry for their mothers, scream and babble out garbled nonsense.

"This is typical," Betesh said.

"Not this. He said the words carefully. There were a lot of repeated phrases."

"Without me picking up the file, can you repeat one for me?"

Ahmed cleared his throat.

"Li'hee...en gah..."

Betesh frowned.

"That sounds like nothing. Something one would say if being struck repeatedly."

"I know, but he said it very directly. Over and over, with other repeated phrases."

"Did you record any of this?"

"No, we did not," Ahmed said. "Not for lack of trying. None of the equipment worked."

"This facility is lackluster and poorly maintained, so that is not a surprise."

Ahmed hung his head.

"No, young man. That is not an affront on you. Just reality. However, the Islamic State is better funded than this place. That is not on you." Betesh put a hand on the young man's head. "I am here now. We shall make the rocks themselves sing. Understood?"

Ahmed nodded.

Betesh removed his hand.

"I have come with my own tools. They are in my vehicle. Set them up in the interrogation room as best you can and bring the prisoner there when ready. I will come when you are finished."

Ahmed stood and gave a salute. He left Betesh in the room.

Betesh took a handkerchief from his pocket and wiped his face. He picked up the file he had dropped earlier with the handkerchief. He looked at it and frowned. He opened it and began to read.

3

The prisoner sat on a folding metal chair with his ruined hands in front of him on a folding table. He held no expression on his bruised face. Betesh watched him on one of the three monitors he had set up in the room. The prisoner simply sat, looking at the room where he had been the subject of brutal interrogation. He seemed almost bored, and this made Betesh smile. He'd have a new expression soon enough.

Betesh wanted to watch the prisoner and see what he would do if he just sat in this room. This in and of itself was a form of torture; being made to wait. And he'd sat in the chair for over two hours now. He'd start yelling something soon, or at least he should have started yelling something by now. A man in his current physical condition should have started at least crying after about twenty minutes. But this man just sat calmly.

All of Betesh's instruments of torture were carefully placed around the room. Betesh insisted that the prisoner not be shackled to the floor per procedure, but the prisoner simply sat, looking on at nothing.

He was also waiting for the prisoner to start praying, but he had been silent.

Betesh picked up his radio and sighed. It was time.

"This is Betesh," he said into the radio. "Bring in the gurney and strap him into it. I'll be there in five minutes."

Betesh watched the monitors as two men came into the room. The prisoner flinched but did nothing else. They had wheeled in the gurney, which was stained and awful looking. The men grabbed the prisoner and picked him up. They flung him onto the gurney and strapped him in. The prisoner gave no resistance at all.

The monitors flickered.

The man cried out in pain as his wrists were cuffed to the gurney, but there was still no resistance. One of the men slapped the prisoner hard across the face. The prisoner said and did nothing but stare at the ceiling. This seemed to enrage the one man and he slapped him again. The monitors flickered again.

"Nog..." the prisoner said. "Nog...nn...shuggnth..."

Betesh's eyes widened as he looked at the monitor. This was the gibberish, and it did sound intentional as it was repeated. The monitors flickered worse now, and ultimately went black.

"Very odd," Betesh said to himself. He stood up and left the monitor room.

It was time to begin.

4

Betesh walked into the interrogation room and the two men were punching the prisoner on the gurney. The prisoner kept repeating what Betesh had heard on the monitor, only pausing when hit.

"Enough," Betesh said. "Leave us."

The two men stopped, spit on the prisoner, and walked out of the room. The prisoner stopped chanting and breathed heavily.

Betesh waited until the door had been closed to walk around the gurney and look at the prisoner, who only looked at the ceiling.

"You were right," Betesh said in English. "I am your new interrogator."

At this, the prisoner looked at Betesh.

"I knew it," he said, almost whispering. "I knew it was you." The prisoner smiled.

"You should not be smiling, young man," Betesh said. "I am not a man who makes one in your position smile."

"But you do..." the prisoner said, smiling even bigger. "The end is soon now. The pain made bearable. You are the one."

"The one for what?"

"You'll see."

Betesh rounded the gurney again and stopped.

"I know your name," Betesh said. "You are Sean Arkady from Arkham, Massachusetts, yes?"

"Yes."

"And you are an American."

"Obviously."

"You are a prisoner of the Islamic State."

"Again, obviously."

"Do you know why?"

"Because I am an American," Arkady said.

"Incorrect," Betesh said.

"Because I'm black?"

"Hardly, no."

"You tell me then."

"No," Betesh said. "You will eventually tell me though. Of that I am certain."

"You're going to try and coerce a confession from me?" Arkady laughed.

"You will talk to me."

"I'm already talking to you."

"You have not talked to anyone else here, in spite of what they did to you. It is only a matter of time before you cease talking to me."

"I will talk to you. I've been waiting for you."

"Is that a fact?"

"Yes. I'll tell you everything you want to know."

Betesh laughed.

"Suddenly you're going to tell me everything, is that it?"

"That's why I'm here."

"You could have spared yourself a lot of pain by doing so earlier, Mr. Arkady."

"Pain is a constant, Mr. Betesh."

Betesh frowned.

"How do you know my name?"

"I am the threshold."

"I do not know what that means. How do you know my name?"

"Nglui n'gha, Mr. Betesh."

Betesh grabbed Arkady's left wrist and squeezed. Arkady hissed in pain.

"What language is that?"

Arkady broke into a laugh.

"The first," Arkady said. "Are you ready to learn?"

Betesh let his wrist free and Arkady gasped.

"And what shall you teach me that I do not already know?"

"Everything," Arkady said.

5

Betesh was not an impatient man. On the contrary, he was extraordinarily patient. Nor was he violent, save for the requirements of doing his job. He was efficient. He didn't waste time, but he knew that time itself takes time and patience is rewarded.

The men who had interrogated Arkady had neither of these qualities, as was evident by the welts and bruises covering Arkady's body. Betesh rarely left marks on his prisoners. His methods were slow and meticulous, marks of a patient and efficient man. But the bruises on this prisoner were the results of sloppy work. No wonder they had called him. The man wouldn't talk because he'd been interrogated by amateurs.

He'd been an interrogator for the last twenty years, and to his own initially disgusted surprise, Betesh found he was quite good at it. The most important lesson he had learned was that the prisoner wanted to talk, whether they realized it or not. His old teacher had once told him something he took to heart.

"Fahti, every man is like a book, written in his own words," he said. "It is your job to translate it in the best fashion available to you." Solemn words from a man who then handed Betesh a red-hot poker for the prisoner in front of them.

But Betesh held those words tightly, and they had served him well.

Now he had Arkady before him, still strapped to the gurney. He decided to begin his interrogation simply.

"Can I get you some water, Mr. Arkady?"

Arkady coughed. "Is this a subtle reference to waterboarding?"

Betesh allowed a rare laugh. "No. An actual glass of water. I imagine you have not had much."

"Water would be nice," Arkady said.

Betesh walked over to the long table where various tools and knives lay. There was a jug of water and a few plastic cups. He poured water into a cup, put in a straw, and brought it to Arkady's face. Arkady turned his head and sucked down the entire cup greedily. He coughed a bit, but he managed a weak smile.

"Thank you," he croaked.

"Would you like more?"

"Later," Arkady said. "I'm sure you have questions."

"Indeed, Mr. Arkady."

"Call me Sean."

"No," Betesh said. "It would not be appropriate, Mr. Arkady. I hope you understand."

"I do," Arkady said. "And so will you."

Betesh didn't understand what he meant, but let it pass. He took his metal folding chair and moved it next to the gurney. He sat and looked at Arkady.

"You have been through quite an ordeal, Mr. Arkady. I would like to spare you further discomfort, if I can. I just want you to talk to me."

"I have been waiting to talk to you, Mr. Betesh. I will tell you anything you'd like."

"Well, that is the problem," Betesh said. "I'm sure you'll tell me anything I'd like, but will it be the truth? I'm sure you see my point."

"I do," Arkady said. "But I have been waiting specifically to speak to you."

"How do you know of me?"

"I dreamed of you. I had the most vivid dream of you, Mr. Betesh. It's how I know your name."

"What kind of dream was it?" Betesh asked. "A good dream or a bad dream?"

"Oh, it was a good dream. It revealed you to me."

"Interesting," Betesh said. "Good dreams come from Allah, and bad dreams come from Shaitan, you know."

Arkady laughed. "I was wondering when Allah was going to come into play here."

"Is that not why you are here?" Betesh asked. "Are you not here to subvert the name of Allah?"

"Why would I do that?" Arkady said.

"There are two reasons Americans arrive here. To blaspheme the name of Allah and to kill our children. You're here for one of these two things, are you not?"

"I guess we'll have to see, won't we?"

Betesh smiled.

6

Betesh decided to let Arkady return to his cell for the rest of the day and the night. This served two purposes. One, to let Arkady think about what would lay in store for him, and two, to give Betesh an opportunity to look up information on his new interrogation subject.

He looked through Arkady's personal items, finding clothes, pictures of whom Betesh assumed was his wife or girlfriend, a few books, a woman's ring, but nothing that stood out. There was a laptop, but nothing on it that would indicate any kind of subversive anti-Islamic sentiment. An internet search turned up nothing to indicate that Arkady was anything more than just an American travelling abroad.

But why in Syria?

He'd never travelled outside of the country before, and there didn't seem to be a connection. It seemed that he simply decided to travel to Syria.

Betesh didn't buy it.

He began to prepare a list of specific questions for Arkady and decided to get some sleep. He'd wake up Arkady early and get to work. He fell asleep quickly.

Hours later, he snapped awake, covered in a cold sweat and screaming.

He forgot the dream almost immediately, but the one thing he could remember were the stars.

So many stars...

7

Arkady was moved from his holding cell to a different room by two guards. It was a larger room, bathed in artificial white light and an odd-looking table in the center of it. The guards picked him up and set him roughly onto the table. They bound his feet and both of his arms by his side. His legs were elevated, and his head rested on the edge of the table. Arkady didn't bother to move. The two guards left the room as Betesh walked in after them. He was carrying one of Arkady's suitcases in one hand.

"Good morning, Mr. Arkady."

"Mr. Betesh," Arkady said quietly.

"Did you sleep well?"

"I did," Arkady said. "Did you?"

Betesh said nothing.

"Any interesting dreams?" Arkady added.

"Today, Mr. Arkady, we will discuss why you are in Syria."

"I thought you'd be waterboarding me."

"Perhaps," Betesh said, walking around the table. "It's not a very pleasant process. I don't like to use it if I don't have to, you know."

"I almost believe that, Mr. Betesh."

Betesh patted Arkady's leg gently as he walked by. "You'll feel differently if I get the impression that you aren't being truthful."

"There is a lot to disbelieve, Mr. Betesh."

"I brought some of your personal items," Betesh said, reaching into his messenger bag. "Perhaps you can explain them to me."

"As you like," Arkady said.

Betesh nodded and set the suitcase on a folding table near the waterboarding table. He popped the latches and opened it up. The first item he pulled out was Arkady's passport.

"You have this passport and I believe what it tells me," Betesh said, holding it up. "This is the only foreign country you've been to."

"Right," Arkady agreed.

"So why come here?"

"Why not?"

"Mr. Arkady, there are currently 195 countries in the entire world. You are an American. You should be in Cancun or Australia or some other godless country. The sentiment of 'why not?' makes absolutely no sense."

"Do you not find your country beautiful?" Arkady asked.

"It is a place of turmoil and strife, mostly due to the invasion of different religions. We are not welcoming of those that would try and subvert us."

"Interesting take. What was it called when you were the invaders?"

"The same thing your country called it. Manifest Destiny."

Arkady laughed. "Touché, Mr. Betesh."

"Why are you here?"

"To see you, of course."

Betesh sighed slowly and deeply. He walked over to the door and knocked on it three times. Two men opened the door and came inside the room. Betesh pointed at Arkady and nodded his head.

The taller man took what looked like a washcloth and dipped it into one of the buckets near the table. The other guard picked up the other bucket and stood over Arkady.

Arkady smiled.

"I see you're ready, Mr. Betesh," Arkady said.

Betesh nodded.

The tall guard took the washcloth and tightly covered Arkady's mouth and nose as the other guard began to pour water over the cloth. After a few seconds, Arkady began to struggle and choke as water began to fill his mouth and nose. The water stream ran steady over his mouth for fourteen seconds and then stopped. The cloth was removed, and Arkady coughed and gasped for air. The look on his face was fresh fear, and his eyes darted around the room. Betesh began to speak.

"You are an educated man, Mr. Arkady. I assume you have looked up at some point how and why waterboarding works, yes?"

Arkady continued to choke and cough.

"Excellent," Betesh said, circling the table. The two guards remained to do their part when told. "I will allow you a moment to collect yourself before we begin again. Why are you here?"

Arkady coughed, turned his head, and spat a wad of phlegm. He looked straight up, then closed his eyes.

"You," he nearly whispered.

"Again," Betesh said, and the waterboarding began again.

Arkady this time almost immediately began to struggle and choke. Betesh watched as he struggled against the restraints with his badly damaged wrists, causing him more pain. He watched the young man struggle to breathe. Arkady's eyes were wild with fear, and Betesh knew it wouldn't take long for him to break.

Betesh waved his hand and the guards stopped. The water stopped and the washcloth was removed.

Arkady choked and gasped, taking huge rasping breaths in between coughs.

Betesh ordered the guards out of the room, and they left without a word. As the door closed behind them, Arkady shook and sobbed on the table. Betesh pulled a folding chair over to the table. He unfolded it and sat down, leaning close to Arkady's face.

"You will eventually think that you'll simply die or pass out from this," he said into Arkady's ear. "But you won't. This will not kill you. But you'll want to die, I promise you. If you came here to see me, then you must tell me why you came to see me. Have we met? Who are you, little man?"

Arkady wept for a moment with his eyes closed. Betesh clapped his hands loudly together twice and the two guards came back into the room.

"You will tell me all," Betesh said and stood up. Arkady's eyes shot open, bloodshot and streaming with tears.

"N'gha," Arkady spat. "N'gha nyth."

Betesh frowned.

"What language is that?"

"The oldest," Arkady replied. "The language of the worm."

"The worm? Like from your gardening book?"

Arkady stared through him and shook his head. "Gardening book? I have no such book."

Betesh smiled. "Granted, I cannot read it. It seems to be Germanic or Latin in parts, and there was a picture of a beautiful girl marking a page. The book you have called *De Vermis Mysteriis.* That I understood... *Mysteries of the Worm*, yes?"

Arkady smiled, but the look in his eyes remained the same.

"It's very simple to read, Mr. Betesh," Arkady said, nearly whispering. "You just need some blood."

"Blood? For an old gardening book?"

Arkady laughed. "I love that you think it's a book about gardening, Mr. Betesh."

"Well, what is it then?"

Arkady closed his eyes.

"Grah'n ai! Mnahn'nnnn nglui!" Arkady screamed over and over again. Betesh looked at the two guards, who didn't look scared, but certainly surprised. Betesh nodded and they began the next round of waterboarding. Arkady continued screaming until the water began to pour over his face.

8

Several hours later, Betesh sat at a worn and grimy desk, reviewing the interrogation of Sean Arkady on a small monitor; well, what there was to see of it. Most of the video was grainy and warped, as if someone were holding a magnet to the video camera that had been in the interrogation room. There were only a few things that could be made out in the footage, and those things were still hard to explain. The audio flipped in and out, but the only voice that Betesh could identify was his own.

However, when Arkady began to scream, something happened to both the video and the audio.

The images became clearer, but as if someone had set the camera to film in the negative. The background and the figures were all dark except for Arkady, strapped to the table. He seemed darker, nearly purple, his image was so black. And the audio, while clearer, did not sound as it had sounded in the room. It sounded as if it were coming from very far away.

It sounded as if it weren't coming out of a small speaker on an old video monitor, but as if it were coming out of the walls.

Out of the air itself.

As Arkady's mouth was covered by the washcloth, the poor video and audio returned, and Betesh had to admit to himself that he was relieved that it was over for the moment.

But it wasn't over at all.

He turned off the monitor and sat there quietly. He looked at his watch. It was quarter after three in the morning. He buried his face into his hands.

Betesh was tired and getting more tired, but he picked up the book off the table and opened it. He went to the section that had been bookmarked by the picture of the girl. He looked at her.

She was standing next to Arkady and they were both smiling. They were outside somewhere in front of the ocean. They were dressed warmly, so it could have been winter. They were holding each other and smiling big for the camera. He flipped the picture over and saw something had been written on the back. It simply said, "Sean and Tara—winter 2014."

He looked at her and frowned. There was something vaguely familiar about her. Perhaps the set of her eyes, the big open smile? He couldn't say why she seemed so familiar. He put the picture on the table and looked at the pages.

It was a mix of English, Latin, and something else. The chapter was titled "The Wyrm That Doth Corrupt," and the text that followed was a configuration of words in impossible places, nonsense words, words that couldn't possibly have any kind of phonetic sound at all.

The words he saw perplexed him on some level, much in the way that what Arkady was screaming filled him with a deep-seated dread.

This was not going the way he had thought it would go. He looked at other chapters, and they did little to change his feelings.

He fell asleep in the chair and dreamed of absolute blackness.

9

The next morning, Betesh had the camera changed in the interrogation room. He also had a microphone placed under the waterboarding table to catch anything that might happen through today's interrogation. He had Arkady brought in and lashed to the table and let him lay there for about an hour before coming in to see him. Arkady made no fuss and just lay there with an odd smile on his face. Toward the end of the hour, he began to lightly snore.

Betesh opened the door and watched Arkady twitch as he suddenly awoke.

"Mr. Arkady, good morning. Are we ready for a productive day?"

"You didn't sleep very well, did you, Mr. Betesh?"

"Does that matter?"

"You were reading the book, weren't you?"

Betesh frowned. "As a matter of fact, yes I was."

"I can tell. You have a very expressive face."

"Do I?"

"Yes, you do."

"What does it say to you?"

"You're frightened."

Betesh laughed, but it was a forced laugh, and it was an obvious forced laugh.

"There isn't anyone else in this room, Mr. Betesh," Arkady began. "And you're the only one who is going to listen to your tapes and watch your videos. Tell me. What did you dream about?"

Betesh walked to the folding chair near the table and sat down. "How do you know I had any kind of dream at all?"

"It's the look in your eyes. I've seen it before."

Betesh blinked a few times.

"In my Tara's eyes. I saw them there once. It didn't last, really," Arkady said, letting his voice trail off.

"The girl in the picture," Betesh said. "Wife?"

"Ex-girlfriend," Arkady said slowly.

"Women are fickle, are they not?" Betesh said.

Arkady said nothing.

"Why did she leave you?"

"She had the same look as you do right now, Mr. Betesh."

Betesh ignored the comment and had an idea. "You miss her, yes?"

"I do."

"Perhaps I can arrange for you to talk to her," Betesh said. "Would you like that, Mr. Arkady?"

Arkady exploded with laughter.

"I'd actually love that," Arkady said, shaking with laughter. "If you could pull that little stunt off."

"Oh, but I can," Betesh said. "I can, you will find, do almost anything I put my mind to. I can get your girl for you to speak with if you just talk to me."

"So, what do you have in mind?"

"You tell me her number in the States, I will arrange a call. It's as simple as that."

"Great plan," Arkady said, chuckling. "But instead of a telephone, how about you get ahold of a Ouija board?"

Betesh blinked. "I beg pardon?"

"You mean to tell me you don't recognize her in that picture?"

Betesh opened his mouth and said nothing for a moment.

"No," Betesh said quietly. "I do not."

"Oh, but I think you do, don't you?"

Betesh sat there for a moment.

"It troubles you, Mr. Betesh, that you cannot remember her. But it troubles you more that you cannot read the book, am I right?"

"Yes," Betesh heard himself say. He frowned because he didn't know where that response came from. It was true. The book bothered him more than anything. The girl? How was he supposed to know she was dead? He didn't know her. But the book.

"Did you bring the book, Mr. Betesh?"

"I did." He reached into his bag and pulled the book out. He did this, but he began to feel as if he were moving in water.

"I can help you to read it," Arkady said. "I can make you understand."

Betesh nodded.

A loud sharp knock snapped Betesh back to attention and he felt an actual wave of nausea as he sprung to his feet.

"What?" Betesh said to no one. He heard Arkady chuckle. "Come in."

The two guards came in looking harried and concerned.

"Sir, are you okay?" one of the guards asked.

"Of course," Betesh said, trying to compose himself.

"You've been in here for three hours, sir," the other guard said. "We watched you through the window, just sitting there next to the prisoner."

"I beg your pardon?" Betesh said.

10

Betesh was entertaining a thought he hadn't had since he was a much younger man. It was something he used to think about all the time, but had been all but driven out of him. He thought of going to Paris. Not to do the will of Allah, or to advance the Islamic State, but just to go to Paris. To take in the beauty, the countryside, the cities, the food, the wine.

The women.

The men.

Ah, to be thirty years younger and less idealistic.

He had enough money, he wouldn't have to work. He could use one of the false IDs he'd had for years, live well and hidden. Safe. Unencumbered. He'd done enough, after all.

Allah would understand.

Betesh laughed.

Of course, Allah would not. It was a silly thought, and it would, of course, remain in his head.

But he thought about it for a few moments more as he looked up the familiar girl in Arkady's picture online.

The first image that appeared caused Betesh to clench his jaw.

***

"Tell me, Mr. Arkady," Betesh said. "What did you think was going to happen? I would discover your little secret and be filled with guilt?"

Arkady was in his holding cell, handcuffed to a wooden cot, half-asleep. Betesh had kicked open the door, furious. He didn't bother to turn on the overhead light.

"Did you think you could come here looking for revenge? On me?" Betesh snarled.

"Revenge?" Arkady said from the darkness. "You think I came for revenge?"

"What else?" said Betesh. "Your girlfriend comes here, selling your Christ to our children. We did what you Americans do when confronted by truth."

Arkady laughed.

"Ex-girlfriend. And not my Christ."

"Of course, your Christ. Why else come here?"

"I came for you. I keep telling you, Betesh. I have come for you."

"To kill me, yes? For killing your girlfriend?"

"No."

"Of course for killing your girlfriend. Your girlfriend comes here for a false missionary trip, trying to subvert the will of Allah, and was caught. I interrogated her and then I had her killed," Betesh snarled. "You will feel the wrath of Allah, Christian."

"No, I won't," Arkady said. "You are going to be enlightened. Sooner than later. Want to start now?"

Betesh stormed out of the room, yelling for his guards.

11

This time, there was no waterboarding table for Arkady. He was brought roughly to Betesh's office and sat in a folding chair in front of a ratty table that served as Betesh's desk.

Arkady wasn't cuffed or shackled. He was left in the room alone with the door locked. Behind the desk, there was a huge window without glass offering a view of the pitch-black night of Syria. There was a slight breeze that offered no comfort.

The end was near. Arkady was exhausted and in constant pain, but he was glad it was almost over. The pain kept him sharp through the lack of sleep. This was worse than he had ever thought it would be, but it was going perfectly well. There would be a finale to this game. And it would be tonight.

At last.

12

Betesh opened the door, entered quickly, and barked an order to the guards outside. He slammed the door shut and sat opposite Arkady. He glared at the young man as he slammed the book hard on the desk.

"You do not want revenge for killing your girlfriend," Betesh said.

"Ex-girlfriend. You keep getting that part wrong."

"So why do you care that I killed your ex-girlfriend?"

"Because you robbed me of doing it myself, Mr. Betesh."

This information made Betesh pause.

"Tara and I were very much in love, but she was...insensitive to a rather large part of my life."

"And what exactly was that?"

"My religion."

Betesh nodded. "What did she believe?"

"She followed the carpenter, of course," Arkady said with near contempt.

"I seem to recall that," Betesh said, almost conversationally. "Yes, she was quite devout. I did admire her resolve."

"That makes one of us," Arkady said. "I did love her, just not her beliefs."

"So, you are not a Christian? What are you then? Jew?"

"There is no name for what I am," Arkady said. "But I want to share it with you. Tonight. It's my last wish, so to speak. It's the completion of something that Tara would not do."

"As a Muslim, that it something that I cannot help you with, Mr. Arkady. I can do a great many things, but you are forgetting that you are a prisoner here. You are being interrogated as an enemy of Allah, and the outcome for you is potentially more dire than you can imagine."

"I don't expect to live. I just have one thing to fulfill. One thing to pass along. But I want to tell you how to read the book before I go."

"Go?" Betesh asked. "Where are you going?"

"You will need to have a small amount of blood to read the book. Can you open the book?"

"I have questions," Betesh said. "And I think you're going to answer them this time, yes?"

"I will answer everything, yes. But the book..."

Betesh put his hand on the book and tapped it three times. "What is this book?"

"It is the answer to every question you've ever had about Allah, Mr. Betesh. The answer to absolutely everything."

Betesh held his hand on the book, and after a moment, it began to feel warm. He looked at it and lifted his hand. He put it back down and, again, it began to feel warm. He looked at Arkady, who looked anxious.

"You...were going to murder your girl—" He paused. "Your ex-girlfriend. For this?"

"Not murder, no. But she was supposed to die. She was an offering of sorts. I had tried to...I guess, make her a part of this. It all fell apart though, and then she was chosen. She ran. She ran here."

Betesh nodded. "To me."

Arkady smiled. "To you."

"To what was she being offered to?"

"The only true power in the universe."

"A one true god? Which one? The world boasts so many 'one true gods,' Mr. Arkady."

Arkady laughed.

"There are many. So many. Not just one true one, but they are all true...all jealous, all powerful."

Betesh's face grew warm. Blasphemy. He'd never heard it displayed or spoken of so casually, but he said nothing. He let Arkady continue.

"Cthulhu, Azathoth, Shub-Niggurath...it's an endless list. This book is for Idh-yah. The bride of Cthulhu. The great and powerful worm. She is whom I worship. She is the key, I am the doorway. I am the threshold."

"The great and powerful worm," Betesh repeated. "This book is about her?"

"Open the book, Mr. Betesh. You know the part I mean. I know you've seen it. I know you've tried to read it," Arkady said.

Without consciously realizing it, Betesh opened the book to the chapter titled "The Wyrm That Doth Corrupt."

"It is unreadable," Betesh heard himself say. His index finger rested under the chapter title and the warmth was growing. Yet, as he was aware of this, it was as if it were happening to someone else. As if he were watching it in a movie.

"You cannot read it as is," Arkady explained. "The pages are of flesh. You need to smear fresh blood on the pages."

Betesh felt himself nod. He tried to pray to Allah in his mind, but the words would not come. He shook as he brought his wrist up to his mouth. He sank his teeth into it and jerked his head to one side, opening a nasty, bleeding wound. He held the bleeding wrist over the page. He watched, amazed, as the blood splashed across the page, but instead of seeing the bright crimson of his own blood, when it hit the page, it ran clear. It was still viscous, but clear, and the words underneath became clear as well. He took his hand and spread the blood across the words.

Betesh became aware that Arkady was mumbling something. Something that became clearer and louder and began to fill the room.

"Ya uln n'ghft, ya uln n'gha."

Betesh was shaking as he saw the very same words he was hearing appear in front of him on the page.

But now, they were translating.

He began to chant along.

"Ya uln n'ghft," Betesh said. "I am darkness."

The poor overhanging light in the room went dark, but Betesh could still see and read as another form of light filled the room. No, not light.

Not darkness. Pure blackness. Betesh had a fleeting thought as his mind began to slip away from him, that the light was like a blacklight in a night club. He'd visited a few nightclubs when he was a younger man, not quite yet committed to Allah.

Allah.

He was forsaking Allah right now and he couldn't stop. His mouth read the next words out loud.

"Ya uln n'gha," he said, beginning to weep. "I am death."

Arkady was chanting on and on, adding other impossible sounding words. Betesh tried to stop reading along, but the chaos of sound and anti-light was overwhelming. He began to see things in the anti-light surrounding him. Things the likes of which he'd never imagined before. Creatures that looked like fish, and dragons, and unspeakable horrors. He felt his mind losing its grip. This was not a reality he had ever heard of, and he was being pulled into it.

"Lost one, born of darkness!" Arkady screamed. "Accept this infidel into your essence! Your threshold has brought you this! Have mercy on your unworthy servant!"

Betesh heard this and realized that Arkady was talking about him.

There was a buzzing in Betesh's head as the madness of the situation took a firmer hold. He tried once more to beg the forgiveness of Allah, but the words again wouldn't come. He tried to say the name Allah out loud, to perhaps break the spell he was under.

"Ah y'hah," Betesh said, knowing that wasn't what he wanted to say.

"Yes!" Arkady said. "Yes!"

Betesh looked at Arkady, who was transforming before his eyes. It appeared as if his skin was disintegrating like a sheet of paper in a fire.

"Thank you, grah'n!" Arkady yelled as he began to dissipate.

Betesh felt his mind finally slip away as he looked down at his own dissipating flesh. He stopped weeping and waited for the unknown to claim the rest of him.

THE LONESOME DEATH OF PHINEAS T. CROUGHLY

All things have a beginning, and most things have an end. For some things, however, there isn't an end, simply another beginning to something else entirely. This is not always a good thing, and the story I'm about to tell you is about one such thing: an incident back in the time of gaslights and horse-drawn carriages, during the Christmas season, a time of picture-perfect joy and wonder.

But underneath the joy and wonder there, always lurks the one lace that threads us all together and makes us all equal.

Man's inhumanity to man.

Phineas T. Croughly was a kind and gentle librarian during this time in the small bustling village of Boonton, New Jersey. The Morris Canal ran right through it, bringing merchandise and goods from all over the world. It was a hub to the rest of the US during its first century of existence and right after the Civil War. Now, Phineas was a very learned man who loved books more than almost anything, and that included people, for the most part. But he did love children. Children had an unquenchable thirst for stories: adventures and exciting history, tales of distant lands and even other worlds. He would arrange story time for any child who asked him to read, and he would fairly swoon at the chance.

He would gather the children right in the center of the small library and sit right on the floor with them, or sometimes, he'd take the book and dance around the room, delighting all who would bear witness.

None more so than a young widow named Penelope Smythe.

Penelope was a sad woman most of the time, as she had lost her husband on the boat from England and her two children under very unusual circumstances. She was also the most beautiful woman Phineas had ever seen.

She would spend hours in the library, every day, losing herself in the volumes of books. And every day, Phineas would watch her, observing her dour expression. The only time her expression would change was when he would read to the children.

Without ever having spoken a single word to one another, they fell very much in love.

It was during the week before Christmas that Phineas began to plan two things. One was the annual reading of Dickens' *A Christmas Carol* for the children. The children were a complete delight to read this to, as it was both positive and just a little bit scary. The other was his plan to finally speak to the beautiful Penelope and tell her how he loved her so.

All things seemed quite right in the world.

This was not to last.

A local landowner named Silas Martin had also fancied Penelope, but not for her good heart or even her good looks. He fancied her money, for she was, unknown to Phineas, a very wealthy widow. And, unlike Phineas, Silas *had* spoken to her—several times, in fact—about the proposition of marriage. Each time, Penelope would tell Silas that her heart was broken and she wouldn't marry again.

However, for the very first time, she gave Silas a different answer.

"I am truly sorry, Silas, but my heart is alive again and belongs to another," she said, and flitted away with a skip in her step.

Silas became furious and hired a man to follow her so he could discover who would dare do such a thing to a man of his caliber.

It didn't take long to discover Phineas and the library.

So, Silas put a horrible plan into motion.

It was two days before Christmas Eve, and Phineas was beginning to close the library for the night. He was excited for the next evening's storytelling and his chance to tell the lovely Penelope his true feelings. As he lifted a large stack of books onto a small unsteady cart, who should walk into the library but Penelope.

He was shocked into silence, but managed to smile.

She smiled back.

He dropped the books, stumbled over them, and nearly ran to her. She beamed.

"Hello," he said, shaking. "I love you,"

"I love you too," she replied and then giggled.

They held hands and looked into one another's eyes, standing in the one place they both loved on all the Earth: a place filled with books with hundreds of thousands of words, and not a single one could describe what the two of them were feeling at this moment. So they didn't try. They stood in silence, saying all they needed to each other. All they had both ever wanted to hear was being discussed without the clumsy intrusion of sound, and it was glorious.

After a moment, they did finally speak, agreeing to meet up at the storytelling the next day. Penelope kissed his cheek and left him in the library, smiling.

He went back to finish his work when he heard the door slam. For a moment, he believed it was Penelope returning, but he couldn't have been more wrong.

It was Silas and two large men entering the library. Having no knowledge of Silas' obsession with Penelope, he didn't flinch or feel threatened in any way.

"I'm sorry, gentlemen and Mr. Martin," he said, still smiling. "The library will be open first thing in the morning. I'm afraid we're closed."

"It seems you're not afraid at all," Silas said, also smiling. "But you very much should be."

Phineas didn't understand the statement, nor did he understand when the two large men grabbed him and began to beat him mercilessly. He managed to get a few licks in, but in the end the two brutes were too powerful for him.

As he lay broken and bleeding in the center of the library, the two thugs began to throw books on top of him. He couldn't move, and simply lay there in agony.

"Oh dear," Silas said, chuckling. "Whoever shall read to the kiddies tomorrow? I expect this to be a very *sad* Christmas, Mr. Croughly."

"Look at him!" one of the thugs said. "Looks more like Mr. *Creeply* than Mr. Croughly!" This indeed was true, for the poor lad's face was a patchwork of blood and dangling skin. Most of his teeth had been knocked out, and both of his eyes had been bruised beyond repair. He gasped for air through a nearly broken windpipe.

"Don't worry yourself about Miss Smythe, old boy," Silas said. "I shall see that she and her fortune are well cared for."

This ignited a burning anger within Phineas, and he struggled to rise, but he was far too weak.

"Enjoy what's left of the Christmas season, Mr. *Creeply*," Silas said, lighting a match. "For however long it lasts."

The two large men left the library, leaving Silas and Phineas alone. Silas laughed and tossed the wooden match atop the pile of books that had been stacked on Phineas.

Silas left Phineas to burn along with his beloved library.

For whatever reason, as the flames began to lick his flesh, Phineas began to croak louder and louder until it almost sounded like laughter...

Six months after the worst fire the town had ever seen, another unthinkable thing happened. The devastated Penelope married the dour Silas Martin. The ceremony was somber, to say the least, with a wedding party of only five people. No one knew what Silas had said or offered to Penelope to change her mind, nor did anyone ask.

However, shortly after the wedding, construction began on a new library.

The goal was to have the library completed by the next Christmas—a near-impossible feat by regular building standards for the time, but where there's a whip, as they say, there's a way.

The Phineas T. Croughly Library was set to open on Christmas Eve, but a small ceremony had been arranged for the day before by the new Mrs. Martin for her husband and his two assistants.

She ushered them inside that evening, and the library was such a sight to behold! It was bigger and quite ornate. It was well lit with gaslight bulbs from every possible angle. It was something beautiful to behold, and yet, it was also sad.

It was missing a librarian.

"You gentlemen wait here," Penelope said curtly, exiting the room and rushing out of the building.

The three men looked at each other and began to chuckle.

"Why did you let her build this...monument to Creeply?" one of the thugs said through a chuckle.

"Oh, the cost was a pittance," Silas said. "She has so much more money than she knows what to do with. Fortunately, I do. In fact—"

They all heard the sound of the lock being engaged from the outside.

Silas Martin was going to say, "In fact, I have plans to build a new mansion!"

But he stopped at "In fact" due to the bright gaslights suddenly fading and going out save for one.

The light was toward the back of the library, and underneath it was a lone gaunt figure who stood in the shadows. The appearance of this figure startled the three men. The shadowed figure began to laugh.

"You had once lamented, dear Silas," the figure began, "'Who shall read to the kiddies?'"

The figure began to move forward.

Not knowing what or who was walking toward them, they began to back themselves up.

"Where d'you think you're going?" the voice said. "It's *story time!*"

A second gaslight came up, revealing the figure to be a man in a burial suit. He resembled a moldered corpse and was smiling a terrible smile of shattered teeth. Silas, of course, knew who it was, as did his two henchmen. And they all began to scream.

All the lights came back on at once, brighter than before, and became brighter still, to the point of blinding. All the while, the figure laughed.

"I know you!" screamed Silas. "I know who you *are!*"

"Of course you do, Silas," the figure said. "I am your librarian. And I don't think you're going to like the story I have for you one little bit! But..."

The librarian moved quickly right next to Silas.

"It's a real *scorcher* of a tale!"

The librarian began to laugh even louder than before as each and every gaslight in the library exploded.

***

The explosion knocked Penelope off her feet and into a pile of snow near the horse carriage. She had dropped the gun she was going to use to shoot Silas; it was a two-shooter, one bullet for him and one for her.

She turned around to see the library she'd built for her one true love burn and burn into the night. Eventually, the fire department arrived and began the chain of buckets from the pond to the doomed building.

Pages from books floated down from the sky in various forms of burning and char. Penelope caught one and saw that something had been written on it.

It was simply a heart, crudely drawn in red.

It was the end of one thing, as I was saying. It was also the beginning of something...*else.*

HIGHWAY 90
A RADIO PLAY

(The theme music begins, and the NARRATOR speaks.)

NARRATOR
The road to hell is paved with a lot more than just good intentions. Take, for example, Peter and Melinda Trotsky. Married for ten miserable years, and now the end is in sight for both. Their Uncle Silas is on his deathbed, much to the joy of both Peter and Melinda, for it is upon his death that they will equally split the old man's estate, left in his will to them both as his sole heirs.

However, once the money is divided, they can end their sham of a marriage; the sole condition for them to receive the money is that they must be married until his death. So, in waiting ten years, they have lied, cheated, and abused each other to the breaking point.

Until now. The end is nigh, but it's a lot longer drive to the hospital than they think. Especially when you're traveling on Highway 90.

(We hear two car doors open and then slam shut.)

PETER
Well, looks like the old bastard is going to finally buy the farm.

MELINDA
Just drive, Peter.

(The car starts.)

PETER
It's my car, and realistically, *my* uncle.

MELINDA
Fine, but I've suffered this marriage for ten years. He's my uncle just as much as he is yours.

PETER
Well, soon enough, we'll be at *our* uncle's funeral, and then we'll split *our* uncle's money and I can get the hell away from you.

MELINDA sighs heavily.

MELINDA
Was it really that bad, Peter? Being married to me?

PETER laughs.

PETER
You're kidding, right? You're the one who hired a private eye to follow me for six months!

MELINDA
Well, he did catch you cheating.

PETER
That was only because I found out that you were cheating.

MELINDA gasps.

PETER (CONT'D)
Yeah, didn't think I knew about that, did you?

MELINDA
You son of a bitch.

PETER
Yeah, yeah, yeah. I'm a son of a bitch. I also married one.

MELINDA
You have no idea.

PETER
Oh, I think I have a really good idea.

MELINDA
Just...stop it.
PETER
Stop what?

MELINDA
This arguing! It's pointless. We're almost out. Why argue?

PETER sighs.

PETER
How about I just turn on the radio for a little while? I think we can spend the next ten or fifteen minutes without yelling at each other, right?

MELINDA
Fine.

(We hear Peter play with the radio, getting static and then finally finding a station.)

RADIO VOICE
Hey, welcome back to ninety-nine point six, WDVL, where the classics keep on comin'...

MELINDA
God, I hate this station.

RADIO VOICE
Comin' up next is an oldie but a goodie! A great song by Chris and the Pres-Tones, from 1963—"New Jersey Surf Story!" Man, this song takes me back...

(We can hear the guitar intro to "New Jersey Surf Story" and listen to about halfway through the first verse before we hear the radio being shut off.)

PETER
Hey, what the hell was that for?

MELINDA
I hate that song.
PETER
You hate the song, you hate the station, what else?

MELINDA
Oh, did you like that song?

PETER
Not really.

MELINDA
Then what's your problem?

PETER
You could have asked.

MELINDA
You could have taken the hint when I said I hated this station.

PETER
Well, what, exactly, the hell do I *care* if you hate the radio station?

MELINDA
I loathe you, do you know that?

PETER
I've known it for ten years now. Know what? I loathe you too.

MELINDA
If it weren't for the money, I'd
have left you ages ago.

PETER
If it weren't for the money, I'd
have killed you ages ago.

MELINDA
You never had the guts to do
something like that.

PETER
Wanna bet? Do you have any idea how close you've come to death,
sweetheart?

MELINDA
Peter...

PETER
With God as my witness, I...

(There is an increasing tire screech. Melinda begins to scream. Peter joins her. The screech of tires is deafening. However, it finally sounds as if Peter has avoided a huge disaster. We hear the car lurch to a halt.)

MELINDA
Oh my God, oh my God!

PETER
It's okay. We made it. Jesus, did you see that?

MELINDA
I thought that truck was going to flatten us for sure.

PETER
That bastard. Did you get his license plate number?

MELINDA
Are you serious?

PETER
Yeah, I'm serious! That guy's dangerous.

MELINDA
That guy? You were the one who swerved into his lane!

PETER
I did not!

MELINDA
Yes you did! I watched you.

PETER
Oh, Jesus…

(Peter starts the car again and peels out.)

PETER (CONT'D)
Let's just get to the hospital and hope that the old man is dead by the time we get there.

MELINDA
If you wanted him dead so bad, you should've just driven him around.

(There is silence except for the sound of the car going faster. We can hear Peter breathing heavily.)

MELINDA (CONT'D)
You okay?

PETER
We could have died back there.

MELINDA
But we didn't.

PETER
You're taking this better than usual.

MELINDA
And you're overreacting to it. People change.

PETER
Whatever.

(He turns the radio on.)

RADIO VOICE
Let's take a quick look at the traffic.

(We hear the traffic music bed begin.)
RADIO VOICE (CONT'D)
There's a bit of a back-up on the 365 this morning, about a half-hour wait at the tunnel. The 410 is running slowly both ways due to construction, but Highway 90 is clear as a bell. Doesn't even look like there's a living soul in sight. I'll be back in ten for the latest traffic right here on WDVL, ninety-nine point six!

(The typical jingle barks out its song.)

JINGLE SINGERS
W-D-V-L! Plays all your favorite oldies! Ninety-nine point six!!

(We hear the beginning of a commercial. Peter talks over it.)

PETER
You know, that's pretty strange.

MELINDA
What?

PETER
The traffic.

MELINDA
What about it?

PETER
Look. There's isn't any.

MELINDA
I don't get your—

PETER
Just look outside.

(There is a pause.)

> MELINDA
> Hmmm. That is a bit strange.

> PETER
> It's eight thirty in the morning. There should be wall-to-wall cars.

> MELINDA
> I haven't seen a car in a while.

> PETER
> Were you looking?

> MELINDA
> No. We were fighting. Again.

(Peter laughs a bit.)

> PETER
> We do that, don't we?

(Now Melinda laughs.)

> MELINDA
> I guess we do.

(Peter sighs.)

> PETER
> Hey, for whatever it's worth, I never came close to killing you. I mean, I did think about it, but I couldn't...wouldn't ever do that.

> MELINDA
> How gallant of you.

> PETER
> No, I mean... Ah, Jesus, Melinda.

(He punches the steering wheel.)

PETER (CONT'D)
I never meant for any of this to happen, you know?

(Melinda sighs.)
MELINDA
I asked you earlier if being married to me was so bad.

PETER
Yeah, you did.

MELINDA
You never really answered.

(There is a pause. The commercial on the radio ends.)

RADIO VOICE
And remember that each one has a thirty-day money back guarantee. Now back to the music. This one's going out to Peter. Watch out for those big rigs, Petey!

(The radio begins to play "New Jersey Surf Story" again.)

MELINDA
I don't believe they're playing this song again.

PETER
No kidding! Thought they weren't supposed to do stuff like that.

MELINDA
Well, that's why this is a crap radio station.

(The radio clicks off.)

PETER
There you go again. Jesus Christ, Melinda...

MELINDA
What? Do you really want to hear that song?

PETER
Leave the radio alone.

(He turns the radio back on. We hear the radio voice and not the song, which by all rights should still be playing.)

RADIO VOICE
You're listening to ninety-nine point six, WDVL. Here's a great tune going out to Melinda. Hey, Mel! How's about leaving the damn radio alone! The Pres-Tones for ya!

("New Jersey Surf Story" begins all over again.)

PETER
Did I just hear that right?

MELINDA
What the hell?

(The radio clicks off. There is silence in the car.)

PETER
That is really weird.

MELINDA
Very.

PETER
I'm going to turn it back on.

MELINDA
Don't!

(Peter laughs.)

PETER
Come on, the guy at the station is having a goof or something. It's just a coincidence.

MELINDA
Don't do—

(The radio is clicked on. The music bed for the traffic report is on.)

RADIO VOICE
And all that traffic on the 410 is running slow due to construction going both ways. There was an accident still being cleared up on Highway 90, but once you get past it, it's a straight clear shot. It's almost like everybody stayed home!

PETER
See what I mean?

RADIO VOICE
Now, let's get back to the music. We've had a ton of requests for this song all morning.

MELINDA
I guess you were right.

RADIO VOICE
This one goes out to Pete and Mel. Hey, guys, try and find an exit! Chris and the Pres-Tones for ya!

(The familiar guitar part kicks on.)

MELINDA
Turn it off, Peter.

PETER
What the hell...

(We hear the fumbling of the control, but the song is playing.)

MELINDA
Peter, turn it off!

PETER
I'm trying...

(More fumbling, then a sound like punches.)

    MELINDA
    Peter!

    PETER
    Dammit!

(Finally, the radio shuts off after a big punch is heard.)

    PETER (CONT'D)
    What the hell do you make of that?

    MELINDA
    Pull over.

    PETER
    Why? The radio is off. It's just a few more—

    MELINDA
    I said pull over!

    PETER
    Okay, okay.

(We hear the car moving, and some tires screeching, but nothing that sounds like the car pulling over.)

    MELINDA
    Peter, did you hear me?

(She sounds frantic.)

    PETER
    Yeah, I heard you, but I can't.

    MELINDA
    What do you mean you can't?

PETER
I mean the car won't let me pull over. I can steer, but it won't let me slow down.

MELINDA
That's stupid. Pull over.
(Peter punches the steering wheel.)

PETER
I *can't*!

(The car tires screech again, and Melinda begins to scream. The car sounds like it is weaving back and forth. We hear the brake pedal being pumped.)

PETER (CONT'D)
See? I can't stop!

MELINDA
Stop weaving! You'll kill us both!

PETER
Okay. I'm sorry…

(The screeching stops and the sound of a normally driving car resumes.)

MELINDA
What the hell is going on?

PETER
I really don't know.

(There is a space of silence and a small swell of suspenseful music.)

MELINDA
What are we going to do?

PETER
We need to call someone to help us. Call the police.

(We hear Melinda dial numbers on her cell phone. A tone indicates that she is out of range for a signal.)

    MELINDA
    Damn, no signal.

    PETER
    You're kidding. This whole highway is a cell relay zone.

    MELINDA
    I'll try again.

(Same thing—all tone, no phone.)

    MELINDA (CONT'D)
    Nope. I'll keep trying.

(Suddenly, the radio springs to life. It's playing the WDVL jingle again.)

    PETER
    What the hell...

    MELINDA
    Oh no...

    JINGLE SINGERS
    You're listening to the oldies!

(The sweet harmony of the singers is replaced with a sinister voice.)

    SINISTER JINGLE VOICE
    W-D-V-L!

(Peter and Melinda scream at the sheer volume and rattle of the voice. The radio voice returns, but it has lost a bit of the fun behind it. It sounds very forced now, almost angry.)

RADIO VOICE
Well, here's the thing about traffic. It happens. If you're on Highway 90, you're alone. All alone. Dead alone. Here's a little ditty for your ride.

(The beginning chords for "New Jersey Surf Story" begin again, but slower and mean sounding.)

MELINDA
Shut that off!

(Peter starts hitting it again.)

PETER
I'm trying.

(The song begins to speed up slowly until it reaches an inaudible version of the song.)
(Peter franticly hits the radio. The radio voice returns.)

RADIO VOICE
Well. Seems like we had a bit of technical difficulty there. That's okay. It happens, right, Pete?

(Peter and Melinda gasp.)

RADIO VOICE (CONT'D)
Like when you tried to sever the brake line on Mel's car. Man, you were so pissed 'cause you couldn't find it. Remember?

(Peter says nothing, but Melinda gasps.)

MELINDA
Peter?

RADIO VOICE
Well, I guess Mel had a bit more luck killing that dog of yours. You know, a dog is just dumb enough to drink antifreeze. A whole—

PETER
I knew it!

MELINDA
That was a dog! You tried to kill me!

PETER
That's not true! He's lying.

(The radio gives off a bit of static, then clears up.)

RADIO VOICE
Looks like our technical problems are a-okay now. Ain't you happy?

MELINDA
I can't believe you tried to kill me! You lousy bastard—and you sat here and lied about it.

PETER
Melinda...

MELINDA
Don't you Melinda me! I'm not through with you, not by a damn sight!

PETER
Melinda, look!

MELINDA
What?

PETER
That sign for Templewood.

MELINDA
Yeah?

PETER
I'm pretty sure we've passed it a few times already.

RADIO VOICE
Here's your song! This goes out to Petey and Mel, my favorite couple!

("New Jersey Surf Story." Again. Melinda screams. Peter starts hitting the radio again.)

MELINDA
(Over the song) I can't stand this.

(We hear her open the car door.)

PETER
Melinda, no!

(We hear her scream in terror.)

MELINDA
Pull me back in! Pull me back in!

(We hear Peter reach for her. We hear struggling until, finally, we hear the door slam shut.)

PETER
What are you, crazy? You could've been killed!

MELINDA
Peter, oh God...

PETER
What happened?

MELINDA
I opened the door and...and...

PETER
And what? What did you see?

MELINDA
Nothing. There was nothing there.

PETER
What? The road was there, right?

(She begins to hyperventilate.)

MELINDA
No. I mean there was nothing there! It was all black and dark.

PETER
But it's sunny out. Surely there—

MELINDA
There was nothing!

PETER
It's...okay, Melinda. It's—

MELINDA
It is not okay! Get your hands off me!

PETER
I just saved your life!

MELINDA
I wouldn't even be in this car if you hadn't insisted on driving.

PETER
I wanted to get there alive.

MELINDA
Great job so far! We're in the frigging Twilight Zone or something, and goddamn it, I HATE THIS SONG!

(Of course, the song has been playing the entire time, in case you were wondering. As she yells, however, the song abruptly ends and the jingle plays.)

JINGLE SINGERS
W-D-V-L! You're traveling Highway 90! You'd better learn to love the things you hate! Better learn but you won't, cause you're screeeeeewed!

RADIO VOICE
And now it's time for a reality check!

(We hear the sound of an explosion and a different voice come on and announce)

ANNOUNCER
It's time for a great big reality check!!

RADIO VOICE
Thanks, Frosty. Here's the reality check. Listen carefully.

(There is silence, except for Peter and Melinda breathing heavily.)

PETER
Well?

(Still silent.)

MELINDA
What the hell is going on?

(There is static now, getting louder and louder.)

PETER
Holy God!

(He starts hitting the dashboard again. Melinda screams.)

PETER (CONT'D)
You're not helping!

(She continues to scream. The static stops suddenly.)

RADIO VOICE
Boy, do I hate it when that happens. Let's do traffic!

(Peter and Melinda start hitting the dashboard together.)

PETER
If I could pull over, I could pull the goddamn stereo wires out.

MELINDA
Can't you just pull the face off and it'll stop?

PETER
Try it.

MELINDA
Okay.

(We hear her trying to remove the face plate.)

MELINDA (CONT'D)
I did it!

(But the radio is still going.)

RADIO VOICE
If you're driving up Highway 90, mind the accident. Nasty one. Semi versus sedan. Guess who won?

(The radio voice explodes in laughter.)

MELINDA
It didn't work.

(The radio voice now sounds totally hostile.)

RADIO VOICE
I SAID GUESS WHO WON?

(Melinda lets out a little scream.)

RADIO VOICE (CONT'D)
That's right. Semi. Always wins. *Always* wins. You hear me?

PETER
There's the sign again.

MELINDA
What sign?

PETER
The Templewood sign we passed a little while ago.

MELINDA
We passed it back there.

PETER
We just passed it again. Don't you get it?

MELINDA
What are you talking about?

PETER
I think...

MELINDA
What?

(The radio voice cuts in.)

RADIO VOICE
So, they're still pulling meat outta that semi versus sedan pile-up back there in the mist, all you Highway 90 fliers. The bodies haven't been identified as of yet... I guess when they wring those two out of the street mop, they should be able to sort out who's who.

PETER
I think...

MELINDA
Come on. What?

PETER
I think...

RADIO VOICE
But I think you can guess who bought the farm, can't ya, Peter?

(We hear Melinda gasp.)

RADIO VOICE (CONT'D)
Oh, you too, Melinda? Good for you! And may I say—

JINGLE SINGERS
It's about goddamned time!

MELINDA
This is impossible.

RADIO VOICE
In an unrelated story...

(The radio voice explodes with laughter.)

RADIO VOICE (CONT'D)
Somebody's nearly dead uncle Silas made quite the miraculous recovery today. I guess being a multi-millionaire has great healing powers.

PETER
Son of a bitch!

MELINDA
He didn't even die?

PETER
Oh, that bastard...

MELINDA
He wants to die, I'll kill him!

PETER
I'd love to wrap my hands...

(The radio voice clears its throat, bringing the couple back to "reality.")

RADIO VOICE
Here's a traffic update. Highway 90 is all yours. Nothing but yours.

(Peter and Melinda start to breathe heavier.)

RADIO VOICE (CONT'D)
Well, enough is enough. Let's get back to that great music. You all know this one. If you don't know the words, trust me, you will. It's only a matter of time, after all. And this one is going out to Peter and Melinda. Just because you're both crispy critters roasted alive in a mashed-up car doesn't mean we've forgotten about you. We'll never forget our favorite married couple! Welcome home, kids!

JINGLE SINGERS
W-D-V-L is your home for the oldies! Forever and ever and ever!

SINISTER JINGLE VOICE
Amen!

(The beginning chords to "New Jersey Surf Story" start. Melinda screams and Peter begins to cry.)

NARRATOR
Peter and Melinda Trotsky drive up Highway 90 to get to a destination they will never ever reach. Or, perhaps, that is wrong. Perhaps they ended up exactly where they were headed all along. Perhaps the highway of life isn't supposed to have a destination for those who don't play by the rules, or can't even find a single shred of decency for their fellow man. Perhaps Highway 90 itself is a destination.
　　A destination known by another name. Jean-Paul Sartre said that "Hell is other people." Maybe, just maybe, hell is something else entirely.

(Music swells and fades.)

HELLO, IT'S NOT ME

One

Let me just say, for the record, that I'm not to blame. I never have been, except for maybe using "I" too often when speaking. Does that mean I'm a narcissist?

I'm open to the fact that it might. No denying it. My thoughts of self—adulation aren't exactly a secret. It's a fault, after all, and isn't there strength in recognizing your faults?

But that being said, this isn't my fault. Not even a little, despite the evidence to the contrary. You want physical evidence? Help yourself. Loads of it. Gallons, in fact, but that isn't actual proof. Not in any conventional sense. I'm telling you, it isn't on me.

For one thing, there isn't any motive, right?

There isn't a single thing to gain from this except maybe a little peace and quiet, and really, at the end of the day, a little peace and quiet is what we fucking all deserve.

Through whatever miracle of happenstance there is free-floating around the universe, this little issue—messy as it may be—is wrapped up in its own little ribbon. It's its own alpha and omega, and why would we want to disturb that? It's DONE. You can't reverse-engineer this sort of puzzle. The pieces don't fit anymore; the design is flawed like that. It's like unmaking a flower—you can't. All you can do is either smash it or let it rot, and someone—certainly not me—has smashed the hell out of this... Well, him.

But it wasn't me.

I'd love to take credit for it, even though it looks indisputable that I did do it. But I didn't. For one thing, it's sloppy. I am not sloppy. Ever. You can all take turns and regale each other with all your perceived views of me—and I know you do have them. Incorrect, by the by... You can say many things, but sloppy isn't one of them.

What's a guy gotta do for a cup of Joe and a smoke in this joint?

Two

I am saddened by this loss, and in no way, shape, or form am I guilty of this heinous crime. I would also like to offer a generous reward for anyone with credible evidence of the actual perpetrator. Please come forward—your identity will be concealed, and if the evidence leads to the arrest and conviction of the killer (or killers), you will be handsomely rewarded.

Three

I'm currently working on a book outlining that if I was going to do this crime—and that's a big IF—I wouldn't have done it this way at all. There are so many things I would have done differently. For example...

Four

I am devastated by the news of his passing. It comes as a surprise to us all that he was met with such an abrupt and violent end. I have no other statements, except a request for privacy for the family of the victim until an investigation is completed.

Five

Yeah, I did it. No kidding. Is there any surprise? None of you assholes are shocked by this; you all saw it coming. Best part is that HE didn't see it coming. Even though he was asking for it, practically begging for it. You don't stalk the earth with that much bile built up in your heart without painting a target on yourself.

I absolutely killed him, and the only regret I have is that I'm unable to repeat it. Christ, I need a drag.

Six

I've only been in this hospital for one day and I hate it.

When I came to this hospital, it was for grounding reasons. I felt like I was losing control. Not in a violent way; at least, I didn't think so. More like...my hold on reality. The air seemed to smell different in some new awful way, like someone was smoking nearby, but you couldn't see where. Like the smell maybe wasn't really there, or whatever was there had just left it lingering.

Or, even worse, was that you just wanted to smoke that bad.

I haven't smoked in years, so that was worrisome to me. I didn't want one. I had smelled people smoking for years, and it never once bothered me until last week.

The car started to smell again, then my clothes. Then the orange nicotine stains on the fingers; I hadn't seen those in years. But I wasn't smoking. I didn't have any, and I had no desire to smoke at all. Even now, I smell them.

I remember checking in to the hospital, telling the admitting doctor that I was feeling a little worried that I was wanting to hurt myself. This had happened twenty or so years ago, and I'd spent a week in a similar facility. Calming down, group therapy, some meds to even me out.

Smokes if you got 'em too.

But I didn't "got 'em."

I went to bed at lights out. Eight thirty. Now, hours later, I hear commotion outside my door. I can hear the orderlies and a few gasps, and then I hear my name in someone's mouth outside.

I have awoken to these entries in my journal. They have been written in my handwriting; they are terrifying in what they imply and what they say. I am afraid...

I'm afraid to leave my room for fear of what is outside my door.

And now, someone is pounding on the door.

HAVE YOURSELF

Go on, then, and have yourself a little drink. It'll help ease the tension of the night. Family gatherings, seasonally appropriate. You just want to get on with it and get it over. A little drink will let it come easier, hopefully make it go a little faster.

It's not a happy time, though. Be honest. The entire year has been a bust. You're not even sure why you're here, standing at the little open bar that your brother-in-law set up in the front room. Bad whiskey and high school gin. After this year, that's what you get? Fucking Christmas with the relatives.

But it can't be light, can it? It's been a year of loss all around. Grandparents dead within a week of each other. Hell of a way to start the year, and then just watch it all follow suit. Everything has been heavy from the get-go.

The entire year has been a fat steamy pile of shit, and not very subtle. Still, you've taken it all on the chin. Your cousin Paul, dying in that oh-so-predictable way you'd all been talking about since high school…"with a bunch of naked dudes." Meant as a joke, but a cold, sad truth revealed all too dramatically. The death of your older sister, allegedly at her own hand.

You stand there with your cranberry and piss-gin, trying to smile at these people. Your family—well, what's left of them anyway. Uncle Yousef standing by the fire, pretending to know how to keep it lit. The house will be filled with smoke in no time, guaranteed, and everyone is smiling at you. It's such shit, isn't it?

Your cousin Amanda sends a group text to everyone (*that she's still talking to, anyway*) saying that she's not coming after all, that something is up with the car and, goddammit, she won't be able to make it. Everyone breathes a sigh of relief. No one really likes Amanda. She would just get entirely too drunk and mean. There'd be enough drunk and mean to go around, thank you very much. You admire her for that; she never ever hid her disdain for the family, and that's why you're glad she bailed. Glad she at least listened to you.

You've been doing this your entire adult life and, to be fair, most of your childhood. It's never been a merry anything, not even once. The only thing to look forward to had killed herself, apparently. You and Marina would sneak out for a smoke or two during the evening festivities. You'd talk about her shitty husband, who for some fucking reason still goddamn showed up here at her house.

You were close when you were both kids, and that never really changed the older you got. Even when you told her not to marry that asshole Jared and she called you an asshole—which you suppose is still true—even then, he just kept proving you right. She was ready to leave him, and you were along for that ride. The years and years of talking about it, until one day, your sister was gone.

Her absence hangs like an open wound this year. She was the only good person in the whole fucking family, and you know it. You look at your niece Tilda, and even at three, she knows it too; this nasty pile of something called your family had one bright spot, and it snuffed itself out. Or allegedly did. Tilda is picking her nose, and what she doesn't ingest, she wipes on the carpet in the large dining room. Or the curtains, or her shithead father's pants. It's the only thing that makes you smile.

Marina is dead. The reason for coming at all is gone, and you won't after this holiday. This is the grand finale, so to speak. You will not set foot in this house again. You make a second cranberry and gin. You see your mother just looking at you, shaking her head. You offer a smile with no feeling behind it. She huffs and looks away. This makes you genuinely smile.

You kid yourself, trying to second-guess your plan. You're going to wear the stain of these people for the rest of your life, but there is no second-guessing. You're never going to see these people again after tonight.

Poor Tilda doesn't have a chance. Jared won't live long enough to die from a prediabetic stroke, but not before ruining this little kid. You can hear his arteries closing. For an absolute know-it-all, he sure doesn't know the reaper has parked her car and is waiting for his dumb ass to drop dead mid-chew.

Mom? You might pretend to be sad for a day, but you need not ever set eyes on her again after tonight. Everyone else? Your sister would have been absolutely eloquent in her thoughts on this: *Fuck 'em all, little brother.*

This awful evening drags on for far too long, as it always does; you're entertaining one drink before you exit forever, but you've come this far. At this point, all you have to do is wait for the sign.

You don't wait too long. Your mother comes downstairs after putting Tilda to bed, and it's simply the adults waiting for the last part of the ritual: a heavy chunk of rum-soaked fruitcake. The fruitcake is as much tradition in this family as alcoholism, diabetes, poor eyesight, and suicide. Or *alleged* suicide.

And how convenient that you decided to take up the honored tradition that your sister held! You are smiling, about to burst that *you* have brought the fruitcake this year.

You bring out the cake that's been soaking in rum all evening and watch the vultures begin to feast.

You watch Jared shovel a piece the size of a fist into his mouth. He's chewing and talking to your uncle Lamar. Lamar, damn near sixty, is eating his cake like it's a bowl of peanuts; you wonder where his goddamn fork is. Your mom is bare-hand eating hers in giant gulps. It's nearly hilarious as you watch her with your aunt Mo, trying to talk through a mouthful. You sip on your cranberry juice; no more high-school gin. Aunt Mo staggers a little, not a lot, into your mom, but it's enough to knock them both over. You hear Jared laugh as the two women collapse. Lamar looks at him oddly as his nose begins to bleed.

In the other room, you hear Aunt Beatrice begin to cough, harder and harder. Missy, your cousin, starts hitting Beatrice on her back hard enough to make you cringe. Eventually even that stops. There are all the thuds that one would associate with someone falling over.

Or several people falling over.

You hear labored breathing. You hear coughs that slowly die down. All at once a great calamity rises up, and then, just as sudden, it sinks and becomes quiet again. With all the quiet, you hear a carol playing softly in the background, and it makes you smile.

Hang a shining star
Upon the highest bough

It took some doing, but getting the rope over the cross beam in the main archway feels like an accomplishment. You've started to sweat a little bit, in spite of the house being a little cold. No matter. You tie the rope around Jared's feet and begin to haul his useless ass into the main archway. His eyes are wide open, the pained look one gets from a chemically-induced throat closure. You pull his pudgy form up high enough so you can look him directly in his eyes one last time. That's the plan, anyway, as you tie off the other end of the rope to the handrail of the staircase. You look at him, gently swaying back and forth, and you smile at him. You'd take a picture, but seeing him like that is enough. Also, you destroyed your cell phone so you wouldn't be traced. However, you do take this time to text Amanda from Aunt Mo's phone, saying that she needs to get there and take care of Tilda. It seems something is wrong with the "frootcake."

You spell almost everything wrong, because Monique Forrest never had patience for spelling shit right. Amanda will show for this.

You have a good chuckle at that as you wipe the phone down and put it back in Mo's hand.

You see the wreath that you and Marina made in grade school together, leaning by the front door where you had left it. Jared always hated it, and was delighted to be rid of it. It was *hers*, after all, and hey, shouldn't it be *yours* now?

You pull two evergreen sticks from the wreath. They're dry, but not *too* brittle as you shove them into Jared's dead eyes. There's a small popping sound as each stick pokes through. You're surprised at how easy they go in, and you smile.

Now you begin to make sure your small footprint this Christmas Eve Eve is eliminated. You take the glass you've been drinking from all night and put it in your pocket. You leave through the back door and through the yard. You walked here from your hotel, since it was a fortunately mild winter night, and no one sees you walking back. The hotel clerk says nothing; it's Christmas Eve Eve. He waves a hand without looking.

Tomorrow you will take the train to Hoboken, and then the path into New York. Everything is still running on actual Christmas Eve, although very limited this year. Which is good for you. You put the glass in the sink in your hotel room and put the evening's clothes in a plastic bag. You shower and dress in the clothes you'll be wearing tomorrow, and potentially for the next few days.

You'll be a distant memory before too long.

You'll start a new life. Amanda will care for Tilda, and maybe she'll have a shot. You wish her well, and maybe regret not taking her, but Tilda was always more Jared's kid.

No matter now, though. She'll be fine.

You stare at the ceiling and think of your sister. *Tilda will be okay,* you whisper to your sister.

You imagine, as you close your eyes, your sister whispering back.

So will you, little brother.

So will you.

A PIECE OF CAKE

1

Isabella looked at the text on her cell phone. She blinked a few times and read it again. Blunt and right to it.

Mom's dead. When can you come home?

Her brother was a lot of things, but subtle wasn't one of them.

She started to write several texts in response, mostly sarcastic, but decided to respond in kind.

Tomorrow morning.

She stared at the phone for nearly a full minute until the response came back.

K

She sighed. She lived in Erie, only about two hours from Pittsburgh, but it already felt like a million miles away. She slumped in her chair and stared at the picture on her office wall. It was her, her brother Edward, and her mom.

Her now dead mom.

She was going to text him back and ask what had happened, but she could probably guess. Too much booze, too many drugs, not enough insulin, and so much more. She really didn't want to know. Isabella had been done with her mother for a while now, and honestly couldn't care less.

What she did care about was the couple of days she was going to lose having to deal with funeral arrangements, her family, and her fucking brother.

She sighed again.

"Death is never convenient," an old girlfriend had told her once. "If it was, wouldn't you pick a better time than 'out of nowhere'?"

She smiled slightly, thinking of her. Marcie. "The Keeper," Isabella had called her, until Marcie decided to be "the one that got away."

She looked hard at the picture. It had to have been at least twenty years old. Her brother, three years younger, just barely a toddler, and

Isabella, a surly-looking five. Their mother was in her early thirties, still beautiful, still present.

Before the divorce. Before it got really bad.

No, Isabella corrected her line of thought. It had always been bad. It was before Mom got stupid.

Isabella looked down at her phone. She was going to have to ask how she died, but she figured she could wait until she saw Edward. She picked up the phone. She had some work to do before driving to Erie, and she got to it.

First, she had to cancel her appointments for the week, save for one: to look at a prospective purchase of some abandoned building that was, oddly enough, in Pittsburgh. Isabella wanted that one in process for buying soon, and wanted to get a closer look at the inside.

The sooner it was hers, the sooner it could get torn down. The sooner she could do what she did best. Make dollars.

The other appointments would still come through. In fact, the delay due to her mother's sudden death would probably add what Isabella called the "sympathy bonus." Real estate folks sometimes kicked in a bit extra if there was a delay for deeply personal reasons. Your mom dying was a big one. Not so much grandparents, but parents, siblings, even kids. That was an easy 10% overage on whatever she would stand to make.

It would help if she could learn to cry on demand. This thought made her smile a little, and then she stopped herself.

Am I that cold? she thought. *Is it all just about money now?*

Somewhere inside of her, something nodded, and a little voice said simply, "Yes."

Isabella nodded to herself and began to cancel appointments.

2

She stood at her mom's front door in Shadyside, but hesitated to knock. There was an oddly overwhelming sense that she should just turn around and go back home. There wasn't anything for her here anymore. She looked at the mailbox. It was the shitty one she and Edward had made their mom one year for Mother's Day. What was she, twelve? Jesus, that was a million years ago.

It was an ugly wooden thing that their mom had immediately put up, replacing the old black one that had hung off to the left of the front door. This ugly thing hung there now like a cyst, all black and yellow with the last name emblazoned in yellow paint, declaring ANTONACCI.

After the divorce, her mom had kept the name, refusing to go back to being the less exciting-sounding SMITH from her maiden years.

"Smith is boring," she had said. "ANTONACCI sounds like you might be, you know...dangerous or connected, you know?"

Isabella fought and won against the smile that almost spread across her face. She knocked twice, hard, on the door.

After a moment, the door swung open. Edward stood there, hair screwed up, in a dirty t-shirt and boxer shorts. He looked at her and sighed.

"You coulda just come in," he said, and walked away from the door, adding, "Come get some coffee."

She grabbed the door handle roughly and yanked it open. She walked in and, out of old habit, dropped her keys in the large ashtray that sat off to the left on a small table. She regarded the old muscle memory with a grunt and walked through the living room and into the small kitchen.

Edward leaned against the kitchen counter with two cups of coffee. He held one out for his sister, who took it.

"Cream in the fridge," he said. "Sugar where it always is."

Isabella said nothing and took a sip. She grimaced.

"Instant?" she said.

He smiled. "I thought it was appropriate," he said, holding his mug out. Isabella grunted and tapped his mug.

They both took a sip and made the same face.

"I never understood how she could drink this crap," she said.

Edward chuckled. "She was high all the time," he said. "She probably couldn't even taste it."

"True," Isabella sighed. "So what happened?"

Edward laughed. "You waited until you got here to ask."

Isabella frowned. "So what?"

"Just typical."

"Your text said, 'Mom's dead.'"

"But you didn't *ask*."

"And you didn't *tell*," Isabella said. "Spill it."

"How do you *think* she died?" he said, suddenly angry. "She was drunk and high. She fell and died on her back, choked on her own puke. Like a rock star. Like we *always knew* she was gonna die."

Isabella joined his anger. "And you couldn't just *say* that, could you? Just had to half-ass it like everything else in your life. A 'Mom's dead' text. Beautiful, Eddie."

He was going to say something else, but stopped.

"Look, I'm sorry," he said finally. "I was the one who found her. It was really messed up to see. I didn't know what to say. Never had to tell anyone someone was dead."

Isabella looked at him and his eyes were wet, but not exactly crying.

"Sorry," she said. "I didn't even think of that."

They just looked at each other for a long moment.

"This is so messed up," Edward said.

"Yeah," Isabella said. "What do we do now?"

"Well," he started, "we have to pick out something for her to wear in the coffin at the wake."

"There's going to be a wake?" Isabella asked. "Who the hell's going to go to that?"

"Well, us, for one."

"She didn't have any friends."

"How the hell do you know?" Edward snapped. "You haven't exactly been around. Or called. Or anything."

"There's a reason for that," she said. "And you damn well know it."

"What, 'cos she didn't approve of your little lifestyle? So what?"

"It's not my 'little lifestyle,'" Isabella said. "I'm a lesbian. It's what I am, it's *who* I am. And I didn't feel like hearing how I was going to hell every time I talked to her."

"That's just how she was," he said.

"Too bad, 'cos this is just how *I* am," she said back.

"You don't even see the irony in that, do you?"

"Oh, I do," she said. "It's just that my little lifestyle isn't going to make me choke on my own puke."

They stood quiet again.

"We used to be close," Edward said quietly.

"We did."

"Why are we angry at each other?"

"I don't know that I'm angry at you."

He laughed. "Yeah, a little bit."

"You angry at me?" Isabella asked.

He nodded.

"Why?"

"Because you left."

Isabella shook her head. "No, that's not true. You *stayed*. Big difference."

"Somebody had to take care of her."

"Wrong. She needed to take care of *herself.* You needed to get out."

Edward looked at her hard, and this time he was crying. "But...it was *Mom.*"

Isabella drank the rest of her coffee in one disgusting gulp.

"*Your* mom, certainly not mine," she said, and put the mug on the counter, hard. "I have to go check out a property. I'll be back in a few hours. We can discuss details later."

"A property? You're *working*?" His face was one of slight revulsion.

"That's right," she said. "I was going to be here eventually anyway. Might as well make the most of it. You'll be here, yeah?"

"Yeah," Edward said, turning away. "Of course. I'll be here. Always here."

"Right," Isabella said, and left the kitchen. She stopped just short of the front door. She looked back at her brother and asked, "Where are you going to live now?"

He sniffed and ran a sleeve under his nose.

"I don't fucking live here," he said quietly. "I live three blocks over in an apartment. The house is paid for. Why, you wanna sell it? Make it more of a work trip? Shit, you could probably just write the whole trip off."

Isabella nodded, said nothing, and walked out of the house.

3

She walked out of the old nine-story building. It was a little run-down looking, but with some work, she could turn it around. Maybe into a really nice, hip apartment complex. It was super close to downtown Pittsburgh, and transportation was right out in front.

She stood outside and leaned against her car. Looking at the building, she felt her brow edge into a frown.

She couldn't believe Edward. How dare he talk to her like that?

It was Mom.

He just didn't get it. And saying it was her "little lifestyle." Bastard. He'd never had to fight for anything, much less work for anything. She was a woman, and a gay woman, no less.

She was also goddamn successful.

Not just a successful woman, but a successful *gay* woman. All obstacles, and she'd beaten them down.

And screw anyone who couldn't respect that.

"Aren't you worried about hell?" Mom would say. "Don't you know it's evil?"

And then Isabella would yell about how she just didn't understand.

"Aren't *you* worried about an overdose?" she'd yell back. "What hell is there for dead junkies, Mom?"

Every time.

The worst part was, her mother would tell her that she wasn't homophobic, she was just worried, but Isabella didn't buy it. She'd say, "I love you, Bells, but I wish you'd just stop being gay."

Like it was a switch.

Isabella was getting angrier.

Well, she was always angry anymore. But happy content people didn't make money. And Isabella Antonacci made money.

She found the anger she always harbored was less when she closed a deal, or had a windfall of cash from a longshot pay off in dividends. Like her mom with drugs, Isabella got high, but on cold hard cash.

She looked at the front door again, and thought she could almost hear the money calling out to her.

4

The funeral was held just two days later. The only people who attended were, just as Isabella thought, her and her brother. Edward only spoke to her in nods and grunts. Barely a sentence had been spoken between them in the last couple days.

After the graveside interment was finished, Edward gave the keys to the house to Isabella. His eyes were red, and he looked exhausted. He began to follow the reverend as the two maintenance men prepared to fill in the grave.

Isabella looked at him and then at the keys. She began to walk to catch up. "Are we going to the house?" she asked.

"I'm going to crash," he said, not looking at her. "Been up for days."

"What am I supposed to do?"

"Go through the house, figure out what you want to do with all that stuff left in there," he said.

"I thought we could go through it together," she replied, slightly taken aback.

Edward laughed at her. "Are you fucking kidding?"

Isabella frowned.

"No, I'm not fucking kidding. That's where we grew up, that's *our* house."

"No, Bells. It's *your* house now. Now that all the hard stuff is done, it's all you."

"You're not even going to help me?"

Edward stopped. "Help you? Your help was needed forever ago. You're great at showing up late, Bells. True to form. It's too late to talk to Mom, but not too late to sell her house and make some cashola, right?"

He turned and began to walk away from her. He turned his head slightly and said, "Let me know what the old place sells for."

Isabella watched him walk away, too angry to follow him.

***

The parking had always been bad on South Aiken, but today for some reason, it seemed especially so. It was eleven o'clock in the goddamn morning—why was everyone home?

The local radio station began to play "Rainbow Connection" from *The Muppet Movie*. She smiled for a moment and then frowned, nearly punching the radio off.

Not that song. Not now.

She opted to take one more drive, looking for a place to park, and found one spot on the street behind the main drag. The house key would get her in through the back door. She'd simply have to walk about half a block more, but it was better than nothing.

Isabella walked slowly, taking in the street she and Edward had called "the alley." It was an actual street, but a dead-end street that no one ever drove on, since the only people who used it lived in the neighborhood. If you didn't live there, you never even knew it existed.

Isabella saw the big brown garage that used to house the family station wagon. She walked up to the dusty window and looked inside. There was no car, just shit strewn everywhere: magazines, old junk, and a bicycle. She thought of that Tom Waits song and smiled.

She walked around to the little metal gate that led to the back door. The gate squeaked, and she left it open. As she approached the back, she saw that the giant tacky red curtains had been pulled shut. Her mother had always insisted that they be open so she could watch the sun rise. Isabella chuckled because that's what her mother had said; it was really to wake her up if she ever passed out on the living room floor, as the sun would fill the room with light every morning. Shaking her head, she put the key into the door and opened it. She walked into the dining room, just off from the kitchen.

As she shut the door, the first thing she noticed was the smell.

Cake.

She heard noise from the kitchen that certainly sounded like someone was baking a cake. She also smelled cigarette smoke.

Cake and cigarettes.

Her mother was baking a cake.

But her mother was dead.

And yet, she wasn't, because Isabella saw her walk into the kitchen, cigarette dangling out of her mouth. She looked at Isabella and smiled.

"Doesn't it smell good, Bells?" she said.

She was in her mother's dining room, all alone with a dead woman.

Her head snapped around and found a cloud of bluish smoke from her mother's cigarette in her face. She coughed a little and waved her hand. Her mother gave a raspy laugh.

"Oh, stop it, it's not gonna kill *you*," Mother said.

Isabella's head was spinning. This was one hell of a hallucination. It was a dream, it had to be. It all seemed so real, but she knew it was a dream.

Right?

"I'm glad you're here," her mom said. "Come sit down. We need to talk."

She reached up and ran her hand along Isabella's face gently. She looked up at Isabella and smiled sadly, then went into the kitchen.

Isabella stood there for a moment.

Just a dream, she thought.

She looked in the dining room for somewhere to sit.

5

Her mother sat next to a window in the dining room. She had her smoke and her awful coffee cup, filled with even more awful instant coffee.

"I need to talk to you, Bells."

Isabella sat at the opposite end of the table. She looked at her mother blankly.

"I know what you're thinking," Mother started. "I'm supposed to be dead. And I am."

"This is just a really fucked-up dream," Isabella said.

"Sure," her mother said, smiling. "Then you're in a consequence-free environment. Nothing to fear. No need to hold back, right?"

"I guess..."

"You're a *very* angry woman," Mother said. "Do you think it's because you're a dyke? I've never really seen *happy* dykes."

This brutal sentiment snapped Isabella back a bit from her daze. "That's a really lousy thing to say. You just called me *dyke*."

"Well, that's what you are, isn't it?" Mother asked. "Is that not the right word? We didn't have them when I was growing up. I wasn't trying to be mean."

"Oh, that's bullshit," Isabella said, getting louder.

"I wanted grandkids," Mother said. "Edward is never gonna have any. All I wanted was that, really. And for you two to be happy."

"You know, you always said that," Isabella said. "But all you *really* wanted was to get high."

Mother nodded. "There was that," she said. "And look where that finally got me. But how could I *not* get high? Look at all I had to deal with."

"Oh, that's right, you're a victim," Isabella said, laughing. "Gay daughter, lazy son, divorced, alcoholic drug addict. Certainly nothing you could have done wrong...except you've *always* been an addict."

"Well," Mother said with an air of indignity, "not anymore."

"Why, because you're dead? That's a shitty way to kick drugs," Isabella snapped.

"True, but it works," her mother replied, and gave a raspy laugh. "I've been clean for a whole four days! Aren't you *proud*?"

Isabella was almost too furious to notice how absurd this all was, and how unlikely. Part of her registered that this was an impossible conversation, but a much angrier part of her didn't care.

"I can see you're angry," Mother said. "And I don't blame you. My death has ruined your routine. How unfortunate. I truly am sorry. But I needed to talk to you."

"So you waited until you were dead," Isabella said through her teeth. "Your timing sucks, as it always sucked."

"Ooh, I have to check on the cake. Come give me a hand," Mother said suddenly. She got up and rushed into the kitchen.

Isabella sighed and got up to follow her.

She walked into the kitchen and watched as her mother pulled the flattish-looking cake out of the oven. She inhaled, and it certainly smelled like cake, but it looked like a flat pile of something. The way her mother's cakes always looked.

"I just don't know why they always look like this," Mother said as she put the cake on the counter to cool. "I follow the directions to the letter."

Isabella laughed. "No you don't," she said. "Does that look like you followed the directions?"

Her mother frowned. "You used to love making cakes with me. And you always ate them."

"Well, they always tasted good, but you always left out eggs."

Her mother looked at her, somewhat shocked. "Eggs?"

"Always. Eggs. Every single time."

"Well, when were you going to tell me?" Mother said. "I mean, I'm dead now, so what good is it?"

Isabella let out a snort. "I always told you. Every single time. You never listened."

"But you always ate it."

"I didn't want you to feel bad," Isabella said quietly.

Her mother sighed. "So you just ate shit cake to spare my feelings?"

"Pretty much. Me and Edward. You seemed to enjoy making it, and really, it was the only time you seemed happy. Why would I ruin that?"

Isabella's mother pushed past her to go back into the dining room. Isabella followed.

"What?" Isabella said. "Why, of all the things, is that the one you feel bad about?"

Her mother sat down hard. She looked up at Isabella, eyes welling with tears.

"You did try to tell me, didn't you?" She slammed a fist on the table. "Why didn't I just listen?"

"Because you were also high and drunk most of the time, Mom. You never listened to us. You never listened to me unless I told you something you couldn't handle. Apparently, putting goddamn eggs in a cake was one of them."

"You watch your mouth. Don't talk to me like that," Mother said.

"No," Isabella said, sitting back down across from her. "I *will* talk to you like this. I'm an adult. I'm a successful adult. I own things. I'm rich, and I did it all responsibly. I don't get high, I don't *not* follow directions, and I've made something of myself. I did *something* and I'm rewarded well for it, in spite of how I was raised or *wasn't* raised by you. All you did was tell me I was going to rot in hell for being a lesbian, but I actually *did* something with my life."

"I didn't want you to be alone like me," Mother said. "I never wanted you to suffer like me, or want for things you couldn't have because of what you are."

"What I am," Isabella started, "is a goddamn *success* story."

"You're not a mother. You can't judge me. You and your brother didn't come with instructions."

Isabella gave a harsh laugh. "That's what you always said. 'You kids didn't come with an instruction manual.' You didn't come with one either. And Jesus, you were just *awful*."

"Why didn't you ever say anything to me?"

"Because you're my mother!" Isabella yelled. "*You* were supposed to be the responsible one. *You* were supposed to take care of *us*. You were supposed to take care of *me*. And what happened? Eddie and I had to peel you off the floor in the morning. We had to clean you up so you could go to work, whenever you actually had a job. Instead of sleepovers and hanging out with the friends we could cobble together, we had to make sure you didn't choke on your own puke when you passed out. We raised ourselves. And frankly, Edward did a lousy job, but he still stayed and took care of you. He paused his whole fucking life to keep taking care of you."

"And you just left," Mother said. "You didn't take him along. He just stayed here."

"That's not my fault," Isabella said. "*None* of this is my fault. You messed up your life, and if I hadn't left, you would've messed up my life too."

"But haven't you messed your life up on your own?" her mother said, crying. "No spouse, no children. Just you."

"I'm rich," Isabella said.

"So?"

"What do you mean, 'so'?"

"You don't have any family. You don't have any friends. You have your job, and you make money. That's your whole thing, isn't it? Money. Are you even still a dyke—sorry, *lesbian*—if you're not with anyone? You have *things*, but what do you *have*? You don't give a shit about your brother, and you sure don't give a shit about me. You have money, but what do you actually *have*?"

"You don't get it, Mom. You never got it."

"No, you're wrong. I think finally I do get it. I was a shit mother. Still am, apparently. Honestly, I was never a good mother. I know that now." There was a hitch to her voice. "No. I've always known that. *Awful* mother. And I can't apologize enough for it. I don't think I *should* apologize for it, because it wouldn't mean anything. I love you and your brother. I always did, but I didn't love myself, because I don't think I should have *ever* been a mother."

Isabella couldn't believe her ears.

"But I *was* a mother. I was just a really shitty one."

Isabella felt a hitch in her throat gathering, but she cleared her throat. "Is this your idea of an apology?"

Her mother shook her head.

"No, not an apology. You wouldn't accept one if I gave it, because even though I admit I was a bad mom, I don't think I did anything wrong. I know I did, but it's much too late for that now. All I can do now is tell you what you already knew, and one more thing before you go."

Isabella had been so wrapped up in what was happening, she had forgotten that this shouldn't be happening at all.

"And what's that?" Isabella asked.

"Don't end up like me."

"Impossible," Isabella said. "I'm *nothing* like you."

"But you *are*," Mother said. "You're filling a large hole that I carved into you because I was constantly trying to feel anything at all. Booze, drugs...nothing I should have been doing with two kids. But I couldn't feel anything except total failure. You, you fill up on *things*. Money, property, stuff, and it feels good until it doesn't and you have to do it again. And again. Sure, you're rich. But when you die..."

Her mother pointed around the room.

"This is where I died. This is where I am now. This is what I built. Remember who came to the wake and the funeral? You and Edward, and you didn't have a single reason other than I'm your mother. I earned that. That's what I made. That's how I go out. A burden in life and in death."

Isabella sat and looked at her mother. There was an expression on her face that Isabella had never seen before.

Acknowledgment.

"So don't you end up like me. You hear? I don't care that you're a lesbian. I never did, I'm just an old asshole. I'm glad you have money, but don't try to fill yourself with anything that isn't good. You can't fill yourself with emptiness. You have people around you already that love you. Don't shut them out, even if it's just your brother. He needs you."

"So you die and suddenly you're fine that I'm gay?"

Her mother laughed. "It's your life, Bells. It was something that made you happy, and I didn't get that. I still don't exactly get it, but it's part of you. Just like I'm always going to be part of you, and that's why you need to stop and hear me. Don't wind up like me. Be happy."

Isabella simply stared at this woman she had hated for most of her life. And for a moment, she hated her more than ever.

Her mother smiled.

"I know," she said. "I'm infuriating. I always have been, but that's done now. I'm not going to see you after this, but I wanted to tell you this before you left. I love you, Isabella."

Isabella began to cry hard and bitter tears. She looked at her mother through them and found she could not speak.

Her mother stood up and went over to her. As Isabella stood up, her mom grabbed her, hugging her hard. The cries from Isabella came in loud wails, and still, her mother held her.

"Shhhh, baby. Let it out," her mother said. "I'm so sorry, Isabella. I'm so very sorry."

Isabella hugged her mother back, just as hard. They stood that way for what felt like a long time. A time, Isabella knew, had to be coming to an end.

Her mother loosened her hold on Isabella and looked at her. "I never saw you cry," she said.

Isabella laughed a little. "I never had a reason to."

Her mother wiped her tears with her fingers.

"You always had a reason to," she said, and kissed her daughter on the cheek. "How about some terrible cake before you go?"

Isabella and her mother laughed.

"Sit down, Mom. I'll go get it."

She started to turn, to return to the kitchen, but her mother gently grabbed her and gave her another kiss.

"I'll be right back," Isabella said, and walked into the kitchen. As she walked to the cake, still sitting there on the counter, she heard the opening banjo chords to "Rainbow Connection" playing on an old record player behind her in the living room.

Isabella stood there for a moment, listening to the song.

There were a lot of things she wanted to say to her mother. There were still things that were going to make her angry. She knew she could possibly never forgive her mother for some things, but for the moment, everything had already been expressed. Unspoken, in a really good hug and a cry.

She looked out into the dining room.

Her mother was gone.

She looked on the counter and the cake was gone too.

The song continued to play on the old record player, and Isabella began to cry again.

6

Edward walked in through the front door and saw his sister sitting on the living room floor. The curtains were open and the soundtrack to *The Muppet Movie* was playing. It was on the real sad song that Gonzo sings right before the end of the movie.

He stood there watching Isabella sifting through a large pile of vinyl records. She looked up at him and smiled.

"Hey," she said.

"Hey yourself."

"When was the last time you looked through these records?"

He looked at her, puzzled. "God... I don't know, years? Mom always played the one already on there."

"Just side one, remember?" she asked, laughing. "Fucking 'Rainbow Connection.'"

Edward smiled and laughed. "I haven't been able to listen to that song in decades."

"Right?"

Edward closed the front door and joined his sister on the floor. They looked at each other for a while.

"I'm sorry I bailed on you, Eddie," she said. "I really am, and I can't imagine how hard it must've been for you. I was selfish."

"Yeah," he said, not unkindly. "But look at you now. You're a total success."

Isabella smiled at him. "I'm rich," she said. "But I left my brother behind. That was shitty."

"Yeah," he said again.

She put a hand on his cheek.

He looked at her and smiled.

"I've missed you, Bells."

"Same."

She got up and reached her hand out.

"I made something for you."

He took her hand and shot up off the floor.

"Oh yeah? What's that?"

She laughed. "Cake!"

He started to laugh. "Well okay, cool, but if there's no eggs in it, I'm out."

She grabbed his arm and started to pull him into the kitchen.

"Of course there's no eggs. Where the hell do you think you are?"

ALL THESE STEPS LEAD DOWN

The door at the bottom of the stairs creaked open and, much to Jerry's surprise, he was in the exact same place he'd started. It had seemed like an eternity that he'd been trying to get out of the staircase. And every time he came to a door...

He looked out in the dimly lit space before him and, like the other times before, had no desire at all to leave the staircase. He wanted to walk back up and just leave.

Except...

He turned around and saw that the same thing had happened again.

His hand was still on the doorknob, and he squeezed.

The stairs behind him had changed again.

It wasn't that he was getting used to it, but he was starting to expect it. He'd noticed that there was a difference. Jerry didn't want it to happen, but after the last two hours, it was becoming hard to deny.

Or so it felt.

The stairs he had just climbed down were gone. The stairs that *were* behind him were quite the opposite, as if he had just climbed up.

These stairs went down.

"Hellfire," he muttered as he looked once again into the vast emptiness before him.

He slumped. He was tired and pissed.

Maybe, the little voice in his head began, *you should man up and take a look.*

He nodded and sighed. *What the hell, right?*

It didn't look like anything dangerous. Hell, it was the basement of a goddamn building. What's the worst it could be, right? Plus, that goddamned stairwell was feeling tight, getting tighter.

He took out his cell phone and looked at it almost sadly. Still no reception. But it did have a light function on it, so that would be helpful.

Jerry engaged it and held it out in front, slowly walking into the dark basement.

The light wasn't very strong, but it would keep him from falling on his ass. He heard a small creak from behind him just before the door slammed shut. He turned around and shined the light on the door.

Except the door was gone.

"Damn," he said out loud to no one.

He turned and began to walk.

There was nothing at all of note in this basement, as far as he could tell. No storage boxes or tools or even garbage. A basement was for things that you didn't need. A basement was where you put things you didn't want to look at anymore, or things that weren't of use to anyone. A place for things unwanted. The attic was for the good holiday decorations and hand-me-down clothes for the kids and such, but the basement?

That was a place for things best forgotten.

But this place had absolutely *nothing*. There wasn't a single thing here. Just him.

"Hello?" he called out, his vague West Virginia accent echoing in the dark place. "Anybody here?"

He heard nothing but his own footsteps and his breathing.

"Hello?" he called again. He shone the light next to him, but still, nothing at all.

He walked a little farther and came upon a door with a sign that surprised him.

It was his first name.

He blinked a few times, but there it was, gold lettering on a black background.

JERRY

All five letters, neatly printed and looking brand new, as if someone had been waiting for him to find it.

Jerry walked closer to it and examined it intently. He took a finger and ran it along the name.

He then knocked.

He laughed nervously. There was no one here. Why was he knocking?

He grabbed the doorknob and hesitated.

The knob was somehow cold and warm at the same time. It made him scared, which wasn't too difficult; he was mostly there already.

But his entire body was screaming for him to absolutely not open that door.

He took his hand off the knob and took a step back. His legs bumped into something, and he whirled around. It was a small school desk: old, worn out, and familiar.

He waved the cell phone light over it, and it *was* there, not imagined. Jerry reached out and touched the chair. The little desktop looked like the one he'd had when he was a boy in school. Third grade, to be exact.

"Mister Paine, please take your seat," a voice from nowhere said.

Whatever was in the voice, which was as familiar as the seat, made Jerry straighten up and sit. To his surprise, he still fit into the desk, even though he was in his late sixties now. He sat and frowned.

What the hell is going on? he thought.

Suddenly, light illuminated this section of the basement enough to see other desks, other students. Some he couldn't quite recognize, but some he knew. The front of the classroom, which was what the basement now resembled, boasted a lone female figure. The teacher, he figured. Missus Jones, except it wasn't Missus Jones. Somehow, it was his sister Roseann.

But Roseann was dead, and she sure as hell hadn't been a teacher. That girl couldn't string a goddamn sentence together to save her life.

"Rosie?" Jerry heard himself say, and his sister shushed him.

"Is that how we talk to our teacher? Is it?"

The voice was filled with a venom he had never heard; she'd always been quiet and docile, like she'd been taught.

"Answer me, *Mister* Paine!"

"Erm, yes, ma'am. I mean, *no*, ma'am," he heard himself say, and became a bit angry at being scolded by his sister.

"Which is it?" Roseann asked sharply, and glared at him.

Jerry wanted to say what had popped in his mind, but instead said, "No, ma'am."

"Good," his sister said, and sat down at the desk in front of the class. She picked up a book. "I'm going to read you all a story now, and I want you to pay close attention. Especially *you*, Mister Paine. After all, we're all here for your benefit."

Jerry went to say something, but stopped. He'd wait. He'd figure out what in the hell was happening. He felt dizzy, angry, and disoriented, but he was at least glad to be sitting. His mind raced. Rosie had been dead for fifteen years. Goddamn drug overdose, which was right up there along with his other siblings. He wouldn't go out like that, no, sir.

Rosie had always been weak. Some of that was Daddy's fault, he figured, but what the hell are you gonna do? That's your daddy.

"*Jerry*," a thin, soft voice whispered.

Jerry's head whirled around in the direction of the voice. There were three children next to him in a row. He couldn't make out their faces, but saw that it must've been the little girl. She wore a dress with apples and flowers on it. That he could make out, but not her face.

He looked at her, and she said his name again.

"*Jerry*."

"What?" he said, and the voice that came out of his was his, but a younger version of it. "Who are you?"

"*Listen to the story*," the girl said.

He squinted at the girl and slowly turned his head back to the front of the class.

Inches from his face was his sister, or the teacher, or whatever this hallucination was—regardless, it was enough to startle him, and he yelled.

"Do you think you could stop your goddamned yammering and pay attention?" she snarled. Her eyes were black pools, and her teeth were a dark yellow from years of smoking and neglect. Jerry pushed himself back into his seat as the teacher glared at him. He closed his eyes for a moment. When he opened them, she was back in the front of the class.

"Your daddy taught you better than that," she said.

Jerry blinked wildly and looked around.

Daddy. Just hearing that made him both angry and terrified.

"As I was saying," the sister-teacher continued, "I am going to read a story."

***

Once upon a time, there was a young princess who lived in a small kingdom. She was a beautiful princess, and although she was young, she was so very smart.

However, she lived with a cruel father, the king of the land. He hated everything, including his wife, his kingdom, and most of all, his beautiful daughter. He never missed an opportunity to tell his wife and daughter how miserable they had made his life. He never once said a kind word to either unless it was in his best interest to do so, which wasn't often.

After years of being told she was useless, ugly, and stupid, the princess told the long-suffering queen that perhaps it would be in their best interests to leave the castle and the cruel king forever.

"But where would we go?" the queen asked. "We're royalty. Our faces are on the money. We'd have to live like common people. Besides, we're royalty!"

The princess shook her head. "Father is a bad man," she replied. "It wouldn't matter where we were, as long as we were away from him."

It took some doing, but the princess managed to convince the queen that they should leave immediately and let the king rot in the castle alone.

Or so the princess had thought. The queen, who wasn't much better than the king in some ways, ran to the king and told him of the princess' plan.

The king flew into a rage and struck the queen not once, not twice, but three times.

He stormed off to find the princess. The queen, who immediately regretted her actions and knew where the princess was hiding, rushed to tell her to leave at once before he found her. Although the princess was upset that the queen had told him, she forgave her mother and ran to flee the castle.

The princess ran to the secret passage that led out to the stables. She negotiated her way in the darkness with a hand out to avoid any sharp turns.

She found the doorknob that led into the stable, turned it, and swung the heavy door open. There stood the king, impatiently waiting for her.

"After all I have done for you, this is how you repay my kindness?" he roared at her, but the little princess stood up straight.

She thought about all he had done for her. All the hitting, all the terrible things he'd said to her, all the awful things that he had done to her behind closed doors, things that she could never ever forget...

"After all you have done for me, which in no way included kindness, I am doing us both a favor," she said.

"You will never leave!" he yelled.

"But why?"

"Because I hate you!"

She looked at him and, suddenly, it struck her.

"No you don't," she said quietly. "You don't hate me or mother. You hate yourself."

The king looked as if he'd been slapped, because he knew, beyond a shadow of a doubt, that she was right. And this simple fact enraged him like nothing else had ever done. His face twisted into a mask of anger, and he ran toward the princess.

He ran fast, but at the last minute, the princess moved to the side and stuck out her foot, tripping the king, who fell into the dark passageway behind her. Quickly, she closed the door. She looked around and saw a large hammer. She grabbed the heavy hammer and began to hit the doorknob until it broke in half. She heard the knob fall on the other side of the door.

"What do you think you're doing?" the king yelled from the other side of the door.

The princess said nothing as she heard the king, who was now alone in the dark passage of the castle, pounding on a door that would never open.

She turned slowly and walked from the stable and never looked back.

The king, however, never made it out of the passageway. He wandered angrily through the passageway for days, realizing that he did hate himself more than anything else in the world. Finally, he fell somewhere in the darkness and never got up again.

The king was presumed dead, and the queen became the ruler of the kingdom. She tried in vain to find the princess, but she was never ever found. The queen wept, but also hoped that if her daughter was still alive, that she was happy at last.

***

Jerry looked at his sister with wild, terrified eyes. *How could she know?* he thought. He realized he was starting to drool and quickly wiped his mouth.

"So, you see," she said after a moment, "the king did things out of his hatred for himself. Isn't that the saddest thing you've ever heard? A hatred that made him cruel and evil."

"But...I don't hate myself," Jerry said quietly.

"Oh, but you do, Mister Paine, you *do*," Roseann said. "And it isn't an excuse either. I'm leaning toward hating you myself, if we're going to be honest. Just like your other sister. And your brothers. And your parents, especially your daddy. And, of course, *your* daughter."

This snapped Jerry out of his stupor, and he glared at his sister.

"Who the hell are *you* to judge me?" he snarled. "You let me out of this goddamn basement right now, you hear me?"

The lights in the little classroom dimmed—except for the light on the teacher, who was also his sister and somehow not either of them. She was smiling terribly at him.

"I'm afraid there's only one way out of this room. There is a door with your name on it. You simply need to walk through. It's obvious at this point."

"What the fuck does *that* mean?" Jerry asked.

"You were never really that bright, but you were never that stupid either."

Jerry got out of the desk, feeling his age return to him, his anger somehow bringing him back to his senses a little.

"I reckon Daddy didn't discipline you enough, did he?" he said, a small smile breaking out on his face. "Maybe you need a little more discipline to teach you a lesson."

The thing that looked like his sister laughed.

"I've learned a lot from Daddy, thanks very much. And from you. And I know for a fact that even you learned a thing or three from Daddy, didn't you? I know you have. I've seen it in your eyes. I see it now. But you have to go through that door first."

"Where are the fucking stairs out of here?" Jerry snapped, taking a step forward.

"What if the stairs are behind that door?"

"Why don't you *tell* me?"

"You're in no position to ask anything, *Jerry,*" the voice said slowly. The light was beginning to dim on her and rise behind him, on the door. "You aren't going to be teaching anyone any lessons today."

"You think you can do this to me, junkie whore?"

The voice began to laugh.

"You all sat around while your father raped your oldest sister. And then again, when he raped your youngest sister. And then, of course, he started raping you boys. It started a cycle, didn't it? And then your oldest brother died first. The only one who came close to having any kind of remorse, but of course, you can't run from it, can you? You either hide, or you succumb to it."

Jerry snarled and walked forward toward the fading light. He held his cell phone in front of him, still shining its light, but now it, too, was dimming. As he closed the distance on his sister, he found himself in front of the door with his name on it.

He punched the door and turned around.

The door was in front of him again.

He walked toward it and kicked it hard. It didn't make a sound, but he felt the door nonetheless. He turned around.

Another door.

"And boy, did you succumb to it," the voice said. "You kept that cycle up even after you moved away after Daddy died. You left and turned right into him, didn't you? Found a woman who was cowed enough to take it from you. And then had a little girl of your own who didn't wind up as *cowed* as you thought."

Jerry tried to swallow, but found he could not.

He began to hear something else all around him. It was music. A girl singing. The girl who'd been whispering to him.

"*The itsy-bitsy spider climbed up the waterspout.*"

That voice.

"What's behind the door?" Jerry said, trying not to sound as terrified as he had become.

"*Down came the rain and washed the spider out.*"

"Stop that singing!" Jerry yelled.

"Just go in the door."

"*Out came the sun...*"

The door in front of him opened slowly. He saw a set of old wooden stairs lit by candles. The smell that wafted up was dank and musty. He heard the voice singing the song become louder now.

"*...and dried up all the rain...*"

"Why are the stairs going down?" Jerry said frantically. He walked through the doorway and dropped his phone. He heard the phone fall down and down. He didn't hear it stop.

He walked down the stairs slowly, the song still echoing in his ears.

"*...and the itsy-bitsy spider...*"

"Jerry," his sister said from the top of the stairs. He turned, and although he thought he'd only taken a few steps, it seemed the door was far away. "These stairs lead down. *All* of these stairs lead down for you. Go say hello to your daughter. She's been waiting for you."

With that, the door slammed furiously shut.

Jerry grabbed the handrail as he watched all the candles that lit the way up to the door begin to cascade and blow out, darkening the staircase.

"*...the itsy-bitsy spider climbed down...*"

Jerry began to wail as he turned back around and saw that the candles leading down were also starting to blow out. The voice of his daughter echoed in his ears. He started to run down the stairs, screaming and screaming, hoping to catch up to the candles.

But he couldn't. He stopped and sat on the stairs, wailing.

His little girl, so defiant against him.

His little girl, who yelled and screamed *no* at him. Again and again. And when she wasn't yelling, screaming *no*, she was singing this fucking song. Again and again.

So he'd start hitting her again and again until she never sang that fucking song again, not once more.

And she had fallen down the stairs right into the basement. So bruised. So beaten up and mangled because the stairs were like these, old and wooden, and no one would have thought to look into the family history.

"*Down came the rain and washed the spider out...*"

He cried bitter, angry tears. He hated his daughter. He hated his sisters and brothers. And he hated Daddy. But most of all, he hated himself. That made him angriest of all. He stood up, defiant in his increasing claustrophobic terror.

"I hate *all of you!*"

Jerry felt himself fall into nothing and screamed.

With a *thud*, he found himself on the floor. He looked around and saw that he was in a stairwell.

It was familiar, that was sure. He stood up and remembered that he'd been trying to get out of this stairwell for a while now. He turned and looked at the door. He put his hand on the handle and turned. The door creaked open and he looked.

"Son of a bitch," he said.

It was the same place he had started.

THE HUMANITY OF *BLADE RUNNER*

One of the challenges of any science fiction film is making sure that the characters are likable enough to carry the audience through the entire story. As the viewer of these films, we the audience experience the events through the prism of the characters, hero or otherwise, based on a certain level of basic humanity.

The multiple *Star Trek* TV series, films, and literature endure mainly due to the beloved, and sometimes hated, characters that carry the storyline. *Alien* and its relentless sequel *Aliens* deliver the goods because they have characters the audience can rally for and worry about even after the end credits. *Star Wars* has a rich cast of likeable characters to choose from, including Han Solo.

It is no small accident that Harrison Ford was cast in the role of Rick Deckard for Ridley's Scott's adaptation of *Do Androids Dream of Electric Sheep?* by Philip K. Dick (replacing Dustin Hoffman). Renamed *Blade Runner*, the film seemed to be set up to become one of the most iconic science fiction films ever made, and although a commercial flop at the time, it did eventually succeed. But why did a film about killer androids being hunted by Harrison Ford tank so badly in the first place?

Sheila Benson, film reviewer from the *Los Angeles Times*, called the film "Blade Crawler" in reference to its slow, deliberate pace. *New Yorker* reviewer Pauline Kael mentioned that the film "...hasn't been thought out in human terms." (References cited.)

This suggests a shallow look at a film that requires a more in-depth consideration. There are parts that contain *much more humanity* when you take a closer look.

From the very opening sequence with the replicant Leon being given the Voight-Kampff test (which measures emotional responses) and being absolutely petrified during the entire process, you can discern that he *knows* he's going to fail. So does the test's administrator Dave Holden. The test proves beyond a shadow of a doubt that Leon is a replicant. But the sequence is full of tension because he's trying so hard to *not* be a replicant. If only for a few moments, his emotional reactions aren't of stealth or subterfuge, but fear: fear of what he is, fear of what he isn't, and fear of being found out. How fitting it is that the question that finally breaks him is in reference to his mother.

If you can recall a time when you've told a serious lie and were on the cusp of being found out, that sick knot that churns and grinds in the pit of your soul was Leon's experience, and is one that many watching can at least identify with for that moment.

The look on his face when he shoots Holden for the first time isn't malice. It's a defensive look born out of an artificial survival instinct based on a genuine fear. Leon wears the same look when he shoots Holden the second time as well. Leon displays considerable malice later on in the film, but that scene reflects a combination of fear and success. Maybe it's for the first time, maybe even for the last. But it's human in any case.

We then meet Deckard, who's the human hero the audience is expected to identify with, and to that end, he's "our" human, our identifier, our hero played by Harrison Ford (for all intents and purposes, both Han Solo and Indiana Jones), the embodiment of bravado, iron will, and guts. Yet, the film subverts our expectations. Deckard doesn't carry the traits we anticipate. Ford plays him perfectly as a flawed character with some less than noble qualities, yet still relatable with arguably the most humanity of anyone in the film.

But he's not alone in having this quality.

Deckard is forced back into the violent career he walked away from, a Blade Runner, and one of some note, as reflected in the variety of cold-sounding nicknames, like "Mr. Nighttime" and "Boogeyman" according to some versions of the script (but we'll stick to the version I am basing this upon: the Director's Cut.)

Deckard is one of the best (if not *the* best) at tracking down replicants, and the toll it has taken on him is apparent. He's already worn out when he meets with Bryant, who coerces him back into "retiring" some "skin-jobs" who have smuggled themselves to Earth. Here we get our official introduction to the main thrust of the film—the hunt for our four villains, and in particular, their leader Roy Batty.

This whole exchange is delivered coldly. After all, it's not actual *people* the heroes are talking about killing, but machines, and Bryant does nothing to hide this fact. Deckard's response is one of weary reluctance, although he accepts the job pretty quickly.

We hear why these four fugitives are wanted so badly: hijacking an off-world shuttle and killing everyone on board. We also see the footage of Leon again, "airing out" Holden for talking about his mom, and here we see it in a different light. Now we have perspective.

Bryant sets Deckard on his path, and for all of his hesitation, Deckard dives right in and goes straight to the birthplace of the replicants: the Tyrell Corporation. We immediately meet Rachael, a beautiful if not a trifle cold woman who introduces us to Dr. Eldon Tyrell himself. Tyrell has Deckard administer the Voight-Kampff test on Rachael, resulting in somewhat predictable results, but with one exception.

Rachael doesn't know she's a replicant.

Now here is a scene worth breaking down a bit, as there seems to be a surprising lack of humanity. To hear Tyrell explain Rachael to Deckard is akin to the way someone describes how a machine works. He's very proud of his work to be sure, explaining why the Nexus 6 models only have a four-year life span. The slogan of his company, "More Human than Human," comes across more sinister and sad than clever.

The film, at its heart, is a detective story. It's not about solving a mystery, per se, but about *detection*. It's a very deceptive one at that, because while Deckard is out looking for skin-jobs, the skin-jobs are looking for something else entirely: a way to stay alive.

Part of the problem with finding humanity in the characters of this film is that the focus is *not* on the magnificence of the human spirit (at least not for the bulk of the film). There's tremendous humanity all throughout, but it's not the kind of humanity we as casual viewers are used to seeing. Up until this point, we have a very real problem in that the human element and the replicant element are both self-serving. They aren't very likable thus far, and there isn't much of a sign that anyone is going to do anything to change that opinion.

That is, until Roy and Leon go to Chew's.

After a brief (but important) exchange between Leon and Roy at the hotel where Leon lives, they go to Chew's, a designer shop that specializes in making replicant eyes.

The reason that the brief exchange between Roy and Leon is important is because, although it appears that Roy honestly doesn't care about Leon's pics, he understands why he went back for his "precious photos" in the first place. The replicants are all too aware that their memories are artificial. Leon may be insufferable, but he's not *insensitive.* The memories are false, but they're *his* memories, and as we learn later, not all the pics are a sham of his memory banks. Also, Roy's exchange about the "police men" isn't to besmirch Leon's pictures, it's to keep Leon focused on what they're trying to accomplish: the all-important mission of extending their lives.

Upon seeing Roy and Leon, Chew knows he is in trouble. The following exchange is one of the best and oddest in the film, but it's absolutely compelling because of what is *not* being said while it's occurring.

Roy looks directly through *everyone* and drops the line that I've heard recited by many people since this movie's release: "Fiery the angels fell, Deep thunder roll'd around their shores, Burning with the fires of Orc." Chew's facial expression tells all. He reacts appropriately by delivering the best "I am so screwed face" since Ned Beatty in *Deliverance.* He knows these are replicants. He made their eyes. And those eyes are firmly upon him.

They want answers and, to his credit, Chew really knows exactly *when* to cave in amidst vague threats of violence. Roy, to *his* credit, doesn't overtly convey these threatening actions, unlike Leon, who lords over the room, randomly placing eyeballs on Chew's person. Chew tries the old "I made your eyes" routine, which deliciously backfires when Roy retorts, "If only you could see what I've seen with your eyes." As it's the first time we've met Roy for more than a glance, we get to know quite a bit about him. The biggest thing that we learn is that he's *not* impatient (at least not yet). He's quite methodical and systematic. Cold? Absolutely, but what is he trying to do after all? He's trying to live. This is a recurring issue, and each time the theme is readdressed in the film, it does so with a bite.

Deckard, meanwhile, makes it home to find Rachael in his elevator. She is a bit concerned by the things Tyrell has told him about her. She opens up to, essentially, a total stranger and what he does next is simply awful.

He tells her the *truth.*

Up until this point, Rachael's demeanor has been nothing short of intellectual flirting with a slight edge. Now, she's damn near beside herself in that she may be something that perhaps she's secretly feared. After her attempts to prove herself human fail, it appears as if Deckard begins to see her in a different light, through *his own* humanity, and he feels suddenly bad. He tries to casually wave it off to her as sort of a "Hey, just kidding" moment, but the damage is already done. Here is where Deckard begins in earnest to be the detective he is, but more out of a real desire to no longer be a Blade Runner. He's hurt someone he's starting to have feelings for, and she is, for all intents and purposes, the enemy.

Deckard enhances one of Leon's pictures and finds a clue to go along with the artificial snake scale he's found. This leads him to the replicant named Zhora, who's been living in hiding as an exotic dancer. Oddly enough, his initial approach isn't full guns blazing. He pretends (poorly) to be an inspector.

This seems to work long enough for Zhora to take a shower and for Deckard to look around her dressing room. It's when Zhora gets semi-dressed that Deckard begins to receive the series of beatings that will plague him for the rest of the film. In fact, she displays a certain amount of pleasure in trying to strangle Deckard before another dancer comes into the room and pushes her to leave at a rapid hike. Deckard manages to pull himself together enough to pursue the half-naked replicant.

In one of the film's most intense sequences, Deckard chases a clearly terrified Zhora through the cyberpunk L.A. streets. This is a far cry from the confident, almost gleeful way she nearly killed him moments before. Pure survival instinct drives Zhora to run as fast as she can, which is considerable. Deckard is waving his gun around and even firing it a few times with little regard for the actual humans he's trying to protect.

If there is any recurring theme with regards to humanity, it is a consistent reinforcement of the raging will to live regardless of the consequences. Deckard wants to live too, but at the same time he wants this replicant dead; not only because it's his job, but also because she just tried to "retire" him.

Two things happen next that are of some importance. First, Deckard kills Zhora after an exhausting chase, concluding with her being shot and crashing through plate glass windows. The look on Deckard's face says it all. Yeah, he's exacted some small revenge, but he's also done his job. This is where his earlier weariness returns. Replicant or not, he just retired someone (or something) in grand fashion and in front of a *lot* of people. It doesn't seem to sit well with him at all.

Second is the reappearance of Gaff, accompanied by Captain Bryant. Bryant congratulates Deckard on his work calling him a "goddamn one-man slaughterhouse." Then, adding coldly, "Four more to go." Deckard frowns, already knowing what this means, but corrects him anyway. It's now four because of Rachael, Bryant explains. The look on Deckard's face is a mixed expression of fear, anger, and quiet resignation. This is not what he needed to hear. Part of this has to do with Bryant's delivery. Bryant isn't inhuman. He's *inhumane*. Here, he represents the not-so-magnificent side of humanity. He even gloats about how Rachael didn't even know she was a replicant before leaving Deckard with this disturbing change in his mission.

He never gets time to let this properly sink in because Leon, who has witnessed the murder of Zhora, finds him first, and he isn't interested in consoling Deckard.

Leon enters the scene in a rage, catching Deckard off guard. Deckard, who hasn't been punched in at least five minutes, begins to make up for lost time. Leon opens his festival of violence by asking Deckard, "How old am I?" You already know this isn't going to go well for Deckard. The beating begins, peppered with banter.

This continues until, just when things seem hopeless and Deckard is literally staring death in the eyes, a shot rings out and a spray of Leon's blood splashes his face. A shocked Deckard is even more surprised when his savior is revealed to be Rachael. She has retired one of her own.

After taking her home for a stiff drink, he finds it's never easy to put yourself together when you're surrounded by so much death. Deckard isn't immune to it, though, and notices that Rachael isn't either. She's shaking. He tells her it's part of the business, and her reply is so stunningly apt, it's chilling.

"I'm not part of the business, I *am* the business."

Again, she's opening herself up to a man who has now been tasked with killing her, but she knows he can't, or rather won't. As he says, he owes her one. She saved his life and he knows why. There's a level of humanity that hasn't been apparent in the film up until this point. Both of these characters are broken. What follows all of this is a widely debated "love" scene.

When I first saw the scene in question, I didn't fully understand it. The reaction I had was that Deckard was trying to force Rachael into having sex. Years later, I found that I may have been mistaken. Looking at it now, I see two damaged people with only the vaguest sense of what it is to be vulnerable, what it is to feel something other than the ugliness that is 2019 Los Angeles, rain and cold and death. Deckard awkwardly shows Rachael how to "desire him," and while it really does look like he's forcing himself on her, in reality it's merely something she has yet to encounter in her short life. It's an actual feeling he's trying to show her, and she picks up on it pretty quickly. This is cathartic for her as much as it is for him. He's teaching her how to feel something, and in that act alone, he's also teaching himself how to feel.

At this point in the film, we've already met Pris and J. F. Sebastian. Their scenes mirror Deckard and Rachael's in an odd way. When we meet Pris, she's apparently setting herself up to *appeal* to J. F. Sebastian. This works without a hitch, of course, because that's what Pris has been designed to do. However, she gets much more than she bargained for, as J. F. isn't seduced by her as much as he is charmed by her childlike demeanor. He doesn't come across as one intellectually armed for what happens to him. He's twenty-five (in spite of his appearance due to Methuselah's syndrome aging him faster than time) with no friends except the toys he's made for himself. It's nearly heartbreaking to see them greet him at the door with welcoming proclamations like "Home again home again, jiggity jig! Gooooood evening, J. F."

At this particular point in the film, Pris seems to be the character we're going to get to allow some, if any, sympathy other than Rachael for the replicants. Almost everything we learn about Pris is done in the presence of J. F.

J. F. is so unbearably grateful to have actual friends (even friends he possibly knows are using him) that he agrees to help them. *He's* going to get Roy in to see Eldon Tyrell. The scenes with J.F. and Pris are almost sweet even though there is a thread of tension, if only felt by the audience, who knows why Pris is there. J.F. certainly does not, and is genuinely pleased to have something more akin to a friend than his "toys."

Thus far, *Blade Runner* is not only the futuristic grand tour of the seven deadly sins, but it's highlighted all the *worst* aspects of the human spirit, which makes it hard to choose sides. As in real life, the choices aren't always black and white. They're not even grey. They're choices that hinge on what you're willing to live with and for how long. In other words, the lesser of two evils. In that aspect, *Blade Runner* becomes a retelling of Lucifer's fall from Heaven, but with *very* different results.

The fall of Lucifer is pretty cut and dry: Lucifer, the favorite of God, became obsessed with his own beauty and cleverness, which resulted in him wishing to become God. Ultimately, God threw him and the other angels like him out of Heaven for their sin of self-generated pride. In this case, however, it is Tyrell, attempting to play God, who is prideful to an extreme. Roy may be the designated "bad guy" in this story, but his motivations are mostly based on his desire to keep on living. Tyrell is simply far too impressed with himself to be bothered to try and repair something he created and already believes to be perfect. Perfection with an expiration date, as it were, and perfection that is self-aware. When Roy kills Tyrell, it isn't out of pride. Roy is killing the devil as well as his god. Roy hasn't fallen as much as he has simply let his anger for wanting to live take him over.

His anger is such that he stalks and kills J. F., thankfully off-screen. Now, it is an extremely human trait to take anger out on those around us, and Roy is no exception to that basic human rule. He murders the one person who had actually helped him out of a bizarre act of kindness. It can easily be explained away that Roy is a cold-blooded killing *machine*. Roy is looked upon as the main villain in this film and he's doing what villains do. So why doesn't it feel right? Why doesn't this sit well with anyone watching this movie?

At this point in the film, we realize that the replicants really *are* slaves who broke free. They could have blissfully gone elsewhere to live out what was left of their lives, but like Leon said, "Nothing is worse than having an itch you can never scratch." Roy had the means to scratch his itch (or so he thought), but once he learned that his expiration date was irreversible, he took it out on poor J. F.

With the deaths of Pris and Sebastian, we come to a climax that isn't so much a climax as it is a reckoning. Once it gets rolling, it's hard to look away.

Deckard encounters Pris at J.F.'s place and it is one of the more unnerving scenes in the film. Pris attacks him with such savagery, it's almost as if we're seeing another character entirely. There isn't really anything in her personality make up that prepares the viewer for what she is capable of doing, and it's reflected in Deckard's face. It's not a long scene, but it's agonizing to watch because of the sheer brutality from Pris. But this violence, again, is a reflection of the desire to live over everything else. She knows she's dead sooner or later, but it is infinitely better to die later than sooner, and on her own terms.

Deckard, desperate to live as well, shoots Pris and leaves her in a heap. He is relieved momentarily because he knows there's one left to go.

Roy finds the body of Pris and he breaks down, not so much with uncontrolled rage as with genuine heartbreak. He is now the last one and he is truly alone. He even howls like a wolf. This sound hits Deckard like a train and invites untold fear upon him. Deckard's facing the alpha now. This is a fight he doesn't want, but he is resigned that it's going to happen regardless. It's part of the business.

During these final scenes, Batty does something the other replicants were only slightly successful in accomplishing. He becomes truly frightening, and he isn't going to go quietly. He's seen what Deckard has done to Pris. It appears that all is lost, including whatever humanity he had developing inside him. He's killed his god/father. His beloved Pris is gone, along with Zhora and Leon, so what is left for him?

All throughout the end chase, Deckard is petrified and functioning on pure adrenaline. His survival instinct is taking over. Although Deckard has come out on top, probably by sheer luck, he knows that there just isn't any more luck left in the tank. The hunter has become the hunted.

As Roy begins his countdown in an effort to be sporting and even more intimidating, he also begins the process of expiration, which gives his countdown a double meaning of sorts. He looks not afraid, but angry. His will to live becomes about something other than survival. It's also about living just long enough to see things come to a proper end, and after much ado on a rooftop, they do. Before this morphology, Deckard finds himself dangling from a beam, once again looking down into the pit of death.

"Quite an experience to live in fear, isn't it?" Roy says, not at all unsympathetically. "That's what it is to be a *slave.*" This is the all-important pivotal moment of truth when this cold, sad, relentlessly *inhuman* film delivers a punch so hard it continues to resonate decades later. As Deckard takes this in, his hands slip, and for a nanosecond, he's falling to his certain death until Roy saves him. In perhaps the most unexpected move in this bleak film, Roy sits down and looks at Deckard, who is now in awe of what he is seeing.

Roy begins to deliver the most raw and emotional moment in the film and possibly the most human scene in *any* science fiction film. "I've seen things you people wouldn't believe. Attack ships on fire off the shoulder of Orion. I watched C-beams glitter in the dark near the Tannhäuser Gate. All those moments will be lost in time, like tears in rain." Deckard is stunned, as are the rest of us. This was the *villain.*

There is no villain now. There are just these two more broken pieces of humanity. Replicant or not, Roy in this moment isn't an artificial anything. He looks at Deckard one last time and says, "Time to die." He does just that, letting the bird he's been holding soar away to live out its life.

The film concludes with Deckard getting ready to hit the road with Rachael, but as they leave Deckard's apartment, we realize Gaff had been there and left behind a little origami unicorn. A voice-over reinforces this fact: "It's too bad she won't live...but then again, who does?" Although overshadowed by the righteousness of the rooftop speech, there is considerable humanity (as well as controversy) in that scene.

Blade Runner contains many examples of the worst parts of the human spirit. The characters are compelling enough to make you worry about what happens to them, especially the replicants. When Roy reminds us that for every dark soul, for everyone who lives in fear, for everyone who knows what it is to be a slave, there is, underneath, one unifying potential we all have and, sadly, often choose to ignore.

The magnificence of the human spirit.

References:
Sheila Benson, The Los Angeles Times, June 25, 1982
Pauline Kael, The New Yorker, July 12, 1982 P. 82

NEGOTIATIONS

Harold Smith sat at his large desk in Folcroft Sanitarium. The sun was peeking through his window, giving him a beautiful view of the green courtyard in the early morning, which he ignored. It happened every day, and therefore, Smith ignored it. He had stopped one day to watch the sun rise, and though he admitted it was pretty, it was also a waste of time, because it would rise quite well without any help from him. He never watched it again.

He sat wringing his hands, aching from arthritis, and waited for his assistant, Mark Howard, to arrive. He looked at his watch. It was 6:45AM. Howard would be in his office any second.

Smith had to admit that he liked the young man. He reminded Smith a lot of himself when he was younger, although Howard possessed the one thing Smith had failed to gain all his life. An imagination. This was precisely why an idealistic young president had chosen the unimaginative but patriotic Smith to be the director of America's secret weapon, CURE.

It wasn't an acronym. It was the job description. The young president knew the worst secret about democracy: it doesn't work. He needed an organization to work outside of the constitution in order to protect it. When the young president was assassinated, CURE continued with Smith at the helm. No one knew about CURE except for Smith and the following president at any given time.

Times, as they always do, changed. And that's what today's meeting with Howard would be about.

Mark Howard knocked lightly on the door and entered.

"Good morning, Dr. Smith," he said tersely, and closed the door behind him.

"Good morning, Mark. Please, sit down," Smith responded, equally as terse. Howard did so, sitting at full attention.

"Mark, this morning I'm going to prepare you for one of the most important functions you will have as assistant director of CURE."

Mark Howard's eyes grew wide, and he couldn't suppress a small grin. Smith's stomach grumbled and he reached into his desk drawer for his antacid tablets.

***

His name was Remo, and he was ready. At least, he *felt* ready. He had done this once before, and wasn't sure if he could do it again. He took a deep breath and held it in. He looked through the window of the cab and took in the beauty of the view of Rye, New York.

It was a beautiful morning, and Remo was dreading his task. He let the breath out slowly and tried to let his concerns leave him as well.

"Are you going to huff and puff all the way there?" a squeaky voice to his left asked. "Some of us are trying to enjoy the silence."

Remo turned and looked at Chiun, the elderly Korean man sitting next to him. He was going to answer the old man, but didn't, and turned back to the window.

"Thank you," Chiun said quietly.

"Thank you for what?" Remo asked. "I didn't say anything."

"Exactly," Chiun replied. "But, of course, you ruin the silence anyway, so why do I bother giving you thanks?"

"Sorry," Remo said. "I'm just a little nervous about this. I've only done this once before."

Chiun nodded. "Yes, and you did fine. Not as well as others before you, but you were...*adequate*."

"You're not filling me with confidence, you know." Chiun sighed.

"No, you are right. I only filled you with Sinanju. How *ungrateful* of me."

Remo didn't reply because Chiun was right. He had been filled with Sinanju for over thirty years until it overflowed. Chiun had turned what he had called a "pale piece of pig's ear" into the pinnacle of human perfection known as the Master of Sinanju.

Sinanju wasn't a form of martial arts, but the sun source for all others. It was the oldest and the best. For thousands of years, Sinanju produced the greatest assassins the world had ever seen. They had no equal, and the House of Sinanju was the most sought-after political tool in the world.

Remo had been chosen to be CURE's enforcement branch. To achieve that goal, Chiun, then the Reigning Master of Sinanju, had been hired to train him. Originally, Chiun was going to teach the white fool a few tricks, collect his money, and move on. No one outside of the village of Sinanju had ever been trained in the deadly art.

Soon after training began, when Remo showed signs of actually *absorbing* the training, Chiun realized that the young American was the fulfillment of an old Sinanju prophecy and stayed on to complete his training.

That was thirty years ago, and in those three decades, Remo himself had become the Reigning Master.

"Little Father," Remo began. "Why didn't we go over anything before we decided to meet with Smith?"

"Why do you ask that now, as we approach our meeting with Emperor Smith and young Prince Mark?"

Remo's face darkened. "And by the way, you can forget me ever calling Smitty and the pipsqueak anything other than that. I mean, why didn't we go over...you know, what we want."

"*You* are the Reigning Master, Remo," Chiun replied. "That's your problem."

"Yeah, but as you like to remind me, I am being judged by all the former Masters on my performance here. The last time I did this, *you* were still Master."

"Perhaps you should have thought of that instead of staring out your window like a stunned halibut." Chiun sniffed. "Besides, we are here."

The cab pulled up to the front of Folcroft Sanitarium. Remo paid the driver, and the two men departed from the cab. They walked into the building and made their way to Smith's office.

"Greetings, O glorious Emperor Smith!" Chiun beamed, bowing slightly. "And salutations to you, Prince Mark."

Smith returned the bow while Mark grinned and looked uncomfortable.

"Greetings to you, Master of Sinanju," Smith returned, and then looked at Remo.

"Hi, Smitty," Remo said. He didn't even look at Howard.

"Remo," said Smith, nodding his head.

"Well," Mark said, "shall we begin?"

Chiun tucked his hands into the sleeves of his brilliant red kimono and descended lightly to the floor.

"Yes, let us begin," he said and looked up at Remo. The three men also sat down on the floor, although Smith, old now and starchy, had a bit more trouble than Remo and Mark. All seated, Chiun pulled a roll of papyrus and a quill pen out from his kimono and handed it to Remo.

"Okay, fellas," Remo said. "Let's make a deal."

Mark cleared his throat and opened his mouth to speak. He never got the first word out.

"Dear Prince Mark," Chiun began. "It would be best for you to heed the emperor during such times of negotiation."

"Actually, Master Chiun, Mark will be the one doing the contract this time around. I thought it would be best that he learn this way."

Chiun stifled a laugh, but Remo didn't. Chiun admonished him in Korean.

"Sorry," Remo said, still laughing. The red look on Mark's face spoke volumes. He cleared his throat again.

"Gentlemen, we have some new procedures we'd like to promote for our new contract with the House of Sinanju." Mark didn't stammer, but his heart was pounding. "In keeping with these modern times, I'd like to suggest that we follow a new contract form."

Mark produced a ream of papers and a pen. He laid them in front of Remo and Chiun to review. Remo looked at the paper while Chiun turned up his nose.

"What's this all about?" Remo asked.

"Well, I thought, this being the 21st century, we should try to keep our paperwork to a minimum by using these standard forms. After we are finished, I can enter them into a database for quick and easy reference." Mark smiled sheepishly, proud of his excellent idea. He looked at Smith for approval. Smith nodded. Remo looked at Chiun, who spoke a single Korean word, to which Remo nodded in agreement.

"What did he say?" Mark asked.

"Well, since there really isn't an English word for it, let's just say he said '*bulldookie*.'"

Mark's face grew ashen.

"I'm sorry?"

"It means no way, Jose," Remo said. "We use papyrus. It lasts longer than paper and computers."

Mark looked down at his ream of contract paper. To demonstrate, Chiun took a single long fingernail and scraped it quickly along the top paper in Mark Howard's lap. The paper ignited instantly, and in a flash, all of the contracts were a small pile of ash.

"See?" said Remo, smiling. Mark was amazed. He only rarely got to see what the two assassins were capable of, so he was always surprised by their skills. Smith tightened his jaw and struggled to his feet. He walked across the room to open a window.

"Um, okay then," Mark said shakily. "Let's move on to payments. What we'd like to do is transfer the currency, presently gold, into gold bonds and hold them in a secure bank account. That way, it can also acquire interest. It also makes it easier on our relations with Korea."

The current contract, as well as all other contracts, insisted upon gold bullion being delivered to the small village of Sinanju, in North Korea, via submarine; dangerous at best, considering the climate of North Korean/American relations at any given point. Remo looked at Mark, but could feel Chiun's glare burning into his head.

"What you're telling me is it would be easier for *you* to just deposit the gold in a bank?"

Mark smiled. "Yes, Remo. *Exactly.* Much easier for everyone involved."

"So, we'd be on kind of like a payroll, where you'd cut us a check and just put it in a bank for us?"

"Absolutely!" Mark was excited. He stole a look at Smith, who knew better; his face was sour.

"Since you're newer at this than I am, I'll tell you a secret, kid. It is something several thousands of years old that has been passed down from generation to generation of Sinanju Masters. It is, in fact, the *most* important code of Sinanju."

Mark was all ears.

"No checks," Remo said flatly. Chiun hid a small grin.

"But wouldn't you rather be assured that your gold wasn't at risk of being hijacked by Korean pirates, or the government?" Mark asked, stupefied.

"The day anyone molests Sinanju payments," Chiun spoke softly, "would indeed be his *last* day. No one would *dare* interfere with our tribute."

"*I* got this, Little Father," Remo said to Chiun in Korean. Chiun looked hurt at the admonishment but understood. He nodded and was silent.

"Sorry, junior. The payment method stays the same." Remo paused for effect, without really being aware he was doing so, and added, "Apart from the increase, that is."

"Increase?" Smith said abruptly. Mark looked at Smith, hurt. Smith looked back at him sternly, but then softened. "I'm sorry, Mark. Please continue."

"Thank you," Mark said, turning back to Remo. "What increase?"

"Well, as I see it, the old contracts were for two Masters of Sinanju. One Reigning and one apprentice Reigning. Now we have one Reigning and an Emri... Um, an Em—"

"*Emeritus,*" Smith said, finding the word. He sighed. This was going worse than he had thought. Chiun had taken the title of Reigning Master Emeritus, which meant that he still held the title of Reigning Master of Sinanju, if only in name. However, it meant he was still a Reigning Master, if not *the* Reigning Master.

"Thanks, Smitty. Reigning and Emeritus. That should reflect in our yearly payments, don't you think?" Remo crossed his arms and waited for an answer. Mark loosened his tie. He was sweating now. He knew he was in over his head, but he refused to back down.

"Just what kind of increase were you looking for?"

"Oh, I'd have to say...double the pleasure, double the fun, and...double the current rate," Remo said casually.

Chiun nodded in agreement.

"*Double*?" Mark nearly yelled. Remo looked at Chiun and winked.

"Each," Remo added.

Smith reached into his suit jacket to pull out the antacid tablets and swallowed six. Remo turned to Chiun.

"Nice touch," Chiun said in Korean.

"Thanks. Should I be writing this down?"

Chiun's expression darkened.

"Were you expecting *me* to write it down?"

"Hey, give me a break. You know you could be writing this down for us. You're not doing anything. And I don't remember writing anything last time."

Chiun turned up his nose.

"The last time was practice, O *Master* of Sinanju," he said.

"Hey, I think I'm doing all right so far," Remo said, and turned back to Mark and Smith, who, in turn, were looking at each other.

"Do you guys need some time to get yourselves together?" Remo asked, reaching for the papyrus. Smith frowned when Mark turned toward him, looking for an answer. Smith's face said it all.

"Er, no, Remo," Mark replied, shakily. "Let's continue."

Remo grabbed the quill and tried to write to no avail. He shook the quill until he heard Chiun sigh heavily.

"Ink," Chiun said finally.

Remo looked at him.

"I know. Where is it?"

"Why are you asking *me*?"

"Well, you brought the papyrus and the quill," Remo said, annoyed. "Why didn't you bring the ink?"

"Why are you assuming I brought the papyrus and quill for *you*?" Chiun sniffed. "This is *your* contract negotiation for the House, not *mine*. That is no longer my concern."

Remo rolled his eyes.

"Then why did you bring this junk in the first place?"

"Not that it's any business of yours, but I was going to write," Chiun said, adding, "Would you like to *borrow* them?"

"What good are they without the ink?" Remo snapped. Chiun produced a small vial of ink from his kimono. Remo went to speak, but Chiun cut him off.

"No thanks are needed, o Master of Sinanju," he said, gesticulating wildly and looking at Smith and Mark. "It is the pleasure of the Reigning Master Emeritus to aid you in your endeavors in the presence of the mighty Emperor Smith and his young charge."

Remo grabbed the vial and opened it, still glaring at Chiun. After a minute of writing, dipping, crossing out, and rewriting, Remo was ready. He looked at Mark and smiled.

"How do you spell 'Emeritus'?" Remo asked.

***

Three and a half hours later, the four men stood up from the floor. Mark was exhausted and Smith felt twice his eighty-plus years. Remo and Chiun might have just woken from a restful sleep, although Chiun's eyes were narrowed and suspicious.

"Well, if that's it, we're outta here, Smitty," Remo said, turning to go.

Smith, seeming to remember something, called for Chiun. "Master Chiun. Just to be clear, this arrangement doesn't in any way interfere with *our* current arrangement."

Chiun bowed to Smith and hurried out the door. Remo was confused.

"What previous agreement?" he asked. "We just made a new one, or weren't you listening for the past three hours?"

Smith removed his glasses and wiped them with the handkerchief in his breast pocket.

"It's a matter that Chiun and I have dealt with personally since your promotion to Reigning Master, Remo. Nothing to be concerned with, I assure you," Smith said in a lemony voice.

"Care to tell me what it is?" Remo asked. Now his eyes were narrowed and suspicious.

"I'm sorry, Remo," Smith replied. "As I said, it's a matter for me and Master Chiun...the Reigning Master Emeritus."

Remo turned to go, but stopped just short of the door. He turned around and looked at Mark, who was leaning against Smith's desk, dead tired.

"Hey, kid," Remo called. Mark looked up at him. Remo was smiling. "Not too bad today. Nice try with the bank account thing," Mark was taken aback.

"Well, thanks, Remo," he said, smiling back.

Remo's face darkened suddenly.

"By the way, you both might want to try '*Master* Remo' from here on in. Have a little respect."

Smith and Mark looked at each other and then at Remo, who was still scowling in the doorway.

"On second thought," Remo started, inching his way out the door, "Smith can call me Remo."

Sounding a little hurt, Mark asked, "Why not me?" Remo smiled again.

"Because that's the biz, sweetheart," he said, and slammed the door shut so hard, it recessed into the frame by half an inch.

Smith looked at the door and then at Mark.

"When you get the chance, Mark, tell Mrs. Mikulka to have the door replaced."

Smith walked to the window and added, "Actually, call her on my phone. We'll be in here until it's fixed."

***

Chiun stood outside Folcroft serenely and calmly when Remo burst through the exit. He was angry, Chiun knew, but then again, Remo was almost always angry about something.

"Okay, Chiun. What deal do you have with Smitty?"

Chiun didn't move, but spoke in a sing-song voice.

"Ah, it is the Reigning Master of Sinanju come to fetch his father after completing his task for the House. O, glorious day."

"Can it, Chiun. I'm not in the mood. What's this deal you and Smith have worked out behind my back?"

Chiun looked at his former student.

"Nothing to be concerned with, Remo. I am merely looking after myself in my dotage. I am, after all, semi-retired."

Remo went to reply to that comment, but changed his mind. "Where's the cab?" he asked Chiun.

"I do not know. Did you call one?"

"Why didn't you?"

Chiun sniffed.

"Is it not in our contract to have transportation provided to us?"

Remo looked at Chiun blankly.

"Here is one now," Chiun said, pointing into the distance. "Behold, my cab."

Remo looked puzzled.

"Little Father, why did you ask if transportation was provided in our contract?"

As the cab pulled up, Chiun glided to the curb to meet it. He turned and looked at Remo, smiling.

"Because it is provided in *my* contract." Chiun opened the back door of the cab and slid inside. He rolled the window down. "Do not forget to pick up fish for dinner. Halibut would be nice."

Remo stood and glared as Chiun's cab drove away from Folcroft Sanitarium. There was no way he was going back inside to call for a cab. He took a deep breath and began to walk. After all, he was the Reigning Master of Sinanju.

He thought of this and smiled.

THE TROUBLE WITH UNICORNS

"The baby should have been the first one to get killed," Reiner said. "Although, I think looking back, if anyone should have gotten killed *at all*, it should have been me or that dragon."

Kimberly Maddox tried to look as passive as possible, but it was tough. He wasn't lying about the dragon. At least, he didn't *think* he was lying about the dragon.

Reiner sat with his back straight against the chair and relayed everything in perfect detail. He even told some things the forensic team had missed. He was being cooperative.

The problem Kim was having was that he wouldn't shut up. And the things he was saying were, at best, insane.

"Now, the unicorns everyone gets wrong," he continued. "You think they're magic, right? Beautiful creatures, so perfect, white, and innocent. Well, who do you think was told to come for my sacrifice in the first place?" He looked at Kim, almost pleading for her to say it.

She cleared her throat.

"The unicorns?"

"The *unicorns*!" Reiner said. "Taking all their orders from that fucking dragon." He began to cry, slowly at first, and then in a steady gurgling rasp. Kim shoved a box of tissues in his general direction across the table in the white mirrored room.

Reiner looked at her and smiled.

"I'm not crazy," he said through his teeth.

"I'm not saying you are or aren't, Mr. Reiner," she said, looking right back at him. "I'm just getting information that is relevant to the case. Are you sure you don't want—"

"No lawyers," he said, waving a hand. "This will all be wrapped up sooner than later. I just want someone to know."

Kim frowned.

"To know how you killed your family?"

He shook his head.

"To know *why* I killed my family," he corrected. "I'm saving the world, you know."

"You killed your family to save the *world*?" She heard anger creep into her voice. When interrogating anyone, emotions must remain flat, regardless of what the asshole did.

"That's right. A blood sacrifice every fifty years. Handed down for generations. Payment in blood, given to the unicorns and delivered to the dragon. Except..." He looked down.

"Except *what*?" Kim responded impatiently.

"I...can't say," he replied.

Kim slammed her fist on the table, and for the first time, genuine fear showed in Reiner's face. He jumped.

"I'm not supposed to tell anyone or my death will be long and painful!"

"Says who? The fucking *unicorns*?" Kim snarled. "Spit it out!"

Reiner slumped and took a deep breath, looking down.

"I killed my family so the world may live," he said. "I'm to start a new family and pass this on to them. But that can't happen now."

Kim nodded, sighing as she did so.

Reiner was going to say something else, but as he looked at Kim, he froze.

Kim wasn't there anymore.

In her place was a snarling, white unicorn.

"Big mouth," the unicorn said, sighing.

REGARDS, ELEANOR

I killed my husband.

Maybe *murdered* is the better word... You'll have to decide on your own. I did something I knew would result in his death. Is that actually murder? To do something thinking, *Well, if this happens, then this* might accidentally *kill him...* Would that be *sort of* homicide?

I crack myself up.

I was never even questioned by the cops. Maybe that's why I'm writing this down. No one is going to read it.

I've been a lifelong wallflower. Even married, I was the last to get *any* kind of attention, and I was *always* okay with it. I'm a mom and a wife...well, *widow* now. When I was younger, I was largely ignored. I had boyfriends, but not for very long. It was a lot of going through the motions. When you're a wallflower with a name like Eleanor, it's almost all going through the motions.

But I told myself I was okay with it all. My role, I felt, was to highlight everyone else. I'd shine someone else's star before even worrying about my own little star. And I did it without complaint until last month. That's when I hit my threshold.

My husband was an awful lover. That's forgivable. But after years of marriage, the one thing that always crawled under my skin was that he *insisted* on calling me Nora. No matter how many times I told him, he'd always call me Nora. It's *Eleanor*. It might be a lousy name to you, but it's *my name.* It's the only thing I ever asked for, and he couldn't give me that one thing.

We had a fight right after the last time we had sex. He called me Nora and I exploded.

"Why can't you ever call me by my name?" I screamed at him.

"Because Eleanor is a stupid name," he said, and walked into the bathroom.

Choosing to take a back seat to other people is different than being put there constantly.

So I bought bees.

Did you know you can buy an entire *hive* of bees? You can. One fake name, a pre-loaded credit card, and a private mailbox later, I was ready. I only got stung a few times—I'm not allergic, so it wasn't too awful. Craig, however, *was* allergic. Deathly allergic. After setting up the hive on the ground in our huge yard that he never mowed (*and another week of begging him*), he finally mowed.

I only regret not being there to see it.

I wonder if he even knew when he ran over the nest that it shouldn't have been there. I wonder if, as the hundreds of bees stung him on eighty percent of his body, he knew that those bees shouldn't have been there at all.

I wonder if he thought of me as his throat closed and he clawed at his neck.

I wonder if anyone will notice this little letter that I'm leaving in his pocket.

Goodbye Craig,

Regards,

Eleanor

MANNERS COUNT

Bethany walked slowly through the receiving line to her mother. It was a longer line than she had anticipated, but it would be worth the wait. The payoff would be huge, if only to her.

Her mother was retiring at the age of eighty-five as the CEO of a large financial institution. She was a pioneer, a legend in her own time.

Bethany hated her guts.

The things that set her off, she had a handle on these days. She could deal with things now; no more booze or drugs to kill the pain. No more cutting herself just to feel anything. No more knocking over drugstores for money or a quick fix, which had landed her in the poke for two years.

Her shit was together. She was clean, sober, centered, and employed. All her past misgivings had finally found peace.

Except for one thing.

Her mother.

She held the small box in her hands firmly, but not as tightly as she wanted. If she hadn't been aware, she would have squeezed the hell out of it and gotten its contents everywhere, including her hands. So, firm but lightly, she slowly made her way up the line.

She heard her mother's voice, and it brought her to a moment in her past that made her angry. The reason she hated her mother.

"Bethany, you should ask people if they want to have the last piece of anything!"

"But why don't they ask instead of looking at it?" the 10-year-old girl had asked.

"It doesn't matter. It's polite."

"But...if they want it so bad, why do they wait so long?"

"They're being polite," her mother insisted.

"But what if I ask and someone comes to take it?"

"Then you hand it over. Because—"

"It's polite," Bethany said, defeated.

Her mother had missed plays, softball games, first dates, suicide attempts, shock therapy—all of it—for her goddamned job. But she insisted on Bethany being polite. Well, she would be *very* polite.

Bethany was next in line, facing her seated mother as she beamed at the room. Her face changed, seeing her daughter, and to Bethany's surprise, it wasn't filled with the anger she had remembered.

It was shame.

Bethany said nothing and held out the box. Her mother, near tears, took it and opened it up.

She looked at her daughter.

"There's only one," she said. "It's for you."

Her mother looked at it and then at her daughter. She handed it back.

"Take it," she said.

Bethany was shocked.

"But...it's the last one."

Her mother smiled.

"And I never let you have the last one, did I? I was never there for you, Beth. I've been a damn lousy mom. Here. You take it."

Bethany couldn't move.

"Just eat it, please. You've earned it."

She looked at the small cyanide-laced peanut butter cup.

Bethany laughed as she put the cup in her mouth and began to chew.

It was the polite thing to do.

MALLORY

Mallory loved the shit out of her boyfriend.

She would burst at the seams just to see him...to kiss him...to hold his hand... She would ache when he wasn't around, and these past few days she had *not* been around him.

Mallory didn't worry. Why would she? They were in love. It's not like he was going anywhere. Some podunk town with little chance of escape. He would work at the Shop and Shop until he retired, just like his dad.

And her?

She'd be his wife, of course. Mallory wouldn't work like her mother always did. How can you raise children like *that*?

You *can't*.

And she wanted children!

As many as her body would allow. If they started right *now*, why, she could have ten kids in *ten years*. That would be amazing!

But she missed Paul.

Paul?

Was it Paul?

No.

Steve?

Yes, Steven.

Not Steve.

She giggled. *See what happens when I don't see my man?* she thought.

It was a clear day, bright and sunny. She held her books to her chest and slowly walked home. Two more weeks and she'd be done with junior year. She'd be a senior! And then she'd be—

Engaged?

Married?

At the very least, engaged.

Steven (?) would marry her. He totally said so, and she believed him.

Her heart knew the real thing when it found it, and Steve (Steven) was the real thing at last.

But...

Paul (*she remembered why she thought Paul—it was only two weeks ago*).

Paul had been the real thing too. Before him, Scott was the one. Brian, Jeff, Martin...

They *all* loved her. She had loved them too, but sometimes...just not *enough.* Mallory, of course, still loved them all. Every boyfriend, every relationship was another step in the right direction. Closer to the *one.*

To Steven.

She picked up her pace to get home and she nearly squealed. She had to see him.

Right *now.*

She yanked the key around her neck and unlocked the front door. Mallory pushed into the living room, slammed the door shut, locked it, and ran for the kitchen. She ignored her father on the floor.

She threw her books on the kitchen table, grabbed a granola bar, and stepped over her mother to get to the basement door. She hit the light switch, threw open the door, and ran down the steps.

She held her breath—she always did when she saw her boyfriend.

When her lungs begged for air, she gasped.

Christ, the smell...

She stopped and took several small breaths; it was easier if she breathed through her mouth. When the nausea had passed, she carefully walked to see Steven.

He was asleep.

She reached up to nudge him awake, but he kept on sleeping.

She nudged harder.

Nothing.

"Steven? I'm back," she cooed. She leaned in closer to kiss him awake, but noticed his eyes were open.

"Hi, sweet love!" she said. "Did you miss me?"

Steve said nothing.

"Aw, baby, are you still mad?" she asked in a baby voice.

Steven remained silent.

Mallory's cute smile faded as she felt the side of his neck.

No pulse.

She screamed. The scream echoed throughout the basement, through Steven's dead eyes, Paul's dead ears, and three other boys, all chained to the wall and all decidedly dead.

No!

Not again...

She had to calm down. For now and for later. It was time to be strong. It was time to be realistic. Finally, she had to face the truth.

Steven *wasn't* the one.

The one—*her* one—was still out there.

And she'd find him.

And when she did, well...

She'd love the shit out of him too.

THE BEST SHOW EVER

I'd been a performing musician for quite some time, either on my own with an acoustic or with a band. There was always an effort made to be in a situation where either I or the band had total control over the material played. Original music, in other words. The only time I can recall not being in that idyllic situation was the two-year stint I had in a wedding/party band.

It was strictly for the cash, and it paid well. Better than average, in fact; I could pull a good grand in a really good month, and most times, the band ate for free in some really great, expensive venues. Lobster and steak on New Year's Eve? Righteous!

The downside was the soul-shattering array of cover songs required by the customers. These ranged from decent cover songs like...well, okay, there *weren't* a whole lot of them. Some Earth, Wind & Fire (*as we had horns, which was pretty cool*), some Commodores, and the occasional "new" songs that were recent enough to not make you want to tear your ears from your head. I'm a rock and roll guy, and although I like other things, these were strictly "the hits."

We were an eight-piece band, and I was one of the singers. I did mostly back-up and some keyboard work, but I was also the "rock" singer. Need a Bon Jovi song? Nelson's got it covered. Bob Seger? Yeah, he can do that, sure. But there were also some songs that no one else wanted to sing anymore, and I got those too. Like "Lady in Red" by Chris DeBurgh. I begged to also be allowed to sing "Don't Pay the Ferryman" since that was a way better song, but really, what part of the wedding party wants a song about being guided across the River Styx by a *huge fucking skeleton*? Exactly. So I sang "Lady in Red."

For the first six months, I attacked every song like I had spent every other show attacking them—like I had something to prove. At the time, I had very long, curly hair and a beard. I looked like either Jesus or Ted Nugent. Or both at the same time. I also sang that way.

My first ever wedding gig required me to take front stage with the wireless microphone and sing "Brick House."

"Go out onto the dance floor and have fun!" Tammi the bandleader had said. She was a very cool lady and a really great jazz singer doing weddings for the same reason I was. Except she was *great* at it. Total showstopper. You would remember if you had her singing at your wedding. She gave the impression of actually caring about you and your wedding party.

I had yet to develop that, as it was my first gig.

So I grab the microphone and Tammi introduces me. The band tears into the song and I follow suit. Now, picture this fun, danceable Commodores song complete with actual horns and played by guys in their mid-forties to mid-fifties in tuxes. Picture the wedding party, ready to dance it up, half-drunk on happiness and gin. Now, picture a gigantic guy with long hair in a tux stepping out in front of the people, holding the microphone like it was a *fucking lightsaber*. His lips peel back in a sneer and the words from the song explode from the speakers in a voice that can only be described as *confrontational.*

The looks of happy revelry fade into looks of confusion and fear as this tall serial killer-looking guy is singing a dancehall favorite like he's trying to kick the living shit out of everyone in the room with his voice and leaving no doubt that he can probably do it as he's done time and time again.

It wasn't pretty.

I prowled the dance floor like a tiger looking for an antelope with a limp. I injected as much soul into the song as I could muster, and frankly, I'm pretty good at that, but because of my height and appearance, it just looked like I was about to mug the bride.

The entire dance floor cleared. There was a circle of people established like a perimeter as I tried to "entertain." It was an absolute fail. *No one* was entertained, except the band, who kind of understood what I was doing. The look of horror on Tammi's face was overshadowed by the look of total joy and amusement of the horn section, who at the halfway point of the song all put sunglasses on and were smiling even while blowing the horn parts. The drummer even started hitting the kit like he was angry at it.

When the song ended, there was a pregnant moment before polite applause broke out. I walked back to the bandstand. It hadn't hit me until the end of the song that what I had just done was tantamount to skull-fucking the bride's mom. Sheepishly, I gave the microphone back to Tammi and said, "Sorry," and took my place next to the drummer. She looked less horrified and offered a smile. We instantly started to play a Frank Sinatra song, sung by the other guy singer—a fifty-something guy.

The drummer and the horns all looked at me, beaming and nodding approval, as I smiled like a douche and played a little keys for effect on "Fly Me to the Moon." People began to forget about the incident and started to dance.

I had a lot of time throughout the course of the night to review and revise how I attacked "Brick House," and I also began to plot how not to attack the rest of the songs I had to sing that night. I still had to sing "Lady in Red" and "Love Shack."

That's right—"Love Shack" by the B-52's.

Some may balk, but the B-52's are one of my favorite bands. I was in love with Kate Pierson, for one thing, and Fred Schneider just flat-out rocks. "Love Shack" is by no means one of their best songs, but I'll take any B-52's as opposed to none.

The problem would be the approach of the delivery for me. There was no way on Earth I was going to attempt to sing like Fred Schneider. Not a chance. He is the only man with that delivery, and to try to imitate it would be silly. I had watched another band cover it, and it sounded like a parody, which sucks. The mistake when covering a B-52's song, I have found, is when the singer tries to make Fred's vocal parts sound *gay,* which is a huge mistake. What makes Fred's vocal style killer isn't the "gay factor." It's there, to be sure, but there has always been a thread of *menace* in his vocals. They are brilliant and matter of fact. They seem to say, "Yes, I'm gay, but I'm also *dangerous as hell.*" If you doubt this, Fred also sings "Planet Claire" the same way. It doesn't matter what he sings, it's awesome as hell.

However, there was no fucking way I was going to try to sing like him. And the lesson of "Brick House" was not to sing like I hated everybody. So I compromised and sang it like I was a 1960s soul singer. Sam Moore, to be specific. I also smiled a lot. Smiling actually comes through vocally and does wonders for making you not sound like an angry bastard.

It sort of worked. No one got scared, and people danced. I also never left the stage again that night, but it was a win as far as I was concerned. Tammi was pleased as well, so that meant I wouldn't be getting fired.

The rest of the night went alright, including a version of "Sweet Home Alabama" that turned into a dirty, Black Crowes-sounding song.

I blame the redhead in the bridal party that danced in front of me. It happens.

Four hours later, it was over. As I helped tear the gear down, I got various reviews from the other seven members of the band; all positive, and one hilarious, as the sax player loved how I had terrified both the bridal party and our bandleader. Tammi was very nice and helpful and never admitted to being frightened, but I could see it in her eyes.

It was, in retrospect, an educational experience, and quite possibly the best show ever. Being in a wedding band is a lot of things, most of which are no fun at all. After a while, you become so jaded about wedding receptions, you lock into auto-pilot. For the first six months, I hit the gigs hard, albeit with a little more finesse. It was fun for everyone, because there was a new kid in town. After a while, I wasn't the new kid, and everyone locked into routine. "Brick House" would get sung while writing a grocery list. It got that way for two years until I quit. I miss the band and the cash, and I learned a lot about performing. I don't slaughter people anymore when I sing, nor do I try.

There are a million wedding band stories, but only one about my first gig. It was a good time while it lasted, and I'll never be able to make an entire room panic again without the aid of a flamethrower and a list of demands.

THE WOLF AND HER WIFE

Vlora Palmeri hissed in pain as the laser seared her skin near her pelvis. She balled her hands into tight fists to keep herself from screaming. It was a struggle she was losing. Tears streamed down her face.

"Just try to relax," Dr. Simpson said, sounding like she had already said this line a thousand times.

"Fuck you," Vlora said through clenched teeth.

Dr. Simpson laughed.

"I probably had that coming," she said. "But remember that you're paying for this."

"So what?"

"That's means when the woman with the laser is burning the hair off your lady bits, you should relax and not say things like 'fuck you'."

Vlora let out a small scream and a chuckle.

"Sorry," she said. "But this really hurts. I mean, this is the worst of it, right?"

"This should be it, yes."

"Thank fuck." She sniffed.

Just then the door opened and a young woman stuck her head inside. She looked at Vlora, then at Doctor Simpson. Her nose turned up.

"Wrong room," she said, adding, "Smells like Auschwitz, for fuck's sake."

The door slammed closed and Vlora looked at Dr. Simpson, who wasn't amused.

"God, people say stupid shit," Vlora said.

"Yep."

"Hope she isn't your next patient."

"Yep."

Vlora was going to say something else, like how if she was she would be getting payback from how badly it hurts, but she said nothing.

Dr. Simpson sighed.

"You're Jewish, aren't you?"

"Yep."

"That stupid bitch," Vlora said.

"Relax. It happens."

"I'm really sorry."

"It's fine," Dr. Simpson said, looking up at Vlora. She was smiling, but Vlora saw that it wasn't a happy smile.

"No, that was super shitty," Vlora said through her teeth. "I can't believe she said that."

Dr. Simpson said nothing and continued her work. Vlora couldn't be sure, but the pain hurt more now, and she felt on some level that she had deserved it.

***

An hour later, Vlora was uncomfortably driving home. She looked at the digital clock and saw that it was just a bit after six. It was still early evening. The sunset looked like she felt: pinkish and on fire at the same time. She shifted in her seat and punched her steering wheel. It was the pain, to be sure, but also what happened to Dr. Simpson. Nothing like that had ever happened in front of her, and although she had said it happened to her a lot, Vlora had never seen it up close.

Tears formed in her eyes; she felt like she wanted to cry, but just couldn't get there. The mere act of how casual the words had come out of that girl's mouth was alarming on some level.

The car's dashboard lights kicked on as the sun continued to set. The headlights blinked on brighter, and Vlora wondered when the world had become filled with such lousy human beings.

She had been damn lucky Dr. Simpson had even been open on a Saturday evening in the first place. The good doctor had been gracious about it, accepting all the apologies Vlora could throw at her. She gave an obvious, forced smile as she ran Vlora's credit card through. She handed back her card and smiled.

"Well, I guess that's all," Dr. Simpson said flatly. "Best of luck to you."

She followed Vlora out of the office and quickly locked the door behind her. Vlora stood there looking at the storefront for a moment. There was no way she'd ever be able to go back without feeling shame.

She thought of this as she pulled into her driveway. She jabbed a finger at the garage remote; the garage light snapped on and the door slowly trudged its way open. Vlora slowly pulled her black SRV inside. Another jab as she parked, and the door began its slow and noisy descent down. She sat for a moment, grabbing the wheel. She took five deep breaths and then opened the car door.

The mere act of getting out of the car was more painful than driving was, but she knew it was worth it. No shaving, no wax, just smoothness in the nethers. This was why she had wine, after all. She pulled herself out of the driver's seat, hissed through her teeth, and stood on her two legs, shaky as they were.

She leaned on the SUV and carefully closed the door. She steadied herself and walked to the door that led her into the kitchen. A quick turn of the key and a careful climb of the short set of stairs, and she was inside. She flicked on the light and dropped her purse and keys onto the tile floor. She resisted the urge to cry; from the pain and from what she had said to Doctor Simpson.

Relax. It happens, Dr. Simpson had said. But *why?* The world was already such a dark, shit-filled place, why make things worse? Vlora thought this as she left the kitchen, made a right to the dining room and into her small bedroom, having shed her sweatsuit one layer at a time.

Thank Christ I wore the sweatsuit, she thought. There were clothes everywhere in her room, as if a suitcase had exploded.

Thank Christ I live alone, she added to her inner dialogue, and let out a harsh laugh. The laugh turned ugly as she took the sweatpants off. Her crotch looked angry and, hey, why not? She'd just had all the hair seared off. But one lucky asshole was going to have an encounter with her one of these days now that she had shed some of her genetic propensity to have hair absolutely everywhere.

Still, it really hurt.

She was told to not shower or bathe for at least forty-eight hours after the last treatment, but she wanted nothing more than to sink into a bath with a bottle of merlot. At this point, she wasn't even sure she had any wine, much less merlot.

She kicked through a pile of clothes and stood in front of the giant mirror opposite her bed.

Vlora was naked with the evidence of her laser treatment exposed, and she sighed. She looked like she had a very bad case of acne in all the worst places. Her legs, normally her favorite feature, were covered in red burn-like marks. *Well, not burn-like...they* are *burns,* she thought. They expanded into her bikini line and probably her ass as well. She lifted her arms slowly and saw more of the same under her armpits. She felt like she was on fire, but also felt good that she had gone ahead and done it. Shaving was the worst, and it seemed to egg on her hair regrowth. She was proud of her Albanian background, but along with that came tufts of hair all over the goddamn place.

But not anymore.

She tried to ignore the pain and the red, irritated blotches of skin and looked herself over.

She looked good for thirty-six. Damn good.

Zumba, yoga, and Thai kickboxing didn't pay off quickly, but dammit, it paid off hard. She thought she looked great, and would look even better once everything was all healed.

She gave herself a big smile in the mirror.

***

She didn't have merlot, but she did have half a bottle of dessert wine that she made quick work of, along with a bland chicken salad and a couple ibuprofen. She threw on some shorts and a t-shirt that simply said *BITCH* in fancy font. As she felt a little better, Vlora managed to straighten up a few things in the house. She called her sister in New Jersey to talk about the procedure (*leaving out the racist part of the story*) and her friend Karen (*including the racist part.*)

Karen seemed indignant at Dr. Simpson's reaction.

"She should lighten the hell up," Karen said. "I mean, she's a customer, right?"

This did nothing to soothe Vlora's chagrin, but she mumbled a half agreement. Vlora walked into her living room with the last of the wine and sat on her sofa.

"I had that done last year, remember?" Karen continued. "Smooth as a baby's ass and holy living fuck it hurts. You'd think your Jew doctor would have a sense of humor about it."

"*Really*, Karen?" Vlora said, suddenly angry. "That's your takeaway? What the hell is wrong with you?"

She heard Karen stammer and then seem to recover with her own anger.

"Hey, I'm on *your* side, remember?"

"That's not my fucking side!" Vlora snapped and hung up.

Vlora squeezed the phone and threw it onto the carpet, where it landed with a light *thud*. This was followed by a loud *thud* that seemed to come from the garage. It repeated twice more.

It sounded like a bull was trying to plow into the garage door.

She got up too fast and hissed at the pain. Still, she managed to get moving toward the kitchen and to the garage door. She unlocked it and threw it open. The motion detector light glared at her, but nothing was in the garage except what was supposed to be there.

She reached around the door and pushed the light switch. It clicked off and she closed the door.

Probably a cat, she thought, and began to trudge her way through the kitchen.

A new *thud* came from the back door. She stopped and looked at the kitty clock on her wall. It was nearly quarter to eight. The clock, unfazed by the second thud, continued to look back and forth in the room, countering the direction with its pendulum tail.

Vlora began to move a little faster through the kitchen and to the back of the condo. The *thud* was now almost a loud rhythmic tapping that was more like someone punching the side of the condo. There was a large sliding door in the space between the dining room and the door to her bedroom. She carefully moved the curtain to try and see the rotten kid (it must be a kid) pranking her like this. She was a little drunk and a bit annoyed.

She was primed to yell, but all she saw was her deck and the lawn. She growled a little and slid the door open. Sticking her head out, she looked left and right. Visibility was good. Great, in fact, as the moon shone brightly.

It wasn't cold, but a little cooler than it had been earlier, and she walked out onto the deck, leaving the door open a bit.

The sky was clear and the moon was stunning.

Vlora walked to the rail and leaned on it, looked up at the sky, and smiled. For a moment, everything was okay. She wasn't a lousy human being at that moment. She wasn't a racist, perceived or otherwise. She was just...

She felt the breath on her legs for a brief moment before it actually registered as something that might be dangerous. She looked down over the railing and saw a pair of yellow eyes reflected in the moonlight.

They were looking back at her.

Her first thought wasn't fear; it was actually practical.

"How'd you get up here, puppy?" she said softly to the yellow eyes, until she realized that it wasn't a puppy and there was absolutely no way anything would be able to get its head level to the deck from the lawn unless it was nine feet tall.

Whatever was looking at her opened its mouth slightly and a long tongue flicked out and licked her foot. Vlora recoiled away from the rail and gasped. She staggered back and nearly fell through her sliding door. She grabbed the sides at the last moment, mouth wide open as she saw two fur-covered clawed things grab the deck.

The puppy/not puppy was coming up to say hi, and now it was panting. She righted herself and stumbled into the condo, slamming the door shut and engaging the lock in time to hear whatever the hell was outside landing on the deck with a loud *thud.*

Vlora screamed as the thing gently tapped on the door. Then scratched. Then struck it hard. She heard the glass splinter, then break as it struck again.

Vlora backed away from the door, but couldn't turn to run. She stepped on her phone and realized she should pick it up, but refused to do so. She was still backing up. And it, whatever *it* was, was coming in, panting.

The first thing she saw was the snout, and the sheer size of the teeth wasn't as scary as the sound it was making. *But,* she thought in a daze, *those are some pretty big fucking teeth.* It seemed to get bigger as it walked into the condo, covered in thick brownish fur. It was standing on all fours like a giant pet, at least four and a half feet tall. The claws on its feet were curved and recessed into the paws. When it was finally inside, it brandished a rather long tail that wagged back and forth almost playfully.

Its entire body was twitching with life, especially its eyes; they were focused on her.

"Good doggo," she said in a soft voice.

It growled at her.

"Nice doggo," she added.

It was inching toward her, and she was quickly running out of room to back away. Vlora smiled at the thing and tried to sound confident.

"Who's a good puppy? Who is a good *puppers*?"

The thing stopped and sat down in front of her. She heard the floor crack under the weight. Its snout, which had been a holding place for huge fangs, suddenly hung open. A large pinkish tongue lolled out as it panted. The tail thumped against the floor.

"You're such a good puppers," Vlora said in absolute disbelief.

The thing on the floor gave a lazy whine of agreement.

Vlora was as fascinated as she was terrified. On the one hand, she wanted to see if this gigantic thing would be interested in the roast that sat at the bottom of the fridge that was a day away from going bad. On the other hand, she hoped it wasn't interested in eating *her*.

"Do you want some water?"

The thing's tail thumped faster as Vlora talked directly to it. Its head went to one side, and it suddenly sprawled itself on Vlora's shag carpet.

Vlora already knew it was huge, but she was getting an eyeful of just how huge it was as it stretched its body out. It wasn't a dog, she knew that, but *it* didn't seem to know that, and for now that was okay. But Christ, it was huge and it looked powerful. The word dancing around in her head was *wolf,* and the more it swirled there, the more it made sense. It was a full moon as well, and although her grandmother had told her stories about such creatures when she was a little girl, she couldn't fully commit to the thought that maybe...

Her eyes noticed several things at once. One, the thing, whatever it was, was a girl. Two, someone had strategically shaved this girl (puppers) to have a bikini line. She looked it up and down and saw that the fur under its front legs was also gone.

The thing rolled onto its back, with all four legs in the air, and Vlora knew what it wanted.

Belly rubs.

Vlora decided that this was, in fact, actually happening. She had grown up around enough dogs to recognize this simple behavior and decided almost on instinct to give this good girl what it needed.

"Good girl," Vlora said, moving toward it, starting to crouch near its massive form, hand extended. The thing let out a friendly growl as Vlora gently began to rub its belly. Her hand grazed against the smooth hairless part of its lower half. The puppers gave a small whine. The whine, Vlora recognized, seemed to indicate discomfort, but not anger.

"Who did this to you, girl?"

Vlora couldn't believe what she was saying, but the instinct of a former dog owner kicked in, and she rubbed the belly higher up and a little harder, which the good little (massive, actually) puppers really liked.

For as fearful and unbelieving as Vlora was, she was also starting to like this giant wolf thing sprawled out on her floor. She smiled genuinely and scratched underneath the thing's chin.

"What the hell am I gonna do with you?" she said, as the thing took one giant paw and gently put it on Vlora's leg.

***

Sunlight spread across Vlora's face and she opened her eyes. She was still on the floor in her living room. Squinting, she sat up and looked around.

Her new friend was gone.

For the smallest moment, she wondered if the combination of pain and wine made her dream it all. That moment was shattered by exactly three things: the pile of broken glass from her sliding door, the large paw prints, and the piles of brownish fur all over the living room. She stood up carefully, wincing a little. She took a step backward and stepped into something soft and wet. Her eyes shot down, and she saw her foot in a rather large pile of shit.

She swore and hopped on one leg into the kitchen.

She still felt sore, but she needed that shit off her foot quickly. Hopping to the sink, she hoisted her foot up and turned on the water. The water, of course, came out cold, and she let out a little yelp. She grabbed the dish soap and shot a blue gob onto her foot. As she hopped to keep her balance, she noticed that she wasn't as freaked out as she should've been. Maybe it was because she had stepped barefoot into her fair share of dogshit growing up, or maybe it was something else. She found that she was a little worried about what she had fallen asleep with on the floor of her living room. Not because it broke into her house, but because it had left.

Satisfied that the shit was clean enough, she turned off the water and set her wet foot back on the floor. There was an entire condo living room to clean, and she needed to figure out what happened last night.

After making some coffee and putting on her sneakers, she began to clean up. The shit would come first, as she needed—and hoped—to get that stink and stain out of the carpet. The carpet was mercifully a deep brown, so the stain wouldn't be as apparent, but the smell...

The rest of the carpet had flecks of fur, glass, and mud that would take a bit of creative maneuvering, plus a much better vacuum than she currently owned. She used a thick straw broom to get all the mess into a larger pile near the sliding door. She could then get it outside and into a thick trash bag. Marveling at her cleaning prowess, she thought of the thing that she wanted to stop calling a thing.

Doggo, she thought. Absolutely not a doggo. And even if it were, wouldn't it be *dogga*? It was a female pupper, after all. She had been avoiding thinking *wolf,* but it was starting to seem that it was possible. She heard her cell phone chime from under her couch.

Must've gotten kicked there, she thought. She stuck her hand underneath and fished it out. The screen was cracked a little, but not too badly. She tapped the screen and saw that she had an email.

It was from Hair to Bare Laser Hair Removal Salon.

She sighed and could only guess what the email had to say.

Ms. Palmeri,

I hope you're not feeling too awful this morning—that was a rather rough session yesterday, and I'd like to apologize for any discomfort, physical or otherwise. Please let me know when you'd like to follow up.
All the best,
Dr. Lynn Simpson

This was the last email she had expected to read this morning, and it made her frown. She was expecting to have to look for a new salon, and frankly, all the self-doubt that she had thrown up had altered her in some strange way. Maybe after she cleaned up the place, she'd swing over there if they were open.

She looked at the condo.

It was going to be a while.

***

Todd, the creepy maintenance guy, asked what had happened to her sliding door. Vlora had decided hours before exactly how to explain it.

"None of your fucking business," she said, and smiled.

He shrugged and got to work.

***

She drove to the salon, a dozen donuts in a box on the passenger seat. She hoped Dr. Simpson liked donuts, and wondered if maybe bagels wouldn't have been better.

She rolled her eyes at that thought.

Everyone loves donuts, she thought. *Stop overanalyzing it.*

She pulled into the strip mall parking lot and found a spot right in front of the salon. She got out of the car, box in hand, and walked inside. The door's little bell chimed and the receptionist smiled.

"Hey, girl, you back for more?" she said smiling.

"Oh, shit no," Vlora said. "I just wanted to drop these off for you girls and Dr. Simpson. Is she around?"

Vlora put the donuts on the receptionist counter, and the box was immediately grabbed and opened.

"Oh damn, powdered cream!"

Vlora smiled.

"Nothing but the best for my hair pluckin' girls."

The receptionist laughed.

"You're the best. Sadly, the doctor is not in at the moment. I think she's not feeling well. She said she'd be back Tuesday, though."

"Oh," Vlora said. "She sent an email this morning."

"Did she? Must be working from home, then. PR and all that."

Vlora stood there watching the receptionist inhale the donut for a few moments longer.

"Well, just tell her I stopped by. You girls enjoy the donuts."

The receptionist smiled, powdered sugar caked around her lips, and mouthed "thank you."

***

The ride back home felt long and uncomfortable. Vlora's thoughts drifted back and forth from her misadventure last night with the wolf-thing to bringing a box of donuts to a woman she watched get insulted. *Living my best life*, she thought.

Later, in her condo, she lit candles throughout the living room, noting that the stench of the shit lingered in a bad way. Not to the point of nausea, but to the point of annoyance. She also opened every window and the sliding door, hoping for a breeze to push the smell outside.

The weather was cool and the breeze felt good. Vlora looked at the time on her phone.

She didn't notice how exhausted she was until she saw the time, and she decided that it was time for a nap. She walked to her bedroom, gently sliding the newly replaced door shut. She looked at it for a moment, then locked it.

She was asleep as soon as she fell into bed.

4:37PM

She woke up shivering and famished. She got out of bed and went around the condo, shutting windows as she went along. The candles had all gone out, and she silently thanked the gods that nothing had caught fire. Turning on a light in the kitchen, she opened her fridge for any leftovers.

Nothing.

She lifted her arm and sniffed. *Could be worse*, she thought. Besides, that's why there are drive-thrus. She didn't want a salad. She wanted a cheeseburger and fries. No. Onion rings. Oh, and a milkshake. Chocolate. Large.

She put on a jacket, grabbed her keys, and decided that dinner was getting *got.*

Thirty minutes later, she had a drive-thru bag of five cheeseburgers and two orders of onion rings along with a large chocolate milkshake. She was hungry but, surprisingly, not *that* hungry. She had no idea why she had bought so much food, but she began to figure it out as she pulled into the parking lot of Hair to Bare. There was only one other car in the lot.

She grabbed the bag and milkshake and went to the door, keys dangling from her jacket. The salon had been closed for hours, but there was a light on in the back. Vlora set the shake on the sidewalk and knocked on the door. She took a deep breath.

Dr. Simpson appeared from the back, squinting at the door. She walked toward the door and began to see Vlora as she got closer. The confused look on her face deepened. She undid the latch and opened the door.

"I'm sorry, but we're closed, Ms. Palmeri."

"I know."

"Well, then...can I help you?"

"I...brought you a cheeseburger," Vlora said.

Dr. Simpson snorted, laughing.

"Yeah, I have no idea why either," Vlora added, smiling.

"Come in," Dr. Simpson said.

Vlora bent down, grabbed the shake, and walked inside.

Dr. Simpson led her down a hallway, past the room where the laser treatment had happened, to a nice cozy office at the end. There was a large wooden desk with two soft-looking chairs in front and a large leather chair behind it. Vlora watched, surprised, as the doctor sat in one of the chairs on the right. She smiled a bit, and sat in the opposite chair, putting the food and shake on the desk.

"Kinda surprised you're still here," Vlora said, sitting down.

"Well, kinda surprised you're here too. With a cheeseburger, no less."

"I...have felt really awful about what happened."

Simpson smiled and started to unwrap her burger. She nodded to encourage Vlora to continue. Vlora sighed.

"Like, really awful. I've been quite off since I left here yesterday, and I wanted to just talk to you about it."

"And give me food," Simpson said. "The donuts were a great start."

Vlora laughed.

"Well, food heals."

"Not really, but it certainly helps," Dr. Simpson said. "But go on. Please."

Vlora looked at the doctor. She was being sincere, as far as she could tell.

"I've been trying to sort out why what someone said to you and not to me affected me so much. My first thought was, I had no idea you were Jewish. Then the second, louder, thought was 'Why would that make a difference'?"

Dr. Simpson, who had taken a bite of the burger, chewed thoughtfully on this last part. She swallowed.

"You know, Miss Palmeri, I'm not that kind of doctor."

Vlora looked at her blankly and then started to laugh. Dr. Simpson smiled at her.

"Listen, I could tell that it bothered you, and that's why I told you I was Jewish. Not so you could feel bad about what was said to me, but to let you know that even though it wasn't okay, it wasn't going to kill me."

Vlora just stared at her, eyes welling. Dr. Simpson continued.

"I've said awful things in my life too. Things I regret, and I can't take them back. She wasn't a bitch, although she was stupid, and she totally felt the wrath when it was her turn on the table."

Vlora chuckled.

"Did you really?"

"No. I canceled her appointment after you left. Nobody says shit like that to me." She smiled wickedly. "Now eat your burger before it gets cold."

Vlora blinked and looked at her burger. She picked it up and started to unwrap it.

Dr. Simpson chuckled.

"Can I have a sip of your milkshake? I don't have cooties."

"Me either," Vlora said. "Besides, you've seen me naked. We're bonded."

"Bonded? You've brought me donuts and cheeseburgers. Where I'm from, we're practically engaged."

Vlora snorted and laughed hard, not really expecting her reply.

"Didn't see that answer coming, Doctor."

"Please, call me Lynn."

"Then you call me V."

"I rather like Vlora. Unusual name. Lovely."

"My dad calls me Vlora."

Lynn smiled.

"He named you, didn't he?"

"Of course he did."

Lynn took another bite and looked at Vlora.

"Daddy's girl?"

Vlora nodded.

Lynn nodded back. "Same."

Then the two sat and ate their cheeseburgers quietly. They looked at each other now and then, not really saying much, just chewing and smiling. This went on for nearly twenty minutes. They passed the large milkshake back and forth between them. They had torn the bag open and combined the two orders of onion rings together and liberally ate them. When there was only one onion ring left, Lynn held it up and offered it to Vlora.

Vlora shook her head.

"That's yours," she said.

"Could be ours," Lynn said back. She looked straight at Vlora with a half-smile. Vlora was struck at how big Lynn's eyes were, a light honey shade eyes that was almost breathtaking.

"I guess it should be then," Vlora said, leaning toward the onion ring, now between Lynn's teeth.

There was a light chime coming from the cell phone on Lynn's desk. Lynn's eyes went wide as Vlora began to close hers. Lynn leaned back and took the onion ring out of her mouth.

"Shit. I'm so sorry," Lynn said, putting the onion ring back onto the greasy paper bag. Vlora recoiled slightly from the sudden shift in mood and action. "I...forgot an appointment."

"Oh," Vlora said as Lynn started to clear the burger wrappers. "Let me help."

Vlora got up and grabbed the Styrofoam milkshake cup. Lynn was already shoving trash into the little trash can on the side of her desk.

"It's fine, thank you, but you need to clear out. I'm so sorry."

She's nervous, Vlora thought.

"Are you okay?" she asked.

"Yes...I just have to get moving. I'm so sorry. Please forgive me. You have to go now."

Vlora didn't know what to say. Lynn grabbed her by the arm and started to escort her out of the office.

"Are you okay?" Vlora asked again, struggling to keep up with Lynn, who had a really good grip on her arm. "What happened?"

"It's not you," came the reply. "Believe me, not you. Just got lost in time there. Forgot myself."

"Well, me too."

"Sorry, have to go," Lynn said as she unlocked the latch and pushed open the door. She started to shove Vlora outside.

"Well, wait!" Vlora said, grabbing Lynn's hand. "It's okay to be nervous. Nothing to be embarrassed about. You know...what almost..."

Lynn gave Vlora's hand a squeeze and removed it just as quickly.

"I know, but I can't explain now. Please, I'll talk to you tomorrow. I'm sorry."

And without realizing how quickly it had all happened, Vlora was outside in the darkened parking lot alone. She heard the door close and latch. She looked inside and saw Lynn practically running to the back of the office.

She pulled out her phone and looked at the time. It was twenty after five.

She sighed and trudged to her car. She sat in the driver's seat, not quite sure what to do for a moment. Sighing again, she started the car and drove home.

***

Vlora stood on the deck outside of her living room, looking up at the moon. The last twenty-four hours had been, at best, insane. At worst it had been...well, still insane. This thought made her laugh.

She looked across the moonlit landscape and sighed, terrified of the wolf coming back and equally terrified of it not returning at all. She also thought about Lynn and how she could explain the wolf to her. This, too, made her laugh, although she didn't really know why.

She'd been going to Lynn (*it was getting hard for her to even think of her as Dr. Simpson after this evening*) for laser treatments for the past eight months. Always pleasant, full of small conversations, but nothing like this evening. It was easy, fun, and flirty. It wasn't anything overtly sexual, but it was very sexy in just how easy it all felt. She couldn't remember the last time she felt that with anyone.

If she had ever really felt it at all.

She looked up at the moon and sighed. She said a little prayer out loud that was simply, "What the fuck, moon?"

She then added, "Sort it out, please."

That was when the growl came from under her balcony.

Vlora's head snapped down and saw the large wolf. *My wolf,* she thought, and gasped. *My wolf.*

The wolf looked up at her and its tail began to wag. Vlora grinned at the wolf.

"Who's a good girl?" Vlora said, smiling like a fool.

She watched the wolf's tail wag faster as she walked in a circle, eyes never leaving Vlora's. Instinctively, Vlora backed up to give the wolf room to jump up.

In a moment, the wolf had leapt up onto the balcony with barely a sound. It looked at Vlora with its gorgeous yellow eyes that seemed somehow...

The wolf gave a playful grunt, tail never stopping as it moved closer to Vlora. Its head was moving back and forth.

"What is it, girl?" Vlora said, holding her hand out. The wolf put her snout into Vlora's hand affectionately, never losing eye contact. Vlora smiled and noticed that the wolf had something in its mouth.

"Did you bring me a present?" Vlora said, smiling. She knew that it may be something disgusting; her dogs growing up dropped off a lot of really appalling things like birds and, once, a stick covered in shit. She was ready for something bad, but she also knew it was something that her wolf thought she might like.

The wolf (*her wolf*) opened her mouth, and a saliva-covered purple rose fell from its mouth.

The wolf looked up at Vlora, pink tongue lolling out and panting.

Her wolf had brought her a flower.

Vlora didn't know what she was thinking, but she smiled bigger and took the wolf's face in her hands.

"You are such a sweet girl," she said softly. "Nobody brings me..."

She was looking into the wolf's yellow eyes and suddenly, there it was.

Not yellow.

Honey.

Just like...

"*Lynn*?" Vlora breathed.

The wolf's tail thumped heavily on the floor upon hearing her name.

"Holy living fuck. *Lynn*?"

The wolf licked Vlora's face.

***

For the next four hours, Vlora and her wolf got to know each other. Vlora found some venison steak from her freezer and defrosted it in her sink while the wolf drank water greedily from a large saucepan on the floor. When the steak had been thawed enough, her wolf sat on her haunches and looked at Vlora like a puppy. Not begging for the steak, but happily letting her know she would gladly accept it from her. Vlora held it out and the wolf carefully took it from her. Vlora was impressed at the wolf's control, but was even more impressed at the size of her teeth.

There wasn't any room to do much, so the two sat on the floor. Vlora had found an old hairbrush and decided to groom her wolf, which the wolf absolutely loved. She was careful around the parts where there was no hair, and she chuckled.

"You're going to have to tell me all about this when you can, *e dashur.*"

The wolf's tail thumped.

"That means *sweetie*, by the way," Vlora said, chuckling. "You know, I'm pretty impressed with myself because I am taking this really well."

When the brushing was finished, Vlora looked at the wolf and smiled.

The wolf's head rested on Vlora's lap, tail gently thumping as Vlora stroked her furry neck.

So many things swirled around in Vlora's mind. So much to process and not a single idea where to even begin. She looked around her living room and then down at the wolf. The wolf looked lovingly up at her, pink tongue partially jutting out of her long snout.

"So this is really you?" Vlora asked. "I know you really can't answer."

The wolf's tail thumped twice.

"We have a lot of stuff to talk about later, don't we?"

The wolf whined.

"No, nothing bad."

The tail thumped three times.

Vlora smiled.

"'Cause you're such a good girl," she said, and scruffed the top of the wolf's head. Tail thumping, the wolf got back to her feet while Vlora stayed on the floor. The wolf licked Vlora's face and Vlora reached up and hugged her.

"Do you have to go?" Vlora asked.

The wolf whined and walked over to the sliding door.

She pushed herself up off the floor and opened the sliding door. The wolf padded onto the deck and Vlora followed. The wolf looked up at the moon and then at Vlora.

"I know," Vlora said, stroking the wolf's head. "Me too."

The wolf's tail thumped twice, and then it sprang up and off the balcony. Vlora watched as it soundlessly ran through the moonlight and into the treeline. She stared out in that direction for a long time, looking at all of it and none of it until she heard it.

She heard her wolf howl.

Her wolf.

A small tear trickled down her cheek.

"What the hell," she whispered to herself and brushed away the tears.

***

Vlora woke to her alarm and glared at the time.

She'd been sleeping through it for twelve minutes, which was something that had never happened before. She slapped the alarm and sat straight up. She looked around and sighed. She didn't really fall asleep until about an hour ago. Her head was in a state of disquiet that was neither bad nor good. It was something else, that was certain. She needed sleep, which she knew she wasn't going to get, so she opted for coffee.

She got up and opened her bedroom door. Immediately, she was hit in the face with a blast of cold autumn air and sunlight. Her balcony sliding door was open wide. She hurried over to it, shaking in the cold, and slid it closed.

She swore a few times at closing the blinds, and silently thanked her real estate agent for finding a condo with really no visible neighbors who'd be able to see a half-naked woman closing her blinds on an early Monday morning.

As she turned to head into her kitchen, she looked at her living room.

It was still a mess, clumps of fur and mud, but as far as she could tell, no big pile of wolf shit. The smell of urine from the previous day was still strong, but she had smelled worse.

She walked into the kitchen and checked her coffee pot. There was enough left from yesterday to microwave. She opened a cabinet and looked for a cup—she grabbed her alma mater wine tumbler and shrugged. It wasn't for coffee, but it was today, and she liked the cute leopard on the side, but she didn't want to use it in her microwave. She sighed and grabbed another mug. This one had a middle finger on it and seemed more appropriate.

As she waited for the microwave to pump out the coffee, she leaned on the counter, thinking of the last couple days. She realized two things at once: she was going to call off work, and she was going to be able to take a shower today. She was itchy and raw and exhausted physically and emotionally. There was going to have to be a nap, and then recon to meet up with Lynn.

She never once questioned her sanity, and that in and of itself made her worry a little. For all of the uncertainty that had been surfacing, she didn't feel out of touch. She felt pretty clear-headed. She heard the microwave ding. She grabbed her coffee and went to the bathroom.

She called her office, taking the rest of the week off ill; "Got the screaming shits," she had said to the poor voicemail of her manager.

She felt no guilt or shame. Vlora had acquired a massive amount of vacation time and unused sick days, to the point that she had once joked that she could bankrupt the company simply by cashing in her time off.

It wasn't funny, because it was partially true.

Smiling at this, she set up her phone to play some music while she showered. She didn't spend as much time as she would have liked, but enough to feel about eighty times better for having showered. She was still a little hesitant around the most sensitive areas of the hair removal, but it felt great.

She toweled off, grabbed her phone and coffee, and went to her bedroom. Once there, she looked at herself in the big mirror on her door. She was still a little red, but her bikini lines looked great. She smiled and then frowned. She thought of her wolf with the same bikini lines and how awkward that must be. Did other werewolves make fun of her for that? She burst out laughing. She really needed to talk to Lynn today.

***

Vlora grabbed her keys to leave the condo when the door was knocked. She frowned and walked over to the door when the knock came again. Just two hard knocks. She looked through the Judas hole and saw Lynn.

She dropped the keys. She unlocked and opened the door just as Lynn was about to knock a third time.

They stood looking at each other, unsure of what to say. Vlora grabbed Lynn's hand and pulled her inside the condo. Without looking, she whirled and closed the door by kicking it.

They stood in the living room, looking at each other, Vlora still holding Lynn's arm. Lynn reached around and grabbed Vlora by the waist and pulled her closer, a small smile on her lips.

Lynn closed her eyes and deeply sniffed Vlora's face. When she stopped, she opened her eyes. She leaned to Vlora's face, their lips gently brushing, and whispered, "Found you."

The two women kissed each other deeply and without stopping for a long time.

***

Lynn and Vlora were curled up together under a blanket on the floor of the living room. They were taking turns nodding off here and there, but as the sun rose higher in the sky outside, they began to rouse more and more.

"Hey," Lynn said, eyes closed.

Vlora smiled.

"Hey yourself."

Lynn pulled her closer and growled a little.

"Oh shit, is it the change?" Vlora said, giggling. Lynn started to laugh as well.

"You're insanely calm about that," Lynn said. "Why is that?"

Vlora grabbed her back, tighter.

"Because I'm fucking awesome," she replied.

"Well, yes, you are."

"And you owe me an onion ring."

"Well, I think we just spent a few hours making up for the onion ring."

"You would think so, but you'd be wrong."

Lynn laughed. She kissed Vlora quickly and looked at her. She closed her honey-colored eyes for a moment and then opened them again.

Vlora blinked and noticed that Lynn's eyes were brighter than they had been just a moment ago.

"How'd you do that?" Vlora asked.

"Do what?"

"That thing with your eyes. How'd you do that?"

Lynn frowned. "I don't know what you mean," she said.

"Your eyes are...*brighter*. You closed your eyes and then... They're doing it now. They're practically glowing."

"Really? I had no idea," Lynn said, sounding genuinely surprised. "Must be you."

Vlora chuckled. "What the hell did I do?" she said.

"I'm feeling very content at the moment," Lynn said, pulling Vlora closer. "Very relaxed and safe. Very...*satiated*."

Vlora looked at Lynn and then saw her eyes had changed shades again. They were still bright, but had darkened just slightly.

"They did it again!" Vlora said. "Holy shit, that's cool."

Lynn laughed and kissed Vlora again. Vlora kissed her back.

Vlora pulled back and looked at her again.

The eyes were brighter again.

"So cool," she whispered.

"Yes you are," Lynn whispered back.

***

Lynn took a shower while Vlora stood in the kitchen in a small robe, looking for something to make for them both to eat. She caught herself humming and cracked up a bit. She was in an extraordinarily good mood as she grabbed the deli roast beef and sharp cheddar block. She opened her bread drawer and pulled out a bag of rolls.

She set these on the counter to get a cheese knife and stopped. She spied the unmistakable flash of mold on the inside of the cellophane bag of bread. She let out a quick curse and tossed the bag into the trash.

"We can eat that roast beef without the rolls," Lynn called from the shower.

Vlora smirked and whispered softly, "Your hearing that good?"

"You bet your sweet ass it is," Lynn said, still in the shower, giggling a little.

Vlora smiled for a moment, but at the same time, found this disturbing. She cleared her throat, hesitated, and then said quietly, "You're a werewolf."

"Would you believe I get more shit for being a lesbian?"

"How many people know?"

"That I'm a lesbian or a werewolf?"

Lynn then cackled loudly and turned off the shower. Vlora laughed a little, but it wasn't because she thought it was funny. She looked at the roast beef on the counter.

Lynn padded into the kitchen, wrapped in a towel. Vlora looked at her; Lynn was smiling. She leaned on the doorway and licked her lips.

"You're the first normal person to know I am both of those things, Vlora. I wanted you to know that."

Vlora smiled back at her.

Lynn looked at the floor.

"I really can't tell anyone about the wolf part. Christ, I hardly tell anyone about the lesbian part. My family knows. I...I don't speak to them anymore."

"I'm so sorry," Vlora said, moving toward her. "That's awful."

"It's infuriating. They're my... They *were* my *pack*. My family. We're wolves. And the thing that gets me *excoriated...*"

"I don't understand. Your whole family are werewolves?"

"Yes," Lynn said. "And I can't continue the pure bloodline properly if I'm not *breeding,* can I?"

Vlora went to say something and then stopped. She had no idea what to say.

"I left when they came for the culling," Lynn continued. "So I ran. Ran very far and started over here. It's been a few years and they haven't found me. Not even sure if they're looking, to be honest. But I haven't smelled them, and I would be able to sense them coming. I go into the woods if I don't make it to my basement to chain up."

"Chain up?"

"Yeah, just to be safe. I'm in control for the most part when I'm a wolf. But during the changes is when I'm vulnerable. I don't need someone to see me. Then the pack may find me and..." She drifted off from that statement.

Vlora found herself oddly moved by this She gently began to weep and grabbed Lynn's hand, kissing it.

"I'll be your pack," Vlora said.

Lynn looked at her and smiled, then wiped away a single tear from Vlora's cheek. She pulled Vlora close, kissed her neck, and whispered, "*Thank you.*"

Vlora pulled back and looked at her.

"Can I be a wolf too?"

Lynn smiled.

"You can, but that is a decision you need to make. And you'd be a different kind of wolf than me."

"How so?"

Lynn kissed her and giggled.

"Weren't there snacks?" Lynn asked. "Your wolf needs snacks."

Vlora laughed.

"Well, I don't want my wolf to go hungry."

After eating their roast beef and cheese, they went back into the bedroom. They fell asleep in each other's arms. Vlora, this time, slept deeply.

And dreamed vividly.

***

Vlora woke up screaming.

Her eyes were wide open and she could only see that she was in her room, bathed in moonlight. She was alone.

She looked around the room, out of breath and terrified for some reason. Her nightmare had already begun to fade, but the dreadful feeling remained, and she found it was because she was alone.

But she shouldn't be alone.

She reached over to the side of the bed where Lynn had fallen asleep. It was cold, so she had been gone for a while.

She had missed the change.

Vlora threw off the covers and turned on the lights.

Her eyes darting around the room, she saw Lynn's clothes neatly piled on top of the dresser. Hopping out of bed, she moved into the living room area. There, she saw the sliding door wide open, a cool breeze flowing through the curtains.

She smiled, seeing that the door hadn't been smashed through, but opened. She was going to close the door, but thought better of it.

She felt a little lonely, but that stopped as she looked into the kitchen. There was a note on the fridge. The moonlight reflected off the stainless steel and the note was the only thing on it. She walked in and turned the light on to read it.

I didn't want to wake you up. Can you leave the door open so I can come back in? But only if that's okay. Do you really want to be my pack? I think that's the most beautiful thing anyone has ever said to me.

XO Lynn
PS
Don't wait up.

The nightmare, now forgotten, was replaced with a smile on Vlora's lips. She was aware of this and smiled even wider.

I think I'm dating a werewolf, she thought.

***

One Year Later

The alarm clock had been set to go off at exactly 6:40 AM, and Vlora was going to beat it today. She was aware of the time not by sight, but by *feel.* She had learned to tell the time by, of all crazy things, the cycle of the moon. Last night was what was called a Corn Moon, which was beautiful.

Her eyes snapped open and her hand shot out to the alarm clock, hitting the snooze button at the exact time before it launched into some classic rock song.

She smiled and sat up.

Lynn would be back, likely sleeping on the floor in a ball waiting for Vlora to join her. The changes were difficult when they occurred during the week, as Vlora still had to hold down a regular job and, of course, Hair to Bare for Lynn, until the pandemic closed it down indefinitely.

But they were adapting. Together, as a couple.

They had moved in together around Christmas time, right before the pandemic. A lovely secluded house with no neighbors and access to the Washington County woods, which meant that Lynn would only need to stay put during hunting season.

She was fascinated in watching Lynn change into her wolf and back again. It looked painful, but she was assured that it wasn't nearly as painful as it seemed.

"Will it hurt when I change?" Vlora had asked.

"Your change will be different if you still want to go ahead with it," Lynn said, smiling. "I'm a pure wolf. A wolf in people's clothing, so to speak. You would technically be the werewolf. Not bound by the moon cycle, but your own will. You would actually have a much easier time. It's still a big responsibility though, and all the things that hurt me would hurt you."

"Like hogging the covers?"

"Like that, but much worse," Lynn said, chuckling.

The year had been wonderful so far, and the future, although uncertain, still looked brighter than it ever had for Vlora. A few concessions had to be made, which weren't really too terrible. Vlora's silverware, for one thing. That part of the mythology was fact; silver had a very dangerous reaction to lycanthropes. Lynn likened it to a peanut allergy, which made Vlora laugh.

"You better not have a peanut allergy, because that's where I draw the line," she said, chuckling.

But the silverware had been made into something a little more useful, just in case.

She got out of bed quietly and looked in the corner of Lynn's side of the bed—the floor where she would always wake. The floor where, this time, Vlora would cover her with a blanket and, of course, herself.

Except, this morning, Lynn wasn't there.

It wasn't unheard of that she wouldn't be there. In fact, maybe she was just up too early. Yes, she decided that could be it. She left the bedroom to put on the coffee.

As she padded into the kitchen, she stepped into something cold and wet, like pudding. She gasped at the sensation and looked down at Lynn's crumpled body, twitching on the floor in the fading moonlight. She was halfway from wolf to human, but seeming to have an issue. Lynn's eyes searched wildly as her mouth was open in a silent scream.

Vlora dropped to her knees and picked up Lynn's partially transformed head in both hands.

"Baby, baby, what happened?" she heard herself say in a panicked voice. "Oh my god, baby, what's *wrong?*"

Lynn's head rolled back and forth, jaws snapping and sharp, quick breaths. A low mewling sound was all that came out. Blood streamed out of her nose, and she began to shudder. She was losing a lot of blood.

Vlora found herself beginning to shake with a deep fear she hadn't thought she'd had in her. She reached up to the kitchen light and snapped it on to get a better look at Lynn.

Most of Lynn's lower half was simply torn away. One leg was gone, and her stomach was torn wide open. Bits of half-human, half-wolf viscera jutted out in a spilled fashion onto the linoleum floor. Huge claw-like gashes told a story of what seemed to have happened here, and her fear turned to rage.

"Vlora," Lynn growled. "I'm...dying."

"Fuck you are," Vlora snapped. "Be quiet. We need to fix you."

"No," Lynn said, the growl fading with each word. "Need to...fix *you.*"

"Who did this?"

Lynn gasped as her features began to return to human.

"Pack," she hissed. "Pack found us."

"How can I fix this?" Vlora said through her teeth. "How can I fix *you?*"

"Dying," Lynn said. "Fix *you.*"

"I don't need to be fixed," she said. "Help me help you!"

Lynn swallowed hard.

"You're my pack," she said. "I love you. My *pack.*"

Vlora understood at last and cried angrily.

"My wolf," she said, and kissed Lynn.

Vlora felt Lynn slowly slip away as they kissed. Lynn squeezed Vlora hard one last time, and a bright coppery taste filled Vlora's mouth.

Lynn finished changing and her body went slack.

Vlora cried hard for hours.

***

One Month Later

Northern Quebec, Canada
Boreal Forest

There were five of them gathered around the fire, tents lit by the fading daylight. They were quiet, all of them just taking in their surroundings. They all looked at each other in quick glances.

The eldest in the group spoke first.

"I told you we should have gutted them both," she said.

"Bullshit," said the youngest male. "The other one wasn't a threat. *Still* isn't a threat."

The eldest woman narrowed her gaze on the young man.

"She is *very* much a threat, Holden. One we will not easily see coming."

"Is that why we're hiding?" Holden replied.

Holden's sister Bethany reached a hand out and put it on his knee.

"Easy," she said softly. "We need to be unified."

Holden jerked his knee and glared at his sister.

"We are unified in our cowardice," he said. "Our mother has betrayed us all, and for what?"

"I'd *love* to hear how I have betrayed you," the eldest said.

"Connor and Bethany don't agree with me, but Fiona does, and Magdalene did until you killed her."

The eldest stood up. Fiona, who had not stopped crying, gasped and cowered.

"I will remind you all, pups, that *we* killed Magdalene. She was an abomination. She threatened the bloodline. She defied us."

"She defied *you*," Holden yelled, standing up.

"*All* of your hands are covered in your sister's blood."

Holden was going to say something else, but Bethany grabbed his hand.

"Please," she said. "We can't come apart now."

"We came apart when we killed Magdalene," he said, beginning to weep.

Holden sat down, hugging Bethany.

The eldest sighed and seemed to take a moment to calm herself. She closed her eyes and sat. She slowly opened her eyes and spoke.

"I am Freya, the pack alpha. And right or wrong, I make the decisions for this pack based on what is best for our survival. Not just mine, but *our* survival. No one is more important than any other, but if one jeopardizes the entire pack, then that one has to be *culled*. That is the way we have survived. That is the way we continue to survive."

"I think we need to leave that woman alone," said Fiona, shakily. "We have enough death on our hands."

"Oh, she speaks, at last," Freya said, causing Fiona to cower again. "And I will say when there is enough death. As long as that woman walks, she is an immediate threat to all of us."

"The way Magdalene *wasn't* a threat to us?" said Connor. "And in spite of what my brother says, I didn't *not* approve of killing her. I did my part, but I disagreed with it, and I disagree with *this*."

Freya laughed.

"It seems that you're all building up to become alphas, is that it? Should we pause in killing your sister's whore until the harvest moon at the end of the month so one of you can try to be the new alpha?"

No one said anything. The four siblings hung their heads.

"As I thought," Freya said. "We will reconvene and kill Magdalene's whore on the harvest moon."

Holden stood up and walked to the pile of wood that was near the treeline. He picked up two chunks of wood. He turned and began to walk back to the fire when there was a gunshot and the front of his white hoodie burst open. He stood there in shock, and the other four looked in horror as red began to seep through the coat. He gasped and fell to his knees.

"No!" Freya screamed as another gunshot came, this time catching Connor in the head. He fell over and died instantly. A third and fourth shot caught Fiona in the shoulder and then the face. A fifth shot caught Bethany in the back as she had begun to stand up to run. She fell forward into the snow right in front of the fire. Freya screamed again. Her eyes, wild with panic and anger, looked everywhere and saw nothing.

"You were right," Vlora said. She sounded close, but not anywhere Freya could pinpoint. "You really should have killed me too."

"Where are you?" Freya yelled, frantically looking in a circle.

Vlora walked out of the treeline, holding a handgun and dressed in dark clothing. Freya saw her and spat.

"You dare attack my children? Are you stupid? We will recover and then we will eat you. No matter where you run, we will find you."

"Gonna smell me out, is that it? Is that why I got so close to you five, because you can find me that easily?"

She cocked the handgun and shot Freya in each leg. Freya yelped in pain. And then, she began to scream.

"That burning feeling is *silver*. So your *children* aren't recovering from a damn thing, I'm afraid."

Freya looked and saw that her leg was beginning to smolder in the cold October air. She looked and glared at Vlora.

"You whore," she barked. "You fucking *whore*."

"Oh, it's even worse than that." Vlora smiled and dropped to her knees. "It's so much worse than that for you."

Vlora gritted her teeth and began to change in front of Freya. Her worst fear had been confirmed: Magdelene had made her whore a wolf.

"You'll never be one of us," Freya said, trying to drag herself backward using her arms. "You'll never have a pack of your own."

"*You killed my pack*," Vlora said in a deepening guttural voice.

Vlora's clothes began to rip and tear at the transformation.

Vlora had watched Lynn change a few times, and it was one of the most horrifying things she had ever seen. It was a slow, painful process to watch. Lynn's entire physical form would change; bones would elongate and snap into different positions, her skin would stretch and break as brown wires of fur would grow and seem to gather in clumps. Her entire face would split into sections while it stretched painfully into a snout. It surprised Vlora how absolutely painful it looked.

Vlora's change was much different, as Lynn had told her it would be. Her body reconfigured itself, but the musculature retained position, for the most part, except they grew thick and more powerful. Thick black fur began to sprout everywhere. With one clawed hand, Vlora began to tear at the rest of her clothes.

Freya, still backing away, noticed that Vlora was missing hair around her changing face and genital area. She stopped and laughed.

"Did Magdalene do *that* for you too? So you can be a ridiculous-looking whore wolf-*thing*? Because you'll never be a real wolf."

Vlora's jaws snapped together. She had two-inch-long fangs, and a thickening glob of saliva dropped from her mouth. She didn't develop a snout like Lynn, but her mouth had stretched wider, revealing lots more teeth.

"*Her name was Lynn,*" Vlora said, growling. Freya's face went pale.

Vlora howled in pain and stood up on her two legs. The transformation was painful, but much faster. It took less than thirty seconds. Freya had been right: she was not a wolf, nor would she ever be.

She was a *werewolf.*

She looked at Freya and snarled.

"*Too bad you can't change at will,*" Vlora said in a low growl. "*It would be helpful for you, I'm sure.*"

She walked slowly toward Freya, who was, again, trying to crawl away.

"You'll never be in a pack," Freya said.

"*Fuck you,*" Vlora said, spittle flying from her maw.

"I'm the alpha!" Freya screamed. "I'm the *alpha!*"

"*Not anymore.*"

Vlora snarled and bit into Freya's neck and began to shake it like a chew toy. The head tore off Freya's body and Vlora threw it aside. She snarled again and tore Freya's body into pieces.

***

Vlora had piled the rest of the wood together to make one large fire, then tossed the bodies of the pack, her torn clothes, and their tents on it to watch it all burn. She sat and howled in front of the fire. When the fire had burned itself out, she went to the treeline and gathered her backpack of clothes in her teeth. She needed to get to her car a few miles away and drive back to Pennsylvania.

She sniffed the air; she smelled the burning bodies, the tents, and a rabbit a half-mile away. She broke into a run, backpack in her teeth. The wind brushed her mane as she picked up speed, feeling everything as if for the very first time, seeing the world with new eyes.

She would never be a wolf, not like her beloved wolf.

But what she was would be enough.

STORIES ABOUT THE STORIES

One of my favorite things about reading collections of short stories is when somewhere in the book, there is a section where the writer explains where the story originated. (*Stephen King does this, and as I am a "child" of Uncle Steve, I'm inclined to do the same.*) There are some people that honestly couldn't care less where a story comes from, and that's okay too. If you read my stuff and like it enough to read the main stories and move along, that's absolutely cool. You'll get no arguments here. Hell, fiction is an *escape* from real life sometimes, and even creative non-fiction is as well. The story behind the evil strawberry protein shake might be enough *without* reading about the shitty-tasting protein shakes of the early nineteen nineties after all. Sort of akin to knowing how hot dogs are made versus just eating them and enjoying them.

I get it.

My first collection, *Everything Here Is a Nightmare Vol. 1* (*Burning Bulb Publishing, 2015*) did indeed have a section about the stories, and if there was one favorite part of that work, it was the section about the stories. And the folks that liked that section?

Mostly other writers.

When authors talk about their work, it is very much like listening to someone talk proudly   about   their children   . It almost doesn't matter what level of writer the person is either. If they've been writing for years or a few hours, there is a joy in listening to a writer simply gush about their work.

There is a very good reason for this: it *never* gets old.

The analogy for stories being children really isn't a good one though, and I hesitate making the comparison. As a parent, we factor in the making and molding of the kid, that's certainly true. But, unlike a story, you can't surgically and strategically remove parts of the kid you don't like or the parts that don't work at all (*although, that is a good premise for a horror story—parenting akin to a violent version of using an Etch A Sketch?*)

Oddly enough, the desire to write about writing only happens when the collection is finished. I look at the finished product as a whole—and it *is* a product—and see if anything is missing. Anything that might be fun past the main course. The cake, as it were.

Well, this right here is the cake. It is optional and does offer a wee bit of insight into my process, but it is, I understand, unnecessary.

I still hope you read it and dig it. At the very least, it's not as bad as learning how a hot dog is made...

Nelson Pyles 9/3/2021

Muerte Con Sabor a Fresa (*Strawberry Flavored Death*)

The idea for this story had been floating around for such a long time, and had begun with a lot of false starts, that I almost gave up on it entirely. For whatever reason, there was an element of the idea that just wouldn't bring it all together.

A million years ago, I was the manager of a health food store. (*I was grossly out of shape and smoked like two packs a day. This is a testament of how well I interviewed...*) We sold a lot of protein powder designed specifically to add muscle mass on folks looking to bulk up. There were a lot of different types of protein you could get and in different flavors. This was key, as most of the powder did, in fact, taste like chalk. The story had a wonderful myriad of titles, like "Gravity" and "Density," but I settled on "Muerte Con Sabor a Fresa" for a really fun reason; in fact, a lot of things in this story are in there for fun.

The main character, Georgie Turner, has a really rich back story, the least of which is that she is Spanish, which, to be honest, never made it into the final draft of the story. Turner is her married name, but her first name is Georgina. I called her Georgie because it's the name of an Elvis Costello song, "Georgie and Her Rival," and my writer friend Georgina Morales was initially who I thought of immediately.

Georgie's personality is slightly based on my friend DJ Jen Nunez, who is, among other things, a vinyl-phile with exquisite taste in jazz and death metal. Originally from Panama, she is a fierce, no-bullshit kind of lady who had a fantastic controlled and vicious reaction to someone who referred to her as "dude." Watching her dismantle the poor bastard who had said it spawned the phrase, "Hey, you remember when Nick called Jen a dude," which brought tears of laughter (*and shame from one*) who was there for it. Jen is also the person who translated "Strawberry Flavored Death" into Spanish for me.

The character of Dr. Phoebe Armstrong is named directly for my friend of the same name. I asked her if it was okay to name the character directly after her, and she agreed, possibly not realizing how serious I was. The character is based a little on her personality, but Phoebe is decidedly much, much cooler. She lent her precious ukulele to my daughter Samantha with a chord chart, and that is how Sam learned to play.

All the things that sneak into a story during its construction...

Mrs. Morrison's Pie

Death is, as you can guess, a common theme in horror fiction. Not fear of what happens after you die, necessarily, but that there may not be anything at all. Even more horrifying to me is that it's not even random, but *scheduled.* There are stories that deserve different takes, and one of them is the old "*Death comes to claim a soul, but is outwitted by someone with grit and guts.*" I absolutely love the idea of someone playing a game to save their own life. I also loved the idea of someone doing it on an annual basis simply because they're *angry at Death.*

One day, Mrs. Morrison popped into my head from a website prompt—only the first sentence was given, and the rest of the story had to be written around it. It was initially rejected by the publication, but I really fell in love with the story and all of the characters. This story is absolutely one of my favorites. It was fun to write, it was fun to *rewrite,* and it was a delight to listen to when it was narrated by the fantastic Nichole Goodnight. The interactions of Mrs. Morrison and Ms. Blake stand as some of the best things I have ever written.

Carol's Christmas

I have had a hate/hate relationship with collaborations. I have co-written a handful of stories and a few scripts, and none of them were any fun. They were miserable experiences. *All of them.* The factor of fun is important, as is the spirit of collaboration. An example of this is writing ninety percent of a piece and then having the other writer swoop down and sprinkle *(re: vomit)* their magic *(re: word barf)* all over it. This is decidedly *not* collaboration.

This story, however, is a great example of when it works and when it's fun.

And really, it's one of the best things I've helped write.

Scarlett is not just a badass editor, she is a badass editor who is also a badass writer as well. She is also a good friend and partner in crime (*along with Cynthia Lowman, for whom this story was written with her voice in mind for the narration*). I started this story while pitching it to Scarlett, who really got what I was doing. She loved the idea so much, I asked if she wanted to take a swipe writing it too. Kind of a "pass it back and forth" kind of thing. She was into it and we kicked this out in, like, no time. It was satisfying to work with someone trying to really add to the creepiness and not lose the humanity of the monster named Carol we made. I think together, we really made a rather terrifying character that, as a reader, you sort of like. Cindy, who had always been in my head for playing Carol, absolutely owned the role. It marks the first collaboration between Cindy, Scarlett, and myself, and really became the start of a pretty badass team.

When the Blood Runs Clear

The idea for this story was predicated on two things: perspective and perception. The idea that the only thing separating a terrorist and a patriot is the individual ideology. There was a responsibility to be careful about how the first characters you meet in this story are depicted, as I didn't want to give off the impression that I was anti-Islamic. Quite the contrary. What I wanted to do was present two sides of the same issue that is described in the movie *Tango and Cash* as "Bad Cop-Worse Cop."

The terrorists, specifically Fathi, know they *aren't* actually representing their religion; that's hopefully abundantly clear. However, I wrote about a much different form of religious terrorism to make the cosmos quake. For as much as Islam is not the religion of terrorists, Fathi finds the existential dread of the Cthultu mythos is *exactly* the religion of terror. There was also a lot of effort to not insult the religion of Islam on my part. I'm friends with folk who are Islamic, and you probably are too, even if you don't know it. My intention was not to draw more unwanted attention to Islam as a "religion of terror," because it simply isn't.

The Lonesome Death of Phineas T Croughly

Ah, the Librarian!

The Librarian, created specifically for *The Wicked Library*, became something he had never really been intended to be, and that was an actual *character*. He was just supposed to be this homage to the EC Comics hosts for titles like *Vault of Horror* and, of course, *Tales from the Crypt*. His similarity to the Crypt Keeper is not a coincidence. However, as the seasons went on, the Librarian began to evolve, until one Christmas, this story popped out. The idea for the Librarian was never one of evil. Quite the opposite; he was always viewed by me as somewhat of an agent of chaos, but not evil. The stories that included him after this one showed him in a more vulnerable and even charming light. He became what the Crypt Keeper could never be: versatile and independent *outside* of his place of origin, capable of being funny and creepy, but also having depth and pathos. (*At least I like to think so.*)

And unlike the Crypt Keeper, we got to see the Librarian as Phineas; a young man in love, then denied that love and his life in the same cruel act. The progression of Phineas to the Librarian seems almost abrupt, but no less tragic. But from tragedy came the opportunity to make the Librarian a lot more fun than just a creepy pun machine. People seemed to really enjoy his evolution. At one point, he had several little spin-off podcasts.

He was a lot of fun to voice, but all good things must come to an end. It was fun sharing him with you all, but alas, it's time for good old "Uncle Creeply" (Daniel Knauf's favorite nickname) to go back from whence he came. There was going to be a new podcast with him, but I think he's ready to retire, poor little sausage...

Highway 90—A Radio Play

Creepshow. Tales from the Crypt. Tales from the Darkside. The Outer Limits. The Twilight Zone. Trick 'r Treat. The list is somewhat endless for anthology shows, films, comics, books, and now, podcasts. Hell, my first contribution to the podcast universe was very much a direct homage to those wonderful EC comics from the 50s. (*The Librarian, was very much a pseudo-tribute to the Crypt Keeper, Zacherley, Elvira, and all the groovy ghoulies from the comic books and late-night TV creep hosts.*)

So being very much a child of spooky and a lifelong disciple of the darkness, I wanted to create something akin to those anthology mediums, and I did with *The Wicked Library*. But before that, there was "Highway 90." "Highway 90" gets its title from a really great song from singer/songwriter/actress Jane Jensen. (*Jane played Juliet in the Troma masterpiece* Tromeo and Juliet, *directed by the legendary Lloyd Kaufman and written by James Gunn.*) I would listen to this song on repeat, and I thought it would be such a great theme song for the untitled project that I figured I'd use the song title as well. It fit the theme of the story of a couple trying to get somewhere and going absolutely nowhere in the most sinister way.

It had gotten to the point where I went to ask Jane if it was cool to use the song, but due to copyright issues out of her control, she advised against it. She's a very cool lady and a very talented performer. (*The song in question is on her album* Comic Book Whore *and it's absolutely fantastic.*)

This was going to be the pilot episode with more to follow, but like a lot of things, it just didn't work out. But it did feed further into the idea that a show podcast like *The Wicked Library* could work. I have also not given up on the idea of producing a full version of the script, even if only for the audio version of this collection.

Hello, It's Not Me

The Horror Writers Association has chapters all over the world, and my transplant hometown of Pittsburgh has, I feel, the mightiest chapter of them all.* During the pandemic, our fun and talented chapter took part in a really fun live-streamed event called *A Night of Haunted Readings.*

See our playbill:

That is one hell of a roster of authors, is it not? I keep this picture, in all honesty, to remind myself how fortunate I am for these folks that I am glad to call friends and cohorts (*And I try not to drop names, but if I were inclined to, this list would be the place I'd start*).

When the idea came about, I volunteered immediately without any idea of what I was going to do. The event was a live-streaming event which was a lot of fun. For my story, I borrowed my daughter's desk lamp, which has a light color controller. Whenever the new personality of the narrator took over, I would click the remote and change the color. It seemed to work. I may try to recreate it down the road. I really do wish there was a copy of that evening somewhere on the interwebs, because it was a really fun time.

Have Yourself

The theme of the last Christmassacre episode for *The Wicked Library* (*at least the final one I've written*) was "Christmas songs," and I chose "Have Yourself a Merry Little Christmas" (*written by Ralph Blaine for the 1944 Judy Garland film* Meet Me in St. Louis). Except it is pretty far and away from a happy little anything. The story—as it is in so many themes in my work, I'm finding—is related to the betrayal of some form within family. The narrator is not *entirely* unreliable, but does fall into the category. I very much liked the idea of a revenge story narrated by the one the revenge itself was being waged for in the first place.

It's a *mean* little story. Probably a lot meaner than I had intended it to be, but at the time I was aware of just how much anger I was starting to put into my work and sort of enjoying the results. It's better, after all, to direct anger in constructive ways rather than blithely taking it out on actual people. You can't hit the punching bag all the time.

A Piece of Cake (*Formerly* "Cake")

This story was originally written for a podcast anthology, and then rewritten specifically for this collection. It is about how much of ourselves we lose by being angry, and how much it affects everything and everyone around us. I've been angry enough to let unresolved issues go to someone's grave, and although mostly I wouldn't change all of those, there is one I wish I could go back and revisit. This story isn't really about the specifics of it, but it's a little close. It isn't about forgiving someone as much as it is about understanding someone and maybe that being enough to, if not forgive the other person, then at least to forgive ourselves.

My friend Laurie Beth Robbins put it this way: "If you do not forgive, you're still attached to them. You're holding onto it as if it means something." This was a tough story to write, and tougher again to re-write, but I think it has more of a heart than it originally did. This version turned out to be a lot more cathartic than the original.

All These Steps Lead Down (*Formerly* "The Basement")

This was another story written for the same podcast as "Cake" and rewritten to exclude the characters and the world of that podcast.

Almost in the same way that "Cake" found more of its heart in the rewrite, this story (*which became the anchor story*) found much more of its teeth. What this story explored for me was looking for punishment equal to the crime and not even coming close, but finding something that would endure. My friend Bret Bouriseau wrote in his fantastic first novel, *Travers McCracken: The Prince of Knocknafay,* "The truly wicked be damned," and I've always loved the totality of that sentiment. Also, it really butters the biscuit, so to speak. I do not feel that it's a story of revenge. It's more justice than anything.

Where "A Piece of Cake" had an element of forgiveness about it, "Steps" does not. This is the exact opposite of any sort of forgiveness and, to be fair, was written before I had felt differently about forgiving someone. As this is a work of fiction, but based on how I felt at the time, I thought it stood better on its own anger than changing the story more than it already had been. And really, the story is sharper and angrier than it was originally. Another argument for rewriting. As they say, "Great writing is rewriting."

The Humanity of Blade Runner

Lou Tambone is a writer and musician that I have known for over half of my life. We were in a band that gigged on a regular basis in the early 90s, cramming gear in and out of whatever vehicles we could caravan for our trio. After leaving the band on relatively good terms, years went by...and somewhere around 2017, Lou, who had become a damn good writer himself, reached out and asked if I would write an essay about a film we both loved and logged a lot of time discussing: *Blade Runner.*

I dove at the chance to write about this movie. Considering my background as a horror writer and general smartass, my first stab at this story came across as very flippant, which garnered a *very severe* edit from one of the editors. Louie was one, but the other editor was absolutely *not* screwing around. "This is a *scholarly essay,*" was one of the notes I remember, and after taking a moment to let the *perceived* scolding sink in, I wholeheartedly *agreed* with it. I'd been taken to task by editors before, but this one really pushed me to be better, and I think it worked.

So when I was thinking of work to include, I wrote to Louie, wondering how difficult it would be to include this essay in the collection. For one thing, *Blade Runner* is arguably one of the most influential science fiction movies ever made. Who the hell was I to ask to include an essay about such an influential and popular piece of modern fiction?

Lou wrote back with an email address for the fine folks at Sequart, a really top-notch outfit, if I do say so, and said to write to them and just *ask*.

My friend Myk Pilgrim had gifted me the audio version of Amanda Palmer's *The Art of Asking* a while back, and that really seemed to resonate with me, so I asked.

Sequart could not have been *nicer* about it. They were, in all honesty, seemingly thrilled that I not only wanted to include it, but were really happy that I had such a good experience writing the essay in the first place. All they asked was that I include the publishing info for the book in the acknowledgements.

Seriously.

That was it.

I think it would have been fair to assume that the right to reprint an article about the **intellectual property** of, arguably, the ***single most influential science fiction film of the twentieth century*** would have been more difficult to get. And I think that line of thought keeps a lot of us from striving to do things. Asking is always better than just *grinding your teeth*, after all, (*and finding solutions to problems is also pretty ideal*).

All that being said, they get a **big** spot in the bibliography page, the acknowledgments, and right now, www.sequart.org. The book is called ***The Cyberpunk Nexus: Exploring the Blade Runner Universe***, and there is a metric ton of great work in there by really great writers, including Lou *"T-Bone"* Tambone. Which also, oddly enough, segues into the next story...

Negotiations

I was fortunate enough to have had my first two published works released at the exact same time in 2002. The first one was a story called "Spring in New York" in an awesome magazine called *Hacker's Source* (*with the words "BANNED IN CANADA" proudly displayed on the cover*), and it later appeared in my first collection, *Everything Here Is a Nightmare*. The other story is this one, and it appeared in an anthology called *Destroyer World: New Blood*. *The Destroyer* is a series of novels written and created by Warren Murphy and Richard Sapir and still going strong with 157 books (*the latest just released, written by James Mullaney*). The series began in 1971, but I didn't discover them until my college days. I worked an overnight security guard gig where I had eight hours to write and/or read. More often than not, I read. In a pinch, I went to a paper store and saw *The Destroyer, Book 86: Arabian Nightmare.* It had a cool cover, and without thinking, I paid the cover price and went to work.

By eight o'clock the next morning, I went on a search for more *Destroyer* books. It took a few chapters to realize that this was the source material for the *Remo Williams: The Adventure Begins* movie from 1985. I was very fortunate to have found this book in the autumn of 1991. Eleven years later, Warren Murphy proposed an anthology of *Destroyer* short stories written by fans of the series. I imagined it would be considered "fan-fiction" and I didn't care. It's one of those stories that was pure joy to write. Every time I sit down to write, part of me wishes to feel the same way I did after I finished that one.

The best part was the email I received from Warren saying that he'd be sending the edits for review in a few weeks and that he liked the story. He sent me the cover art signed (pictured) which is now framed in my house. He remains one of my favorite writers. I was very sad when he passed away in 2015.

A very huge thanks to Devin Murphy for letting me reprint this story. You can dive right into the amazing books by going to https://destroyerbooks.com/.

The Trouble with Unicorns

There was a now-defunct publishing house that released a collection of flash fiction from a lot of the writers that were on their roster at the time. I had written a total of four stories, and two made the collection, but I'm going to include them all because I really like them. That being said, the stories are all a little weird; in particular, "Unicorns." I love the idea that the much-beloved unicorn is actually just a really beautiful, pointy-headed asshole. My favorite version of a unicorn is the one stabbing soldiers at the end of *Cabin in the Woods.* And this one.

Regards, Eleanor

This idea was inspired by three things: an internet search to see if you could buy a beehive online (*you can*), one of my favorite names ever, and the revenge of a woman who was really annoyed at the way people said her name. The name of my friend who inspired this is Heidi. We were talking and she said how angry she would get at the many ways people would shorten her name or abbreviate it, like *Hide* or *Hidey-ho*. She also included that people would butcher the pronunciation of her name, which still baffles me. So this story remains for her and doesn't reflect anything she had ever planned. She was in between her first and second marriage at the time, and I didn't want anyone to think she was plotting something, or worse, that I was *helping her plot something*. I wasn't. Honest.

Manners Count and Mallory

I'm combining these two as there really is no need to write stories about two flash fiction pieces that risk being *longer than the actual stories themselves*. "Manners Count" always surprised me at how, in a very short span of words, the plot actually changed in the last segment. The original idea was a revenge-fueled quickie where the payoff was always going to be off-page. I wanted to kill this old lady. I mean, I *really* wanted her dead, until, at the last minute, the infusion of her having this sudden flash of magnificence, self-awareness, and regret changed it all. That's what happens sometimes in storytelling, because that's how it happens off-page in real life. Things change in a second. Sometimes it's very satisfying to have a plot go sideways because it adds something that never would have surfaced.

Then again, "Mallory" ends *exactly* where I wanted it to end. And that is also really satisfying. "Mallory" was an experiment in delusion that I didn't want to be another "*weak, psychotic girl*" story. There is already so much of that these days. You also may have noticed that a lot of my stories feature women as the protagonists, and "Mallory" was an attempt to have my protagonist be delusional, but not *weak* because of it. Part of me roots for good old Mal. Part of me will always be afraid of her too.

The Best Show Ever

I used to have a website, and it was a repository for a lot of writing. Different stuff, mostly non-fiction, and it was fun, but it ultimately needed to be put down like a sick animal. (*Okay, that was too dramatic.*) What survived is a handful of essays, and this is one of my favorites.

The Wolf and Her Wife

This story turned very much into a labor of love, which is odd, because where it started was a joke concept. The main character is named after my very good friend Vlora. She contributed exactly two things to this story. One, her name, which neither of us has ever seen anywhere else and was almost too perfect not to use. I've known her for an extraordinarily long time and thought that the name should get out there. The second thing was the idea, as she was telling me about her experience of laser hair removal and the *smell* that goes with it. We then started talking about the hilarity of a werewolf who, while in human form, gets hair removal surgery, and then turns into a werewolf. It's a very funny visual. So I started writing it that way, and then my favorite thing happened: the story decided to go elsewhere. This happens when you've been writing a while and the story *behind* the story comes out. "Fiction is the truth inside the lie," as noted by Stephen King, and the truth of this story is that it became a love story. A tragedy, for sure; horror, certainly, and on occasion, funny. But its engine, it's heart, is a love story, albeit an unconventional one.

I sent the story to Scarlett immediately upon completion and did the agonizing "wait until she reads it" part.

As of this writing, I'm still waiting.

I'm pretty sure she's going to like it.

(Note from the editor: obviously I did!)

PUBLICATION HISTORY

Muerte Con Sabor a Fresa (*9th Story Publishing—Thirteen Wicked Tales, 2019*)

Mrs. Morrison's Pie (*The Wicked Library Extra Wicked, 2017*)

Carol's Christmas—with Scarlett R. Algee (*The Wicked Library—Christmassacre, 2019*)

When The Blood Runs Clear (*Burning Bulb Publishing—Fiends of the Flesh, 2017*)

The Lonesome Death of Phineas T. Croughly (*The Wicked Library—Christmassacre, 2015*)

Highway 90—A Radio Play

Hello, It's Not Me (*Performed Live—A Night of Haunted Readings, HWA Pittsburgh, 10/24/2020*)

Have Yourself (*The Wicked Library—Christmassacre, 2020*)

A Piece of Cake (*appeared originally as "Cake" in The Lift—9 Stories of Transformation ,based on the podcast of the same name. 9th Story Publishing—Altered and expanded for this collection*)

All These Steps Lead Down (*formerly "The Basement," adapted from the podcast "The Lift"—Altered and expanded for this collection*)

The Humanity of Blade Runner (*An Essay—Sequart Publishing, 2018, The Cyberpunk Nexus: Exploring the Blade Runner Universe*)

Negotiations (*appeared in Destroyer World: New Blood, edited by Warren Murphy, Ballybunion Press, 2002*)

The Trouble with Unicorns (*Appeared in 88 Lies by 44 Liars, Post Mortem Press, 2016*)

Regards, Eleanor (*Appeared in 88 Lies by 44 Liars, Post Mortem Press, 2016*)

Manners Count (*original to this collection*)

Mallory (*original to this collection*)

The Best Show Ever (*Essay from the old nelsonwpyles.com website, 2006*)

The Wolf and Her Wife (*original to this collection*)

ACKNOWLEDGMENTS

This collection took a bit of putting together. The writing part, as always, is the most fun. The part when the stories wind up where they're going to be is the second best part.

It's the bit in between that usually holds the most sighing and hair tearing moments at least for me. The edits, rewrites, re-rewriting...rejections, re rejections...gah! Tedious....but I might be lying.

Okay, I'm *totally* lying.

I absolutely love it all.

It's cliché to mention the parts about writing to dislike being edited and rejections, but honestly, I love all of that stuff too.

However, the part I don't like too much is the acknowledgements page because I *know* I am going to miss some people. I will do my best and here we go!

Scarlett R. Algee is absolutely one of my favorite people and also one of the finest editors in the business. "To write is human, to edit, *divine*," is what one of my favorite writers once said quite correctly. *(I bet it was there simply to make their editor smile, and I bet it totally worked.)*

Scarlett is also one of the best writers I know personally. I'm not gonna lie, we're friends but we also work really well together. The evidence of that is the story included here, in print for the first time, "Carol's Christmas." The concept was strikingly simple: a first person modern take on the old Dickens classic with a hell of a juxtaposition. "What if Ebenezer Scrooge was a female serial killer *(and, also simultaneously, all three ghosts)* and there really *wasn't* a moral at the end?" This book and about half of what's in it wouldn't be here or as good as it is if it weren't for you. Thank you!

We both agreed that the voice for Carol should be performed by Cindy Lowman *(who is another top notch editor, author and voice actress. She performed the hell out of the character in all three incarnations— teenager, burgeoning murderer and the final serial killer who narrates the story.)* Cindy and Scarlett are both incredible creative partners and I am very fortunate to not only be able to work with them both, but to call them both friends. I appreciate that more than absolutely anything. Cindy also keeps me honest as we both check in on our health—mostly mental—and that seems to work to keep everything cool. Thanks! *(Also, this shit ain't gonna write itself! You're a badass.)*

I'd like to additionally thank Lou Tambone, Joe Bongiorno, and all the folks at www.sequart.org for allowing me to reprint my essay on *Blade Runner* from the book *The Cyberpunk Nexus.* You should do yourself a solid if you're a sci-fi aficionado and check out the other works they have at Sequart. Lou has made quite a name for himself over there and has skin in a lot of those books. He's also a super talented musician as well, so check him out on www.loutambone.com and tell T-Bone I sent ya!

Devon Murphy is the son of the late Warren Murphy, who along with Richard Sapir, created *The Destroyer* series of books and was crucial in allowing me to reprint my own Remo Williams and Chiun story for this collection. Thank you, Devon! Find that book and all of the books in the series (*including stories written by the fantastic Will Murray*) at https://destroyerbooks.com.

Gary Lee Vincent has published a lot of my stuff and subsequently resides as one of my favorite people to work with. He's what most industry people should aspire to be: kind, honest and above board. I appreciate all that you do for the writers under the banner of Burning Bulb Publishing, found at www.burningbulbpublishing.com.

Huge thanks to Don Noble for the amazing cover! Check out his work and other fun stuff over at https://roosterrepublicpress.com.

Massive thanks as always to Deb, Declan, and Sam. I love you three and this would not be possible without your love and support. And by this, I mean absolutely EVERYTHING. And of course, those of you reading this part. I'm glad you're still here. There's a word for folks like you.

Appreciated!
Thank you!
Nelson W Pyles
8.2.22

PS—Update 3/12/23
Has there been an update in an acknowledgment for a book?
Well, now there is!

Anyhoo, I'm less than a month away from open heart surgery and as of this writing, I'm very much alive. Kooky, right?

I should be very much alive by the time this comes out. However, if I am not...INSTANT COLLECTORS' ITEM!!! I'll see if Scarlett can put something in here to make it an actual collector's edition!

Or maybe a *curse*?

Nah...Just promise me if you read this and like it, give it someone else that may like it. Secondhand store this guy. Pass it around. Even if it's signed. Do this with all of your books, especially with ones from independent authors like me. Know what our advertising budget is?

A whole lot of not enough.

But I have YOU, reader of this book! Spread the word if you like the stories in here—even if you like only one.

The idea of being a writer isn't about being "the next Stephen King." There won't be a next Stephen King. We have one Steve and when he's gone, well...his books will still be here but we only get one. **You only get one.**

I am fortunate to be a writer among a group of extraordinary writers, some of which are mentioned throughout this book. I am not lucky by any means (*especially if I'm dead when you read this...wouldn't that be hilarious?*).

Not lucky, but fortunate. Fortunate for the friends I have made among my peers, among some of my favorite writers, poets and creatives. I'm grateful to you all.

Also, pretty sure I'll still be alive if you're reading this and if so, I look forward to thanking you all in person.

NWP

Scarlett—look into making haunted books just in case...

PSS—3rd Update

Sorry kids, I'm still alive. Anna (*now Declan*) took the photo for the back cover, which was the decoy cover for the reviewers' ARC that Scarlett and I put together. The picture is from the very top of the stairs at the Warhol Museum in Pittsburgh. Thank you, A-Ball! (*Now Declan— brief side trip. In the time of this original acknowledgment, my oldest kid has begun to transition to a he/him lifestyle and is now going by the name*

we picked had he popped out a biological male—Declan. It was his own decision as a legal adult and he is super supported by his family.)
My heart still works—even better now, believe it or not!
Thank you all again!

N
7/6/23

Last update:

Writing a book really doesn't take a long time if you have the thing loaded in your head. A collection, even less so, but this book became its own time vacuum. I had read the anchor story during a Halloween reading on 2021 along with some spooky pals at Chatham University. And really, everything for this book was written and waiting for a solid edit and to be uploaded.

But real life laughs at you when you try to make plans. Like, a lot. If, for example, you have the Uncorrected Proof of this book, you'll notice the original publication date was to be October 31st, 2023. If all the fruit lines up, this will be officially released and available October 29th, 2024 (fingers crossed).

I am writing this little missive on Scarlett R. Algee's birthday in hopes of courting some kind of luck. Last night, she caught a really glaring edit missed during the first pass. As she put it, "If I have to choose between being slightly behind schedule and being correct, I will choose being correct."

Preach, sister.

Thank you all again for not only your patience, but your continued readership.

Nelson
9/13/24

ABOUT THE AUTHOR

Nelson W. Pyles is an author, musician, podcast creator and actor born and raised in New Jersey. His introduction to horror (other than his childhood) was seeing the original "Nosferatu" on television when he was five. He wrote his first short story in sixth grade to impress his teacher and continued from there. He became a performing musician and a stage actor while continuing to write. He created *The Wicked Library* podcast in 2012 and in earnest began to focus more on writing. He has written two novels; "Demons, Dolls and Milkshakes" and "Spiders in the Daffodils" and is currently working on his third. His second collection of short stories, essays and articles "All These Steps Lead Down" will be released in 2024 from Cold War Radio Press. He

now lives in Pittsburgh. For more information, visit his website
www.whatnelsonwrites.com